LAKE OF DREAMS

Cañas y barro (Reeds and Mud)

Vicente Blasco Ibañez
Translator E M Armstrong

ISBN-

To my wife, Katie, for her patient support.

CONTENTS

FOREWORD

Lake of Dreams, (or to use its Spanish title “Cañas y barro”, meaning Reeds and Mud) is the last of the series of “Valencian Novels”, all of them in the genre of social realism espoused by authors including Charles Dickens, Honoré de Balzac and Émile Zola, which were published by Vicente Blasco Ibañez between 1890 and 1903. Born in in 1867 in Valencia and a lawyer by education, he was a socialist politician and journalist during a time of turmoil in Spain. While the political system stagnated under a corrupt, but constitutional monarchy, the country wrestled with the social pressures of a late and uneven industrial revolution, a disastrous war with the United States of America which resulted in the loss of Cuba, the Philippines and Puerto Rico and the influence of liberal and revolutionary ideas. In this novel, Blasco Ibañez charts the effects of these forces on an ancient family of fishermen on the Albufera, a freshwater lagoon south of Valencia. Now a National Park of some 50,000 acres and a major tourist attraction as a wildlife habitat, it was originally a saltwater lake ten times that size that became gradually enclosed by a vast sandbar. By the 16th Century, the sandbar was complete and the shallow lagoon, fed by the Torrente and other smaller rivers, became freshwater. Rich in fish and a haven for wildfowl, the lake was bordered to landward by a rich coastal plain which was irrigated by the Arabs during their six-hundred-year occupation and is today one of Spain's principal fruit and vegetable growing areas. Ditches and dykes enabled farmers to encroach on the shallow edges of the lagoon, a process which accelerated in the nineteenth century with the growth of demand for staples such as rice, and Valencia became, for a time, one of the west's principal rice-growing areas. The huge seaward sandbar, The Dehesa, became a pine covered wilderness and an effective buttress against the Mediterranean. As in all his Valencian novels, the geography and history of their setting is a key element of both character and plot and the reader is encouraged to explore the wealth of online images of the area. A map will also help, as all the locations that Blasco-Ibañez mentions are real and can be found around the present-day Albufera. The main site of the action, El Palmar is a small village in the southeast corner of the lake. Among its other attractions, it has a Cañamel restaurant (spelt Canyamel in Valenciano). The village of El Saler, in the northeast corner has preserved the Casa de la Demaná as a museum, and while Catarroja, in the northwest corner, now finds itself distanced from the water by reclaimed land, and is a suburb of Valencia, it still has a fine waterfront on its canal. The lateen-sailed *laudes* and smaller punts that Blasco Ibañez describes are still seen, and the abundance of waterfowl makes the lake a major attraction for ornithologists. With his journalistic eye for detail, Blasco Ibañez takes trouble, too, to anchor the action in real time, early in the narrative. In chapter 2, old grandfather *Paloma* describes his role in aiding the "escape" of General Prim and later shooting expeditions with him when he was back as head of the government. This would suggest that the latter encounters took place about 1868-70. Juan Prim, born in 1814 was a major figure of 19th Century Spanish politics who gained military prominence early in the first Carlist war, 1833-40. A staunch liberal, he was exiled and returned to power several times in his career. He was finally forced to move in 1868 against his increasingly tyrannical former patron Queen Isabella II, in a successful rebellion which saw him promoted Marshall and appointed to government as President of the Council. He led the establishment of a constitutional monarchy but was assassinated in 1870. The queen herself figures in the narrative, as does her childhood friend, Eugenia de Montijo, a famously athletic young lady, who was Empress of France following her marriage to the last Emperor, Napoleon III. To the modern reader the events described may seem lost in distant history, but it is notable that in the episode in which the "hero", Tonet, returns from the Spanish American war as a survivor of the siege of Santiago de Cuba, the author is describing the disastrous defeat which finally ended the Spanish colonial era only four years before, in 1898. In a short period of hostilities from March to August of that year, US support for local rebellions in Cuba, Puerto Rico and the Philippines resulted in the destruction of Spanish naval and military power, the loss of all their territories and the end of a process which had commenced with the loss of their major Latin American Empire to independence movements following the Napoleonic period. Blasco Ibañez was a member of the "Generation of ´98", an informal group of Spanish artists and writers who set out to build a new Spanish cultural identity out of the rubble of this era. Following a failed attempt to set up two new colonies in Argentina in 1909, Blasco Ibañez moved to Paris in self imposed exile where he witnessed the early stages of Worl War I and, in 1916, wrote the enormously successful *Cuatro Jinetes del Apocalipsis*, (Four Horsemen of the Apocalypse), a bestseller in the United States and filmed to great acclaim in 1921, directed by Rex Ingram and starring the then unknown Rudolph Valentino. Several of his works have been used as the basis of film scripts and Spanish TV series. He died at Menton in France in 1928.

Although he wrote in Spanish (Castellano), Blasco-Ibañez was of course equally familiar with the local Valenciano language, a variety of Catalan, with which he liberally adorns the text, particularly in the speech of local working people. I have left occasional examples untranslated where I do not think the general reader will have trouble in construing their meaning. One particular problem for the translator was his use of Valenciano and old local names for the variety of wildfowl found on the Albufera. I am most grateful to John Muddeman at Spainbirds Nature Tours (www.spainbirds.com) who, with the help of local colleagues, very helpfully researched and deciphered these for me.

E M Armstrong.

Plymouth, Devon, UK. December 2022.

CHAPTER 1

As on every afternoon, the mail boat announced its arrival in El Palmar with a couple of calls on the post horn.

The boatman, a skinny little man, with one ear missing, would make his way from door to door picking up deliveries for Valencia, and at every vacant space along the town's single street, would blow the horn again to advertise his presence to the cottages scattered further along the edge of the canal. A sort of admiring swarm of semi-naked children followed him. They felt deep respect for this man who crossed the Albufera four times a day, carrying to Valencia the best fish in the lake and bringing back from this mysterious and fantastic city, a thousand and one delights for the little urchins, brought up on an island of reeds and mud.

A crowd of agricultural labourers, over for the

harvest, surged out of the Cañamel Tavern, the number one establishment in El Palmar, with their bags over their shoulders ready to catch the boat back to their own side of the lake. The womenfolk made their way to the canal, as to one of the streets of Venice, its banks lined with cottages and the tanks where their fishermen kept the eels.

Like a great coffin loaded with people and packages, its gunwales almost awash, the mail boat lay motionless on the still waters glinting like a sheet of tin in the light. The triangular lateen sail, much adorned with dark patches, was topped by a bleached-out scrap of cloth which had once been a Spanish flag, signifying the official designation of this ancient hulk.

An insufferable stench hung around the boat. Its planking was impregnated with the stink of the eel baskets and the dirt of hundreds of passengers: a nauseating mixture of slimy skin, the scales of fish that spent their lives in the mud, mucky feet, and filthy clothes whose constant rubbing had ended up polishing the boat's seats to a brilliant shine.

The passengers, mostly farm labourers from Perelló at the far end of the Albufera on the seaward side, called loudly to the boatman to get under way as soon as possible. The boat was already full! It couldn't take more people!

And neither it could; but the little man, turning the formless stump of his missing ear towards them so as not to hear, slowly distributed around the boat the packages and baskets that the women kept on passing down to him from the bank. Each of these new additions provoked a stream of protest; the passengers huddled up or changed seats, and the Palmar folk who were boarding received the torrent of abuse from those already settled with beatific smiles. A little patience, friend! You'd be lucky to find as much space in heaven!

The boat seemed on the point of sinking under such a load, not that the boatman displayed the slightest concern, used as he was to dodgy crossings. Not a seat remained unfilled. Two men stood on the gunwales, clinging to the mast; another perched on the prow, like a figurehead. Yet once again, amid general protests, the implacable boatman sounded his horn. Christ! Didn't this rogue have enough already? Were they to spend the whole of the afternoon there with their backs toasting in the September sun which hit them full on?

A sudden silence fell as the folk in the boat saw a man approaching along the canal bank, supported by two women, a spectre, white and trembling, his eyes burning, wrapped in a thick blanket. The waters seemed to boil with the heat of that summer afternoon, everyone in the boat was pouring with sweat, making every effort to avoid the inevitably sticky contact with their neighbour, but the lad was shaking, his teeth chattering with continuous shivering, as if the world had turned to continuous night. The women supporting him protested forcibly, in crude terms, seeing the people in the boat keep their seats. They ought to give him a seat; he was ill, a labourer. He had caught a fever harvesting rice, the cursed tertian fever of the Albufera, and was going to Ruzafa to recover with some relatives. Maybe they weren't Christians? For pity's sake! A seat!

And the ghost, shuddering with fever kept mumbling, like an echo, as the rigors gripped him:

- Pity's sake… Pity.

He elbowed his way in without any help from the selfish huddle but, finding nowhere to sit, slid down between the passengers' legs, stretching out in the bilge with his face stuck in the nauseating stench among the mucky sandals and mud-caked shoes. People seemed used to scenes like these. That boat was used for everything, for provisions, as an ambulance, as a hearse. Every day it would take the sick aboard, ferrying them to the suburb of Ruzafa where the Palmar folk, lacking anything to treat them with, had some squalid rooms rented to let them recover from the tertian fever. When some poor soul without his own boat died, the coffin would be placed under a seat and the mail boat would set off with its load of passengers unconcernedly laughing and chatting and banging the box with their feet.

As the sick man sank out of sight the howls of protest rose again. What was that earless wonder waiting for? Was someone still missing? But guffaws from the whole boat greeted a couple who emerged through the door of *Cañamel's* tavern next to the canal.

- Old Paco! they roared, old man Paco Cañamel!

The tavern's owner, an enormous man, swollen even to his belly with dropsy, whined softly like a plaintive child at each step as he made his way along in little hops, leaning on his wife, Neleta, tiny, with wild red hair and lively green eyes which seemed to caress him with a velvet-soft look. The famous *Cañamel*, sick and bleating, while his ever more beautiful and desirable wife reigned from her counter over the whole of El Palmar and the Albufera. What he was suffering from was the disease of the rich: too much money and too much good living. You only had to look at his belly, his heightened complexion, his large round nose and piggy eyes almost hidden in the greasy folds of his cheeks. Fat chance of them complaining of what ailed him! If he had to make his living in water up to his waist harvesting rice, he wouldn't even be thinking of being ill!

Cañamel got one foot into the boat, painfully, with soft little groans, still hanging on to Neleta, grumbling under his breath about the people making a joke of his infirmity. He knew what it was all about! Oh, Lord, yes, he did! He settled himself into a seat which they vacated for him with that fawning concern that country folk feel for the rich, while his wife, unconcernedly faced down the jibes of those who complimented her on looking so good and in such good spirits.

She helped her husband unfurl a huge parasol, placed at his side a wicker basket of provisions for the voyage, which would not be more than three hours, and finally recommended the boatman to take the best possible care of her Paco. He was going to spend some time in his house in Ruzafa. Some of the best doctors would visit him there; the poor man was ill. She said this with a smile, all innocence, caressing the heap of flab trembling like a jelly as the boat began to rock gently. She paid no attention to the mischievous winks of the passengers, to the knowing glances and jibes which seemed to slip by her to find their target in the innkeeper doubled up under his sunshade, wheezing in painful grunts.

The boatman heaved with his long pole against the steep bank and the craft began to slip along the canal followed by the cries of Neleta, who with her unfailingly enigmatic smile continued to urge all her friends to look after her husband.

Hens scuttled along among the dead leaves on the bank following the boat. Flocks of ducks flapped around the prow disturbing the canal's mirrored surface reflecting, upside down, the images of the village cottages and the black punts tied up to the fish tanks, their straw roofs at surface level, adorned at each end with a wooden cross as if wishing to place the eels in their bosom under divine protection.

Leaving the canal behind, the mail-boat began to glide among the rice paddies, huge fields of liquid mud covered in deep golden ears of grain. The reapers, wading deep in the water moved forward sickle in hand, and long black punts, narrow as gondolas gathered to their breast the sheaves which they were to convey to the threshing floors. In the midst of this watery world of vegetation, indistinguishable from the canals, one would see, from time to time, little white houses surmounted by a chimney, built on islets of mud. These were the pump houses for the machinery which flooded and drained the fields as demanded by the cycle of cultivation.

The high banks hid the network of canals, wide "*carreras*" through which could sail boats loaded with rice. Their hulls remained invisible, but their great triangular lateen sails slipped through the green fields in the silence of the afternoon like ghosts over the ground. The passengers cast an expert eye over the scene, voicing opinions on the harvest and lamenting the misfortune of those whose fields had been poisoned by nitrates, killing the rice.

The boat slid along tranquil passages, the water yellowish, its reflexions as golden as tea. In the depths, the aquatic plants inclined their swaying fronds at the touch of the keel. The silence and the stillness of the water augmented every sound. At intervals when conversations ceased, one clearly heard the laboured breathing of the sick man lying under a seat and the persistent grunts of *Cañamel* with his beard sunk on his chest.

From distant and almost invisible boats came sounds, magnified by the calm; the crash of a pole falling on a deck, the squeal of mast blocks, the shouts of boatmen warning each other to avoid collisions at turns in the canal. Their earless skipper cast his pole aside, and leaping over the passengers' knees, ranged from one end of the boat to the other sorting out the sail to make best use of the faint evening breeze.

They had entered the lake itself, that part of the Albufera strewn with reedbeds and islands, where one had to navigate with a certain care. The horizon widened out. On one side was the dark wavy line of the Dehesa pinewoods, separating the Albufera from the sea, mostly virgin forest running for miles and miles, where wild bulls graze and great reptiles live in the shadows, beasts which few see but which are much and fearfully talked of in the watches of the night. On the opposite side the immense flatlands of the rice paddies stretched away, losing themselves in the horizon in the direction of Sollana and Sueca, merging with the distant mountains. Ahead were reedbeds and little islands hiding the open lake, among which the boat now glided, its prow submerging the water plants and its sail brushing the reeds hanging over the banks. Thickets of black slimy grasses rose like sticky tentacles towards the surface, entangling the boatman's pole and one's gaze uselessly searched the dark miasmic growth, throbbing with the life of the creatures of the mud. Every look expressed the same thought; anyone falling in there would only get out with difficulty.

A herd of bulls was feeding among the rushes and pools on the Dehesa shore. Some had swum over to the nearest islets and, sunk in the ooze up to their bellies, were rooting among the reeds making great splashes as they moved their heavy feet. They were huge animals, filthy, their backs covered in scabs, their horns massive and their muzzles forever dribbling. They gazed balefully at the loaded boat gliding among them, scattering, as they moved their heads, a cloud of fat mosquitos which immediately fell back onto their curly locks.

A short distance away, on a bank which was no more than a sliver of mud between the waters, the people in the boat saw a man squatting. Those from El Palmar knew him.

-It's *Sangonera*, they cried, *Sangonera*, the drunk.

And waving their hats they shouted to ask where he had got tanked up that morning and if he was thinking of spending the night there too. *Sangonera* remained where he was but, tiring of the shouts and laughter from the folk in the boat, got to his feet, and turning a gentle pirouette, sneered and gave himself a few good slaps on the backside before gravely squatting back down on his haunches.

Seeing him get to his feet, the laughter had doubled, excited by his bizarre appearance. He was wearing a hat adorned with a tall plume of flowers from the Dehesa, and around his chest and waist were coiled several bunches of convolvulus tendrils from the plants growing among the reeds on the bank.

They were all talking about him. The well-known *Sangonera*! There was no one like him in all the villages around the lake. He held a firm belief in not working like other men, saying that work was an insult to God, and he used to pass each day in search of anyone who might invite him to share a drink. He used to get drunk in Perelló in order to sleep in El Palmar; he would drink in El Palmar so as to wake up the next day in El Saler. And if there was a fiesta in one of the landward villages, he would be seen in Silla or Catarroja searching out some good soul among the folk who tilled the fields around the Albufera who might invite him for a drink. It was a miracle that his corpse had not turned up in the bottom of a canal after so many trips around the lake, completely drunk, following the edges of the rice paddies, thin as an axe blade, wading across breaches in the drainage ditches with water up to his chest and getting through areas of liquid mud which no one else would dare attempt, except in a boat.

The Albufera was his home. His instincts as a son of the lake, got him out of danger and on many a night when he turned up in the *Cañamel* tavern to beg a glass he was as slimy to the touch and stinking of ooze as a veritable eel.

Hearing what was being said, the innkeeper muttered between his grunts. "*Sangonera*! Shameless scoundrel!" He had barred him entry a thousand times from his pub! But people laughed as they recalled his wild vagabond's accoutrements, his mania for covering himself in flowers and crowning his brow with garlands like a savage, pretty much as soon as a drop of fermented wine reached his empty stomach.

The boat was getting into the lake itself. Between two great clumps of reeds, standing like breakwaters to a port appeared a huge expanse of flat open water, glittering, pale blue. It was the *lluent*, the true Albufera, the open lake with its little clumps of reeds scattered well apart, refuge for the birds hunted by the wildfowlers from the city. The boat coasted along the Dehesa side where several muddy enclosures were slowly being converted into rice paddies.

In a little lagoon walled off with mud banks a well-muscled man was emptying baskets of earth out of his boat. The passengers looked at him in admiration. This was Tono, son of "old *Paloma*" and himself father, in turn, to Tonet, "*El Cubano*". As they mentioned this last name many glanced mischievously at old *Cañamel* who carried on grunting away as if he heard nothing.

There was no harder worker in the whole of the Albufera than Tono. He had set himself the task, basket by basket, of becoming a landowner, to have his own rice paddies, not to live by fishing like the older *Paloma,* the oldest boatman on the Albufera; and all on his own (for his son, easily tiring of the size of the task , only helped him occasionally) he continued filling with earth, carried from a great distance, the deep pond let to him by a rich lady who otherwise did not know what to do with it.

It was a work of many years, perhaps of a lifetime, for a man on his own. Old *Paloma* used to joke about it; his son helped him from time to time, only to declare how tired he was after a few days; but Tono just carried on, his faith unbreakable, aided only by la *Borda,* a poor little kid that his dead wife had got from the orphanage, fearful of everyone, but ready for work as much as he was.

Hi, Tono, no rest for the wicked! Let's hope you get some rice soon from your field...and the boat slipped away without the stubborn labourer so much as lifting his head for moment to reply to the sarcastic comments.

A little further on they spied old *Paloma* himself, in a little punt no bigger than a coffin, next to a line of stakes, setting his nets for hauling the next day.

The passengers were discussing whether the old chap was ninety or nearer the hundred. What that man had seen without ever leaving la Albufera! The great personages he had done business with! And they went over his cheeky repartee, much enlarged in the popular imagination, with General Prim to whom he acted as boatman on shoots on the lake, his bluntness with great ladies and even with queens. The old man, seeming to guess what was being said but a bit fed up with talking about his former glory, remained bent, examining his nets, showing his back to them. He was wearing a large-checked blouse and a black soft hat pulled down to his rather leathery ears which seemed to stick out from his skull. As the mail boat passed, he raised his head, showing the black abyss of his toothless mouth and the ruddy lines of wrinkles circling the deep-set eyes twinkling with a mischief.

The wind was beginning to get up. The swelling sail shook in the freshening gusts and the boat heeled enough to wet the backsides of those sitting on the lee rail. The bubbling song of the surging bow wave was more and more obvious as they swept along. Now they were in the real Albufera, in the immense *lluent*, blue and flat as a Venetian mirror, reflecting the inverted images of boats and the soft undulations of the distant shoreline surrounding them. The clouds seemed to roll over the depths of the lake like white tufts of wool. On the Dehesa shore the outlines of some hunters, walking head down with their dogs, were mirrored in the water. On the landward side the bigger towns around la Ribera seemed to float over the lake, their surrounding fields hidden by the curve of the earth.

The freshening breeze changed the surface of la Albufera. The swell was felt more strongly, and the lake bottom disappeared, while on the shore of coarse shell sand, the waves began to throw up a yellowish line of foam, glittering with all the colours of the rainbow from the soapy bubbles glinting in the sunlight.

The boat swept along the length of la Dehesa, passing swiftly by the sand dunes with the game wardens huts on their summits, the dense thickets of brush, the clumps of twisted pines, whose fearful shapes suggested bunches of tortured limbs. The passengers, fired up by the speed and excited by the peril of being in a boat dragging its rails in the water, shouted greetings to boats passing in the distance and held out their hands to feel the shock of the surging waves. The water churned around the rudder. A short distance away two cormorants sat on the water, dark birds which could submerge and then resurface after a long time under, amusing the passengers with this method of fishing. Further away, in the "matas" the great islands of water reeds, coots and mallards took to the air as the boat approached, slowly, as if knowing that these people came in peace. Some folk flushed with excitement at seeing them. What a great shot! Why do people have to prosecute any chap that shoots without a permit, as they see fit? And while the more fiery got their tempers up, the moans of the sick man still could be heard in the boat and the childish whining of old *Cañamel*, bothered by the rays of the setting sun hitting him under the edge of his parasol.

The woods here seemed further away towards the sea, leaving between it and the Albufera a wide expanse of low ground covered in rough vegetation dotted at intervals with the limpid waters of little lagoons.

This was the plain of Sancha. A flock of goats guarded by a little boy was grazing among the shrubs and seeing him reminded the sons of the Albufera of the tradition that gave its name to the plain.

The folk from inland, who were returning home after making a good rate at the harvest, asked who was this "Sancha" that women spoke of with real fear, so the lake folk told the outsiders the simple legend which they all learned as children.

A little shepherd boy, like the one now walking along the shore, in former times used to pasture his goats on that same plain. But this was many years ago, lads, so many that not one of the old boys still living on the Albufera knew the chap, not even old *Paloma*.

The lad used to live like a savage in the solitude, and lake fishermen would hear him calling from far away on calm mornings:

-Sancha! Sancha!

Sancha was a little snake, the only friend he had. The evil beast would come to his calls and the shepherd boy, sorting out his best goats, would offer him a bowl of milk. Later, at the height of the day, the boy would fashion a pipe by cutting a couple of stems from a reed bed and would play softly while the reptile at his feet would partly raise itself up and sway as if it wanted to dance to the gentle rhythm of the music. On other occasions the boy would amuse himself by undoing Sancha's coils, stretching him out straight on the sand and taking delight in the nervous impulse that impelled him to coil up again. When, tiring of these games, he would take his flock to the other side of the great plain, the snake would follow him like a little puppy, or coiling himself round his feet slithered up to his neck and lay there still, as if dead with his eyes, glittering like diamonds, fixed on the shepherd boy's, making the fluff on his face stand on end with the caress of his forked tongue.

People around the Albufera thought the lad was a magician, and more than one woman stealing firewood from la Dehesa would cross herself as if it were the Devil himself when she saw him coming with Sancha coiled round his neck. So everybody understood how the goatherd was able to sleep in the woods without being frightened of the huge reptiles that swarmed in the undergrowth. Sancha, who must be the Devil, was guarding him against any danger.

The snake grew and the goatherd was already a man when the inhabitants of the Albufera stopped seeing him around. It was known that he was a soldier and was off fighting in the Italian wars. No other herd had gone back to graze the pastures of that wild plain. Fishermen making a landing did not like to venture among the tall reed beds covering the pestilential lagoons. Without the milk which the goatherd used to so freely give him, Sancha now had to pursue the countless rabbits in the Dehesa.

Eight or ten years had passed when one day the inhabitants of El Saler saw a soldier come down the road from Valencia leaning on a stick, with his pack on his back, a scrawny, pallid grenadier with black gaiters almost up to his knees, white greatcoat with red cloth bobbles and a mitred cap over his plaited locks. His great moustaches did not stop people recognising him. It was the little goatherd, back to revisit the scenes of his childhood. Keeping to the lakeside, he set off for the woods and got to the boggy plain where in former times he had looked after his flock. No one. Softly buzzing dragonflies darted among the tall reed beds and frogs, startled by the grenadier's sudden presence, croaked in the hidden ponds under the thickets.

-Sancha! Sancha! The former goatherd called softly.

Absolute silence. The drowsy song of a fisherman toiling in the middle of the lake drifted over him.

-Sancha! Sancha! He called again with all the breath he could muster.

Only when he had repeated his call many times did he see the tall grasses waving and hear the crack of broken reeds as if a huge body were dragging itself along. Among the reeds gleamed two eyes, level with his own, as a flat head advanced, flickering its forked tongue with a sudden ill-humoured hiss that seemed to freeze his blood and still his heart. This was Sancha, but now enormous, raising himself to the height of a man, his tail coiling away into the depths of the undergrowth until lost to view, his skin gleaming with every colour of the rainbow and his body as big as a tree trunk.

- Sancha! cried the soldier, stepping back in fear, how you've grown, how big you are!

He tried to flee. But having got over his initial surprise his old friend seemed to recognise him and looped around his shoulders, his rough skin shuddering with nervous excitement and squeezing him tight in his coils.

-Let me go, Sancha, let me go! cried the soldier, struggling, You're too big now for these games.

Another coil gripped his arms, pinning them. The reptile's flickering tongue caressed him as in former days; its breath stirred his moustaches, making him shiver in fear, while the coils relentlessly contracted and tightened until the soldier fell to the ground, asphyxiated, his bones cracking, completely enveloped in the painted coils.

Some fishermen found his body a few days later, a formless mass, every bone broken, and the flesh crushed by Sancha's irresistible grip. And so, the little goatherd died, victim of an embrace from his old friend.

The outsiders in the mail boat roared with laughter on hearing the tale while women shifted their feet in some disquiet, with the feeling that what was stirring around their skirts was Sancha hidden in the boat's bilge.

They were coming to the end of the lake. Once more the boat entered a network of canals and in the distance, in the far distance the houses of El Saler were standing out above the flat immensity of the paddy fields, the nearest little town on the Albufera to Valencia, with a port full of countless small boats and large vessels whose great wooden masts standing like stripped pine trees, filled the horizon.

Evening was falling. The boat slipped ever more slowly along the still waters. The shadow of the sail passed like a cloud over the paddies, reddened by the setting sun and the silhouettes of the passengers stood out on the bank against the orange background.

People returning from their fields passed continuously, punting along in little boats, tiny craft with their gunwales at water level. These punts were the work horses of the Albufera. Everyone born into that lake-dwelling tribe learned to handle one from childhood. They were essential for working in the fields, for getting to a neighbour's house, for making one's living. No sooner would a child pass, when it would be a woman and then an old man, all effortlessly using the pole, pressing on the slimy bottom to make the tiny shoe which served them as a boat slip through the still waters.

In ditches alongside, other small boats slid by, invisible behind the banks, but above the reeds their boatmen moved them forward, standing motionless, driven by the gentle working of their hands.

From time to time the folk in the mail boat would see wide breaches open in the bank through which, soundlessly and with no apparent motion, the canal water flowed, sleeping under a blanket of clinging floating vegetation. Eel nets hanging from stakes closed off these entrances. As the boat approached the paddies, enormous rats would leap into the water to disappear into the mud along the ditches.

The people who had earlier risen to the thrill of the chase on spotting the wildfowl on the lake now felt their pulses race again, seeing those rats along the canals. What a great shot! What a lovely dinner!

Amid laughter and protest from the folk from the Albufera, the landlubbers could only spit disgustedly at the thought. A delicious mouthful! How could they comment without ever having tried it? Marsh rats ate nothing but rice; they were the food of princes. You only had to see them in the market at Sueca, gutted and hanging in dozens by their long tails on the butchers' stalls. Rich people bought them; the nobility in towns in la Ribera ate nothing else. And *Cañamel,* in his capacity as a rich man himself, felt it necessary to say his bit. He stopped whining to pronounce gravely that he knew of only two creatures in the whole world that were devoid of any bitterness, the pigeon and the rat; and with that nothing more remained to be said.

Conversation became livelier. The outsiders' expressions of disgust served as a wake-up call to the Albufera folk. The physical debility of the lake dwellers, the miserable condition of people deprived of meat, whose only acquaintance with animals was with those seen running off into the distance in la Dehesa, who lived condemned to a diet of eels and coarse fish, resulted in a visible desire to outrage, to boast, to astonish the outsiders by spicy tales of their daring dishes. Women recounted the delights of rat paella;

many had eaten it without being aware they were doing so, simply astonished by the flavour of this unknown meat. Others recalled snake stews, the well flavoured soft white slices, much better than eel, and the earless boatman broke the silence he had kept throughout the voyage to talk of a certain cat which had just given birth, which he had eaten with some friends in the *Cañamel* tavern after it was ordered by a seaman, who, after sailing all round the world, would have paid anything for such a dish.

It was starting to get dark. The fields were sinking into blackness. The canal took on a whitish lustre, gleaming like tinplate in the faint twilight. The reflections of the first stars, glinting in the depths of the water, trembled with the boat's passing.

They were nearing El Saler. Over the roofs of the cottages rose the great bell on its two pillars fronting the *Casa de La Deman*á, the historic building where shots and their boatmen gathered on the eve of shoots to draw pegs for the following day.

Next to the building was a huge diligence, the stagecoach ready to convey passengers from the mail boat into the city of Valencia.

The breeze faded; the sail hung loose along the yard and the earless one seized his pole, leaning on the banks to punt the craft forward.

A small boat laden with earth passed, heading back towards the lake. A girl poled vigorously in the prow aided, from the opposite end by a young man with a wide straw hat.

Everyone knew them. They were Tono's kids, taking earth to his field: *la Borda,* that indefatigable foundling, who was worth more than any man, and Tonet, *El Cubano*, grandson of Old *Paloma*, the handsomest lad in the whole of the Albufera, a man who had seen the world and something to say for himself.

- Cheers, *Bigòt,* some called familiarly.

They gave him this nickname on account of the moustache shading his dark-complexioned face, an old-fashioned adornment in La Albufera, where everyone else was clean shaven. Others asked, in mock astonishment, since when was he doing any work.

The little boat made off with Tonet, who only managed a rapid glance at the passengers, seeming heedless of the joking remarks.

Many of them looked over rather insolently at *Cañamel*, giving vent to the same vulgar comments common in his tavern. Watch out Old Paco! You're heading to Valencia, while Tonet would be spending the night in El Palmar!

Initially, the innkeeper pretended not to hear them, until, tired of putting up with it, he raised himself with a start, a flash of anger in his eyes. But the greasy weight of his body seemed to bear down on his will, and he crumpled back on the seat, as if crushed by the effort, whining pitifully again, and muttering between groans:

Indesents! ...Bastards!

CHAPTER 2

Old Paloma's cottage was erected at one end of El Palmar. A huge fire had split the village and changed the look of it. Half was consumed in the flames. The thatched cottages quickly turned to ashes, and their owners, wanting to live from then on without the constant fear of fire, built brick houses on the razed plots, many of them using up their meagre fortunes to bring in the materials which ended up costing a lot after having to cross the lake. The end of the village which suffered in the fire was covered in little houses, their fronts painted in pink, green or blue. The other part of El Palmar retained its primitive aspect, with the roofs of the cottages rounded front and back, like boats placed upside down on the mud walls.

From the little church square to the end of the village towards la Dehesa, the cottages lay scattered at random, well separated from each other for fear of fire.

Old *Paloma's* was the oldest. It had been built by his father in the days when not a human soul could be found on la Albufera who did not shake with fever.

The brush in those days came right up to the cottage walls. As Old *Paloma* used to tell it, the hens would disappear through the cottage door, and when they reappeared a few weeks later they would bring after them a clutch of recently hatched chicks. Otters were still hunted in the canals and the lakeside population was so sparse that boatmen did not know what to do with the fish that filled their nets. For them, Valencia was at the other end of the world, and the only person who came from there was Marshall Suchet, appointed Duke of La Albufera by the King, lord of the lake and the forest with all their riches.

The memory of this man was the earliest that Old *Paloma* could recall. The old man even thought he had seen him, with his hair awry and his wide sideburns, clad in a riding coat and broad round hat, surrounded by men in splendid uniforms carrying his guns. The Marshall used to shoot from Old *Paloma's* father's boat while the little lad, perched in the prow gazed on admiringly. He used to laugh at the broken Valencian the

Caudillo used to express himself, lamenting the backwardness of the country or commenting on events in a war between the Spanish and the English of which people on the lake had only the vaguest notion.

One time he went to Valencia with his father to present the Duke of la Albufera with an eel notable for its huge size, and the Marshall himself had received them, smiling, wearing a wonderful uniform, glittering with gold braid, in the midst of officers who appeared as satellites of his heavenly splendour.

By the time Old *Paloma* was a grown man, with his father dead and himself owner of the cottage and two boats, the Dukes of la Albufera were already no more, and Bailiffs ruled over the lake in the name of the King, their master, excellent gentlemen from the city who never came near the lake, allowing the fishermen to roam the Dehesa and freely hunt the birds which lived in the reed beds.

Those were the good times, and when old Tio used to recall them in his cracked old man's voice during discussions in the *Cañamel* tavern, the young folk would shiver with excitement. They used to fish and shoot with no fear of guards or fines. People would return home at night with dozens of rabbits ferreted in the Dehesa, not to mention baskets of fish and strings of birds shot in the reeds. It was all the King's, and the King was far away. It wasn't like nowadays, when the Albufera belonged to the "State" (whoever this gentleman might be!) and there were permit holders for the shooting and tenants on the Dehesa, and poor folk couldn't fire a shot or gather a bundle of firewood without a keeper jumping out on them with his badge on his chest and his carbine pointing at theirs.

Old *Paloma* had hung on to his father's privileges. He was Premier Boatman on the lake and no great personage arrived on the Albufera that he did not convey among the islets pointing out the curiosities of land and water. He remembered Isabel ll as a young woman, filling the entire stern of the much-decorated little boat with her ample skirts, her budding breasts rising in time as the boatman poled it through the water. People laughed when they recalled his trip over the lake with the Empress Eugenia, she forward in the bow, slim, dressed like an Amazon, with her shotgun always at the ready, downing birds which skilful beaters put up for her in droves from the reed beds with sticks and shouts, while at the other end of the boat stood wily, mischievous old *Paloma*, his ancient fowling piece between his legs, knocking down the birds that escaped the great lady while alerting her in his uniquely fantastic Castellano , to the appearance of any mallards: Look out, your Majesty, behind thee cometh a Milord !

All these great personages were very appreciative of the old boatman. He was admittedly insolent, with all the rough manners of a son of the lake; but however much his rough tongue might fail to attract compliments, it was all more than compensated for by his gun, a venerable weapon, so much repaired that it was difficult to discern what remained of the original construction. *Paloma* was a prodigious shot. Story tellers around the lake could embroider tales at his expense, to the point of alleging that on one occasion he had downed four coots with a single shot. When he wanted to flatter some great man who was just an average shot, he would position himself behind him in the boat and fire at the same instant with such precision that the two shots rang out as one and the client, seeing the game fall, stood amazed at his prowess while the boatman at his back slyly ground his teeth.

His best memory was of General Prim. He got to know him one stormy night in a passage across the lake. Those were the days when he was out of favour. The militia was patrolling nearby. The General was disguised as a labourer and was fleeing Valencia after having unsuccessfully tried to raise the garrison. Old *Paloma* conveyed him to the sea, and when, years later, he saw him again he was head of the Government and the idol of the nation. He would escape Madrid sometimes, abandoning the life of politics to shoot on the lake, and old *Paloma*, boldly familiar after his past adventures, would give him a proper telling off, as if he were just any lad, if he made a mess of a shot. Human greatness was not an issue for him; men were just divided into good and bad shots. When the hero fired but missed, the old boatman would get so angry that he dropped the formalities and started using a familiar form of address. "General...rubbish! Were you the brave lad that did such great stuff in Morocco? Look! Look and learn!" and while his glorious pupil laughed, the boatman would fire his blunderbuss almost without aiming and a coot would tumble into the water in a ball of feathers.

All these stories added to old *Paloma's* standing among the people of the lake. What a man he must have been to open his mouth and speak that way to his customers! But he carried on, forever rough and foul-mouthed, treating the great and the good like pals at the bar, making them laugh at his insolence in ill-humoured moments or with his tortured use of phrases in Castellano and Valenciano when he wanted to appear more amiable.

He was content with his lot, even when it became

harder and more difficult to bear as he got older. A boatman, just a boatman, always a boatman! He despised the people who cultivated the rice paddies. They were "labourers" and for him that word was the greatest of insults.

He was proud of being a waterman and would often prefer to follow the twists and turns of a canal rather than cut the distance by walking along the bank. He did not willingly set foot on land other than on the Dehesa, and then only in order to fire a few shots at the rabbits before making off at the approach of the keepers, and by choice would have eaten and slept on the boat which was for him like the carapace of an aquatic animal. The old man kept well preserved the instincts of his primitive ancestral lake dwellers.

To make his happiness complete the only thing missing was to be free of his family, to live like a fish in the lake or a bird in the reeds, making his nest today on an islet and tomorrow on a canal. But his father had taken steps to get him married. He did not want to see that cottage, built with his own hands, lying abandoned, and the bohemian waterman found himself forced to live in society with people like him, to sleep under a thatched roof, to pay his dues for the maintenance of the priest and to obey the island's mayor, always some good-for-nothing, according to him, who sought the protection of the big boys in the city in order to avoid having to do any work.

Of his wife, he now retained in his memory only the vaguest image. She had rubbed along with him over many years without leaving any impression other than her skill at mending nets and the stylish way she kneaded the weekly bread every Friday before taking it to the round, white-domed oven, like an African ant heap, erected at the far end of the island.

They had had many children, very many; but apart from one, all of them had died "appropriately enough". They were pale creatures and sickly, bred with their thoughts fixed on food, to parents who coupled solely from a desire to feel each other's heat, shaking with malarial rigors. They seemed to be born carrying in their veins the cold fluid of tertian fever instead of blood. Some had died of consumption, weakened by the insipid diet of freshwater fish, others drowned after falling into canals around the house, and while one survived, the youngest, it was only by clinging stubbornly to life in a mad panic to stay alive, standing up to the fevers and sucking from his mother's flabby breasts the meagre sap of her diseased body.

Old *Paloma* found these misfortunes logical and indeed necessary. Praise was due to the Lord, ever mindful of the poor. It was awful to see destitute families growing ever larger in misery; without the goodness of God, who cleared out this plague of kids from time to time, there wouldn't be enough food in the lake for everyone and they would have to eat one another.

Old *Paloma's* wife died when he was already an old man and father to a lad of seven. The boatman and his son, Tono, stayed on their own in the cottage. The boy was wise and a worker like his mother. He cooked the meals, made repairs around the house, and learned from the neighbours so that his father wouldn't notice the lack of a woman in the home. He did everything with gravitas, as if the terrible struggle required to simply exist had left in him an indelible streak of sadness.

The father was always clearly happiest heading for the boat with his son at his heels, almost hidden by a bundle of nets. The boy grew quickly, becoming stronger by the day, and old *Paloma* was proud seeing how he could whip the eel nets out of the water or punt the boat smoothly over the Albufera.

- He's a man among men in the whole Albufera, his friends would say, what he is today comes from what he suffered when he was small.

The Albufera women found no less to praise in

his steady ways. No nonsense with the young folk who would meet in the tavern, none of the inevitable losses in the card games which, with fishing finished for the day, would be held lying on the ground behind some cottage, making the most of a measly hand.

Always serious and ready for work, Tono gave his father not the slightest cause for disapproval. Old *Paloma*, a man who could not work with anyone else, because at the slightest mistake he would fly into a rage and lash out at his companion, never used to get into any disputes with his son, for if ever he tried barking out an ill-humoured order, the lad, guessing what was needed, would already have set his hand to the task.

When Tono was a grown man, his father, this enthusiast for the wandering life, for throwing off the shackles of family ties, suddenly felt the same anxieties as the older Paloma, his father, had. What were these two men doing, living, cut off on their own in this old cottage? He felt awful seeing his son, this big strong man crouching over the hearth in the middle of the dwelling, blowing on the fire, preparing the meal. Often times he would feel a pang of remorse looking at his hairy hands with their stubby fingers of steel, scrubbing the pots or scattering the stiff, iridescent scales of some big fish with a knife.

On winter nights they were like two shipwrecked mariners on a desert island. Never a word between them, not a laugh, no woman's voice to cheer them. The cottage was sunk in gloom. In the centre of the floor burned the cooking fire, a brick-bordered square of earth. Opposite was the kitchen bench, with its meagre stock of pots, pans and old tiles, and on each side the wattle and daub partitions of two rooms, made of reeds and mud like the rest of the house. Above these partitions which were only up to head height, stretched the whole interior of the roof space, black with layers of soot laid down by the smoking fires of many years which had no means of escape other than the gap in the peak of the thatch through which the gusts of winter gales whistled. Hanging from the roof was the two men's waterproof gear used for night fishing; heavy stiff trousers, jackets with a pole stuck through the sleeves, the canvas greasy, glinting yellow and well rubbed with olive oil. The wind coming through the hole that acted as a chimney made these strange rag dolls swing to and fro, reflecting the red light of the fire from their oily surface. It looked like the cottage's two inhabitants had hung themselves from the rafters.

Old *Paloma* was bored stiff. He liked to talk; in the tavern he would swear away to his heart's content, make fun of the other fishermen, enlighten them with his memories of the great men he had known, but at home he didn't know what to say, his conversation didn't warrant the slightest reply from his son, silent and obedient, lost for words in the respectful but boring, boring silence. With rough good humour the old boatman would declare it at the top of his voice in the tavern. That son of his was a very good man but not like him at all, always silent and submissive. His dearly departed must have put a spell on him!

One day he confronted Tono, his expression brooking no opposition, a true father in the Roman style, who considers that his children have no free will and disposes of their future and their lives without consultation. He had to get married; that was what was wrong; they lacked a woman in the house. Tono received this order just as if he had been told to get the boat ready to go to el Saler and pick up a shot from Valencia. It was all good. He would try to comply with his father's order as soon as possible.

So, while the lad cast around on his own account, the old boatman put his proposal to the womenfolk of El Palmar. His Tono wanted to get married. Everything he owned would be the boy's; the cottage, the big boat with one new sail and one old one which was even better, two punts, nets, he couldn't remember how many nets and, more than all this, the characteristics of the boy himself, a serious worker, with no vices, not liable for military service as a result of getting a good number in the draft. In all, it might not be a great match, but his Tono wasn't a pig in a poke! He was worth something and given what was available among the girls in El Palmar.... Well!

With his disdain for women, the old man felt like throwing up, as he looked round the young ladies among whom lurked unseen his future daughter-in-law. No; they weren't any great shakes, those virgins of the lake, with their clothes washed in the putrid canal water, smelling of mud, their hands impregnated with sticky slime that seemed to penetrate to their very marrow. Their hair bleached by the sun, dull and colourless, provided sparse shade for their scrawny, sunburned faces, in which the eyes burned with the fire of fever that came back every time they drank the lake water. Their angular profile, the artful, slippery movements of their bodies and their animal smell, like shepherdesses, gave them a certain resemblance to eels, as if the constant monotonous diet over many generations had ended up embedding in them the traces of the very creature that sustained them.

Tono chose one, any one, the one that offered the least resistance to his timid advances. The marriage was made official, and the old man had one more human soul to talk to and tussle with. He took a certain satisfaction in finding that his words didn't just disappear into the ether, and that his daughter-in-law resisted his ill-humoured demands.

But there was a downside to this satisfaction. His son seemed to be forgetting the family tradition. He was turning his back on the lake to seek a way of life among the fields, and in September, when they were harvesting the rice and the rates were high, he abandoned the boat, becoming a day labourer like so many others who aroused the ire of old *Paloma*. It was for the outsiders, for folk that lived well away from the Albufera, this job of working in the mud, of suffering the torment of the fields. Sons of the lake were unbound by such slavery. God had placed them next to that blessed stretch of water for a reason. Food lay in its depths, and it was nonsense, a shame, to spend all day in mud up to your waist, your legs eaten alive by leeches and your back burnt in the sun, cutting grain which in the end did not belong to you. Was his son going to turn himself into a "hired hand"? In putting the question, the old man infused his words with a sense of complete astonishment, of the virtual impossibility echoing unspoken in the notion, as if suggesting it was as likely that one day the Albufera would dry up.

For the first time in his life Tono dared to go

against to his father's thinking. As always, he would continue fishing for the rest of the season. But now he was married, and he had bigger concerns at home, so it would be foolish to turn up his nose at the terrific wages paid during the harvest. And they paid him even better than others on account of his strength and enthusiasm for work. One had to take opportunities as they arose; more rice was being grown all the time around the lake, the old ponds were being filled in and the poor were making themselves rich, so he wasn't going to be so stupid as to miss out on his share in this new way of life.

Grumbling under his breath, the old boatman accepted this turn around in the way the house was run. His son's common-sense and seriousness inspired a certain respect, but he still complained, leaning with his pole on the canal bank, chatting with other boatmen of the same vintage. They were going to transform the Albufera! No one would recognise it in a few years. Down by Sueca they were setting up some huge iron contraptions among groups of little houses with huge chimneys, and boy, did they belt out smoke. The quiet, friendly old water mills with their rotting wooden wheels and black conduits were going to be changed for infernal machines that chucked out water with a racket like a thousand devils. It would be a miracle if all the fishing wasn't completely spoilt by such innovations and driven out to sea. They were going to end up farming the whole area, piling more and more earth into the lake. In the little time left to him he might even have to watch the last eel, with no more space left, waving its tail as it headed down the Perelló channel to disappear into the Mediterranean. And Tono was up to his neck in this piratical enterprise! That he should have to see his own son, a *Paloma*, turned into a "hired hand". And the old man would laugh out loud at the thought of such an unlikely eventuality.

Time went by, and his daughter-in-law gave him a grandson, Tonet, whom his grandfather would carry on many an afternoon down to the canal bank, tilting up the pipe clamped in his toothless jaws so the smoke wouldn't upset the little boy. What a devil of a lad, and so good looking! His ugly, lanky great daughter-in-law was like all the women in the family, the same as his own dearly departed, producing children that in no way resembled his parents. Cuddling the child, the grandfather's thoughts would turn to the future as he showed him off to the diminishing group of his boyhood friends, predicting that:

- This chap will be one of us; he'll have no home but his boat and before he's lost his first teeth, he'll already be handling a punt pole.

But before the teeth were out, what happened to old *Paloma* was the thing he least expected in all his life. They told him in the tavern that Tono had taken a rent on some rice paddies near Saler, the property of a lady from Valencia, and when he confronted his son in the evening, was astounded that he did not deny the crime.

When had a *Paloma* ever seen himself as a proprietor? The family had always lived in freedom, as befitted any self-respecting son of God, seeking their sustenance in the air or the water, by shooting or fishing. Their masters had been the King himself or that Froggy warrior, who was Captain General of Valencia, proprietors who lived far-away, who didn't impose themselves and could be tolerated on account of their high standing. But a son of his, tenant of some lanky city bitch, every year handing over part of his labour in ringing coinage. Come on, man! He was just ready to set off to have a talk with that lady and undo the contract. *Palomas* served no man as long as there remained in the lake something to put in their mouths to eat, be it even frogs.

But the old man's surprise was even greater when he faced resistance from Tono. He had thought long and hard on the matter and felt he had nothing to regret. He was thinking of his wife and that tiny child she carried in her arms, and he was ambitious for them. What were they after all? Beggars on the lake, living like savages in that cottage with nothing to eat but the animals in the ditches and having to flee like criminals from the keepers whenever they shot some bird to liven up the stew pot. Parasites on the wildfowlers, who only ate meat when those outsiders allowed them to dip into their provisions. And this miserable existence just carried on and on, from father to son, as if they were stuck forever in the Albufera mud, with no more aspirations in life than the toad who thinks himself happy in the reedbed because he finds plenty of insects on the water.

No, he was having none of it, he wanted to lift his family from this miserable servitude, to work not only to live but to save. You had to focus on the advantages of rice as a crop; little work and plenty of reward. It was a true blessing from heaven: nothing in the world gave a better return. It was sown in June and harvested in September: a little fertiliser and a little labour and that was all; three months; once the harvest was in, the lake water, swollen by the winter rains, would cover the fields and then it was on to the next year. The profits would look after themselves and there was fishing in the clear light of day and a bit of shooting at other times to see the family through. What more could he want? Grandfather had been poor and during a dog's life was only able to build that cottage where they lived in a fug of eternal smoke. His father, whom he greatly respected, had not managed to save so much as a crust for his old age. Just let him work his will and his son, little Tonet, would be a rich man, working fields stretching out of sight, and perhaps on the site of the cottage they would, in time, build a house better than any in the whole of El Palmar. His father was doing the wrong thing, getting angry because his progeny was tilling the soil. It made more sense to be a farm labourer than to live wandering the lake, often hungry and at risk of being shot by a keeper on the Dehesa.

Old *Paloma*, pale with rage as he listened, was staring fixedly at a pole lying along the wall, and his hands moved towards it ready to break it over his son's head. Had such rebelliousness happened in other times, he would certainly have done so, considering himself within his rights as an old-fashioned father.

But he became aware of his daughter in law standing with his grandson in her arms and the pair seemed to make his son grow in stature, putting him on the same level. He too was a father and his equal. For the first time he realised that Tono was no longer the little boy who tended the stew, as in former times, lowering his head in terror at one of his father's glances. So, trembling with rage at not being able to hit him as he used to when he made some stupid mistake in the boat, all he could do was to let his breath escape in a groan of protest. It was fine, each to his own, one to the lake and the other to flatten his fields. They would live together, given there was nothing else for it. As he dragged out an increasingly rheumaticky old age, he no longer was able to sleep in the middle of the lake, but apart from that why should they not get along. Oh, if the patriarchal *Paloma* were to raise his head, that old boatman from Suchet, and see the family thus dishonoured!

The first year was one of incessant torment for the old man. Getting back to the cottage of an evening he would find agricultural tools lying among his fishing stuff. One day he fell over a plough that Tono had dragged back to *terra firma* to put back together in the evening, which he could easily have mistaken for a huge dragon lying in the middle of the cottage floor. These steels blades brought him out in a cold fury. He only needed to see a scythe dumped within a few feet of his nets to feel that the curved blade could move on its own and slice its way through his precious kit, so he would give his daughter in law a telling off for her carelessness, shouting at her at the top of his voice that she should get those "labourer's tools" out of the way, far out of the way. There was farm stuff everywhere! And that in the *Palomas'* very cottage, where up till then, folk had never known anything about steel other than the gutting knife for cleaning the fish. Man, it was enough to make to you burst with fury!

At sowing time, when the fields were dry for the ploughing, Tono would come back sweating having spent the whole day following the hired team. His father would roam about him sniffing in mischievous satisfaction before rushing off to the tavern where his comrades from the old days were found dozing with a glass in hand. Great news, gentlemen! His son smelt like a horse! Ha-ha! A horse on the island of El Palmar! The world had turned upside down.

Such cheeky behaviour apart, old *Paloma* maintained a cold and distant attitude in the bosom of his son's family.

He would come into the cottage at night with a *monot* in his arms, a net sack with wooden rings containing some eels, and would kick his daughter in law aside to give him some room at the hearth. He prepared the meal himself. Sometimes he would slice them up with a blade to grill them on an *ast*, or griddle, patiently browning them on all sides over the flames. Other times he would go off to the boat in search of his ancient and much mended pot to cook some enormous tench in its own juice, or to make a *sebollo*, a stew of eels and onions enough to feed half the village.

That scrawny little old man had the appetite of all the ancient sons of the lake. He only ate a proper meal at night, on returning to the cottage, when, sitting in a corner with the pot between his knees, he would pass whole hours, in silence, his jaws masticating like an old goat, taking in enormous quantities of food such as seemed impossible for the human stomach to contain.

He ate his own food, what he had taken during the day, taking no notice of what the young people were eating not offering them any from his own pot. Let everybody eat their fill from their own labour. His eyes would gleam with malign satisfaction when he saw that the only food on the family's table was a meagre bowl of rice, while he gnawed the bones of some bird shot in the middle of a reed bed when he saw the keepers were well away.

Tono left his father to do as he wanted. He did not have to think any more about giving in to his father, while the distance continued to grow between the old man and the family. Little Tonet was the only thing keeping them together. On many occasions his grandson would go over to the old man, as if attracted by the good smells coming from his cooking pot.

-Tin, pobret, tin, have some, ye poor wee thing, have some! his grandpa would say lovingly as if the little chap was in a really piteous state, handing him some rich, filling, coot thigh, smiling as he watched the little chap devour it. When he put together some *all y pebre*, eels with garlic and peppers, with his old drinking buddies in the tavern, he would bring some home for his grandson without so much as a word to his parents.

Other times there was more to celebrate. In the early morning, old *Paloma*, itching for adventure, would be stepping out of the boat in the thickets of the Dehesa with some companion as old as he was. There would be a long wait, lying flat on their bellies among the bushes, spying on the keepers who were completely ignorant of their presence, so that when the rabbits came out, hopping around the stalks of the undergrowth, Bang! Bang! Two in the bag and run, into the boat, and then a good laugh from the middle of the lake, watching the keepers on the shore vainly casting about for the poachers. These capers made old *Paloma* feel young again. You should have heard him in the evening, cooking up the game in the tavern with his buddies, who were paying for the wine; how he revelled in his deeds! No lad nowadays was up to anything like it! And when the more prudent among them mentioned the law and its penalties, the old boatman would proudly straighten his ancient frame, bent by years of working the pole. Those keepers were lazy bums who took wages because they couldn't stand working, and the gentlemen who rented the shoots were a bunch of robbers who wanted everything for themselves. The Albufera was his, with all the fishermen. Had they been born in a palace they would be kings. When God had decreed that they should be born there, it was for a purpose. Nothing else was true, people just made it up as they went along.

And after dinner, when there was hardly any wine left in the *porrones* old *Paloma* would look at his grandson asleep on his lap and show him to his friends. That little lad would be a true son of the Albufera. He was taking charge of his education, so he wouldn't follow his father and step out of line. He would handle a gun with astonishing ease, he would get to know the depths of the lake like an eel, and when grandad died everyone coming to shoot would find a boat with another *Paloma*, but looking younger, rather like him when the queen herself came to sit in his little punt and laugh at his witty remarks.

Such tenderness apart, the animosity between the boatman and his son continued under the surface. He had no wish to see the detested fields he was working, but they were always in his mind, and he laughed with devilish glee on learning that Tono's affairs were going badly. The first year, nitrates got into the soil just as the rice was setting seed and he almost lost the crop. Old *Paloma* talked with delight about his bad luck but when he saw the resulting unhappiness at home, and the penny pinching because of the costs, which were all for nothing, he felt a certain softening of his attitude, to the point of breaking his silence with his son to give him some advice. Wasn't he convinced now, that he was really a waterman and no farm labourer? He ought to leave fields to the folk from up country who, from way back, had spent their lives working them. He was the son of a fisherman and nets needed to be drawn.

But Tono's reply was a couple of ill-humoured snorts, making clear his determination to carry right on, so the old man sank back into hateful silence. The stubborn so and so! From then on, he wished down every sort of calamity upon his son's fields as a means of overcoming his stubborn pride. At home he said not a word, but out on the lake, when he came across some great hulk making its way from the direction of El Saler he would find out how the harvest was going and felt a glow of satisfaction on learning that it was to be a bad year. His stubborn son was going to die of hunger. In order to stay alive, he was even going to have to beg on bended knee for the keys to the old fish tank with the collapsed straw roof which he still had near El Palmar.

The storms at the end of summer filled him with joy. He prayed for the cataracts of heaven to open, for the Torrent gorge, which discharged into the Albufera to be filled from side to side with surging waters, that the lake should burst its banks, flooding the fields as it did sometimes, drowning the grain ready to harvest. The farm workers would die of hunger but that was no reason to think that for him the fishing would fail, and he would have the pleasure of seeing his son gnawing his knuckles and begging his protection.

Fortunately for Tono, the perverse old man's wishes did not come to pass. The following years were good ones. A feeling of well-being reigned in the cottage; there was enough to eat, and the energetic farm labourer, in bliss beyond his wildest dreams, began to think about the possibility of one day tilling fields that were his own, with no obligation to go into the city once a year to hand over the takings from almost his entire harvest.

Then something happened in the life of the family. Tonet was growing up and his mother was becoming depressed. The boy would go off to the lake with his grandfather and later, when he was older, he would accompany his father to the fields while the poor woman spent all day alone in the cottage. She thought about the future and the prospect of this life of solitude filled her with fear. If only she could have other children! Her fervent prayer to God was for a daughter. But no daughter came and indeed couldn't come according to old *Paloma's* opinion. His daughter-in- law was all out of sorts: women's troubles. Her neighbours in El Palmar had assisted her in labour, leaving her in a state that meant it was one thing after another, according to the old boy. This was why she always seemed to be unwell, pale as chewed paper, unable to keep her feet for long without a whimper, her step some days so faltering as to be on the point of falling headlong, holding in her tears and groans so as not to upset the menfolk.

Tono worried about how to get what his wife wanted. He had no objections to having a little girl in the house; she could be useful as a help to the sick woman, so the pair made a trip to the city, returning with a little girl of six, a timid, ugly little surly beast, that they got from the foundlings' home. She was called Visanteta, but so they wouldn't forget where she came from, and with the unfeeling cruelty of the common herd, they called her *La Borda*, the Gunwale.

The old boatman grumbled angrily. One more

mouth to feed! Little Tonet, now ten, found the little girl much to his taste, someone to suffer the capricious demands of the much-loved only son.

The only succour La *Borda* found in the cottage was from that sick woman, who became weaker and more racked with pain every passing day. In the unhappy woman's mind, the illusion began to grow that she actually had a daughter and, getting her to sit down of an afternoon facing the sun in the cottage door, she would comb her red curls, well lubricated with olive oil.

She was like a little puppy, lively and obedient, who cheered the house with her running to and fro, never tiring, putting up with all Tonet's mischief. With a supreme effort of her little arms, she dragged a pitcher of clean water from the Dehesa, as big as herself, all the way from the canal to the house. She was really frightened of old *Paloma*, with his silences and fierce glances. She would run to the village at all hours on errands for her new mother, and at table ate with her eyes down, not daring to put her own spoon in the pot until everyone was almost half finished the meal. Since the two little rooms were occupied, one by the married couple and other by Tonet and his grandfather, she slept at night next to the hearth, on a bed of mud seeping through the tiles which served for her bed, covering herself with nets to ward off the gusts of wind that blew down the chimney and under the door which was falling to bits and well gnawed by the rats.

Her only time to relax was in the afternoon when, with everything quiet in the village and the men out on the lake or in the fields, she would sit at the cottage door sewing sails or weaving nets with her mother. The two of them would chat with their neighbours in the great silence of the single, winding street, covered in grass among which strutted hens and squawking ducks, stretching their damp white wings to dry in the sun.

Tonet wasn't going anymore to the village school, a damp hovel paid for by the city authorities, where an evil smelling confusion of boys and girls would spend the day reciting the alphabet and intoning prayers in the nasal accents of the schoolroom.

He was, according to his grandfather quite a man now, slapping him on the chest as he tested his arms to see how strong they were. By his age, old *Paloma* had been able to live off what he caught and had shot every type of bird that lived on the Albufera.

The boy enthusiastically followed his grandfather in all his expeditions by water and on land. He learned to handle a pole, slipping like a breath of wind along the canals in one of *Paloma's* little punts, and when shots from Valencia came for the wildfowling, he would crouch in the prow of the big boat to help his grandfather manage the sail, or jump onto the bank in tight passages to grab the painter and haul it along.

Later there were masterclasses in shooting. He came to handle his grandfather's gun with relative ease, a veritable blunderbuss whose "boom" marked it out from every other weapon on the Albufera. Old *Paloma* used to use a big charge, and those first shots knocked the boy back on his heels, so he almost fell flat on his back in the bilge. But little by little he got the better of the beast and was able to bring down coots to his grandfather's great satisfaction.

That's how boys should be brought up! By choice Tonet would have eaten nothing but what he had shot with his gun or caught with his own hands. But during the year of this rough finishing school, old *Paloma* noted a growing slackness in his pupil. He liked shooting and took great pleasure in catching fish. What did not seem to please him so much was getting up before dawn, spending a whole day punting with the pole or hauling the boat along on the end of a rope like a horse.

The old boatman saw it clear as day; what his grandson hated, with an instinctive revulsion which roused his very soul, was any actual work.

In vain the grandfather would talk to him about the great fishing they would have the next day in *el Recati*, *el Rincon de la olla* (Stew pot Corner) or some other favoured spot on the Albufera. But as soon as the old boatman took his eyes off him, he would be off. He preferred roaming the Dehesa with the local lads, lying under a tree listening to the sparrows sing in the round tops of the pines or watching the fluttering white butterflies and brown bumble bees buzzing around the woodland flowers.

His grandfather threatened him without effect. He tried a slap, but Tonet retaliated like a cornered beast, grabbing stones from the ground to defend himself, so the old man just resigned himself to carrying on working the lake on his own as before.

He had spent his life working; his son Tono, was stronger than him when it came to getting things done but had lost his way in his commitment to farming. So, who was he like, that whippersnapper? Lord! Where did he come from with his insuperable resistance to every form of physical work, his desire to just hang out, to spend hours on end lying in the sun, like a toad by a ditch.

Everything was changing in that world, which the old man himself had never left. Man was transforming the Albufera with agriculture and changing for the worse the way families lived, so that the lake's old ways might be lost forever. Boatmen's sons were becoming slaves of the land: grandsons raised a fistful of stones against their grandfathers; barges full of coal were to be seen on the lake; rice fields extended in every direction, encroaching on the lake, gulping up its water and consuming the wild woods with huge clearings. Oh Lord! To see all that happen, to witness the destruction of a world he had thought eternal, he would be better off dead!

Cut off from his own family, with no feelings other than his deep love for his mother, the Albufera, he examined and inspected it in detail every day, as if his old eyes, the lively, wise old eyes of a still strong old man, could take in and keep safe all the waters of the lake and the countless trees in the Dehesa.

Not a pine did they fell in the Dehesa, but he would notice it from a distance, from the very centre of the lake. Another one gone! The gap left by the fallen tree in the leafy canopy surrounding it would cause him deep feelings of grief as if he were seeing there the emptiness of a tomb. He cursed the Albufera tenants as insatiable robbers. The folk in El Palmar robbed firewood from the Dehesa: no logs burned in their hearths that did not come from the Dehesa, but they were happy with brushwood, with dry fallen logs. But those invisible lords, the only evidence of whose existence was their keepers' carbines, would fell one of the old boys in the forest without batting an eye, a giant which had seen him crawling about boats as a baby and was already enormous when his father, the original *Paloma*, lived on the untamed Albufera, beating to death the snakes which abounded on the banks, beasts he thought more likeable than the men of the present day.

Depressed in the face of the ruin of his old way of life, he would seek out the roughest corners of the lake, the ones as yet untouched by any hint of redevelopment.

The sight of an old watermill made him shudder as he tearfully gazed at the black and rotting wheel, the broken-gated sluices, dried up and full of grass out of which tumbled packs of rats on his approach. These were ruins of the dead Albufera, mere memories, as he was himself, of better times.

When he felt the need for a rest, he would go ashore at Sancha Flats with its limpid algae-covered pools and tall reed beds and, gazing into the dark depths of the lush verdant undergrowth, in which seemed to rustle the coils of the creature of legend, it would gladden his heart to think that there still existed somewhere that was beyond the greedy reach of people today, among whom, yes, he had to include his son!

CHAPTER 3

When old Paloma finally gave up on his grandson's rough upbringing, the boy breathed a sigh of relief. He was also bored of going with his father to the fields in El Saler and, contemplating him stuck in the mud among leeches and toads, with his legs soaked and his back grilling in the sun, was not looking forward to doing it himself.

The boy's instinctive laziness rebelled against it. No, he would not do as his father did and work in the fields. To be a gamekeeper lying on the sand by the shore, or a *Guardia Civil* like the chaps who came from the market gardens of Ruzafa, with their yellow cross belts and the white sunshade protecting their necks at the back, that seemed better than growing rice, sweating away in the water, your legs swollen with insect bites.

The first few times he went on the Albufera

with his grandfather he had found that way of life acceptable. He liked just wandering about the lake, sailing without any particular objective, going from one canal to another, stopping in the middle to chat to other fishermen.

Sometimes he would jump ashore on little reed islets to rouse the solitary bulls with his whistles. On other occasions he would make his way into the Dehesa to pick blackberries in the bramble patches, and poke about in the warrens, hoping for a nice young rabbit at the bottom.

His grandfather would applaud when he spied a coot, or a mallard sleeping on the surface and took them with a well-aimed shot.

He also liked spending hours on end in the boat, lying on his back listening to his grandfather talk about things in the past. Old *Paloma* would recall the most notable events of his life, his dealings with the great and the good, some smuggling in his far-off youth with a certain amount of shooting, and, enlarging on his own memories, he would talk about his father, the original *Paloma*, going over what he in turn had been told.

That old boatman of former times had also seen great things without stirring from the area. So old *Paloma* would relate to his grandson how Carlos IV and his wife had come to the Albufera, before he had even been born, a fact that did not stop him describing to Tonet the great tents with their waving pennants and fine rugs that were put up among the pines in the Dehesa for the Royal Banquet; the musicians, the packs of dogs, the servants in their powdered wigs looking after the food wagons. Dressed for the hunt, the King did the rounds among the rough wildfowlers of the Albufera, semi-naked by comparison, with ancient blunderbusses, commenting admiringly on their shooting prowess while Maria Luisa strolled through the leafy groves of the forest, arm in arm with don Manuel Godoy. Recalling this famous visit, the old man would always end up intoning the *copla* his father had taught him:

Underneath the forest green
Said unto the King his Queen,
"You I truly love, Carlitos,
But much more, I love Manuel!"

As he sang, his tremulous voice would take on a mischievous tone, and every verse would be accompanied by nods and winks, as if it were only days before that the Albufera people had come up with this *copla* as a way of getting back at an expedition whose conspicuous ostentation had seemed an insult to the settled misery of the fisherfolk.

But this happy period for Tonet did not last long. His grandfather began to show that he could be demanding and tyrannical. As soon as he saw that the boy had got the hang of handling the boat, he stopped just letting him sail about as he liked. He would take over his whole mornings with the fishing. He had to take in the *mornells*, great net sacks, laid the night before, emptying their blind ends of writhing eels, before setting them again; these tasks took a lot of energy standing on the gunwale with your back baking in the heat of the sun.

His grandfather would be there with him, but doing nothing, not even giving him a hand, and on the way back to the village, the old man would be laid out in the bottom of the boat like an invalid, allowing himself to be driven along by his grandson, gasping for breath as he worked the pole.

Other boatmen would hail *Paloma* from afar as he stuck his wizened head above the gunwale "Well, well, lazybones, spending the day in comfort are we, relaxing like the priest in Palmar and your poor grandson poling away there covered in sweat!" To this the grandfather would reply with all the gravity of a master craftsman: "That's how you learn how to do it. I taught his father the same way!"

Later there was the fishing at *la ensesa*, the trips on the lake after the sun was down, setting off into the blackness of the winter nights. Tonet, in the bow would watch over the bundle of dry grass burning like a torch, lighting a great red bloodstain on the water. His grandfather stood in the stern grasping his *fitora*, a forked iron fish spear with barbed teeth, a terrible weapon which, once stuck well in, could only be removed with great effort and horrible destruction of flesh. The light reached down into the bottom of the lake, revealing beds of shells, water plants, a whole world unseen in the light of day, through water that was so clear that the boat seemed to float unsupported in mid-air. Fooled by the light, fish were attracted to the rosy splendour when, Zap! *Paloma* never struck with his *fitora,* but he pulled from the depths a fat specimen hanging in desperation from the sharp points of his trident.

At first, Tonet loved this kind of fishing, but little by little an entertainment morphed into a kind of slavery so that he came to hate the lake as he looked back longingly at the little white houses of El Palmar sticking up over the dark outlines of the reedbeds.

He thought back nostalgically to his earlier days when, having nothing else to do but attend school, he would run about the village street to the compliments of neighbours congratulating his mother on what a handsome lad he was.

There he was master of his own destiny, his sick mother would excuse all his childish pranks with a weak smile while la *Borda*, an inferior being who admired his strength, meekly looked after him. The kids that swarmed around the cottages looked up to him as their leader and they would stroll in a gang the length of the canal throwing stones at the ducks which fled squawking, to the protests of the womenfolk.

The break with his grandfather meant a return to this leisured way of life. He would no longer set off from El Palmar before dawn and stay out on the lake until nightfall. The whole day was his to spend in that village where the only men were the priest in the Presbytery, the schoolmaster and the OC of the Coast Guard with his fierce moustache and his red alcoholic nose wandering along the canal bank, while the womenfolk stood in a knot around their doors leaving the street at the mercy of the little people.

Freed from his labours, Tonet now renewed his old friendships. He had two pals born in cottages next to his, Neleta and *Sangonera*.

The little girl was fatherless, and her mother was an old eel-wife in the city market who loaded her baskets in the middle of the night onto the carrier's barge known as the "eel wagon". A pale woman of overflowing obesity, she would get back to El Palmar in the afternoon, worn out by the daily trip, and the haggling and squabbling in the *Pescadería* fish market. The poor woman was in bed before nightfall and up again with the stars to carry on this far from normal way of life. It left her no time to look after her daughter, who grew up with no one to care for her except the neighbours, especially Tonet's mother, who fed her on many an occasion and treated her as an extra daughter. But this little girl was far less docile than la *Borda* and preferred following Tonet in his escapades to spending hours on end learning the finer points of netmaking.

Sangonera had the same nickname as his father, the most famous drunk on the Albufera, a little old man who seemed to have been pickled in alcohol for many a year. When he lost his wife, and with no other children than little *Sangonereta,* he surrendered himself to permanent drunkenness, so that people seeing him avidly supping away at the drink, compared him to a *sanguijuela,* a leech, thus dubbing him by his nickname.

He would disappear from El Palmar for weeks on end. From time to time, it would become known that he was wandering about in the villages on the landward side, begging alms from the well-off agricultural labourers in Catarroja and Masanasa and sleeping off his bouts in straw lofts. If ever he stayed very long in El Palmar, the net traps in the canals would disappear during the night, the *mornells* would be emptied of eels before their owners got to them and more than one housewife counting her ducks used to raise a wail to heaven on finding one missing. The Coast Guard officer would look sideways at old Sangonera as if he would like to poke him in the eye with his bristling moustache; but the old drunk used to protest his innocence, calling all the Saints in heaven to witness for lack of anyone more creditable. It was just people's ill-will towards him, wanting to get rid of him, as if he hadn't enough misery to bear, by which he meant he lived in the worst hovel in the village. So, to pacify this fierce Representative of the Law, who on more than one occasion had spent time drinking with him, but who recognised no friend outside the tavern, he would set off again on his wanderings on the other side of the Albufera, not returning to El Palmar for several more weeks.

His son refused to go with him on these jaunts. Born in a dog kennel with never a crust of bread thrown his way, he had had to fend for himself since childhood to get anything to eat but rather than follow his father, he tried to go on his own, so as not to have to share the fruits of his adventures.

When the fisherfolk would just be sitting down

to table they would see at their door a sombre shadow pass to and fro until it came to rest by the jamb, head down and gazing up at them, like a young bull ready to charge. This would be *Sangonereta*, chewing on his hunger with a well-practised expression of shy embarrassment, while there burned in his thieving little eyes the desire to grab everything he could get.

But the apparition usually produced the desired emotional response in the family. Poor little boy! So, by getting his hands on a nice half-eaten coot thigh, a bit of tench or a crust of bread he filled his belly by going door to door. Seeing dogs called by a low whistle towards one of the taverns in el Palmar, *Sangonereta* would head in the same direction, as if in on the secret. There would be wildfowlers there with their *paella* pan, gentlemen from Valencia who had come to the lake to sample the *all y pebre*, the famous garlic, pepper and eel stew of the region. The visitors seated at the tavern's little table, plunging in their spoons, would have to fend off the famished dogs as they pushed in on the feast and would find their efforts aided by this ragged little lad who, thanks to his smiles and ability to instil fear in the hearts of the ferocious pack, would end up the owner of what was left in the pan. A coast guard had donated him an old forage cap, the village bailiff had given the trousers of a wildfowler who drowned in a reed bed and his feet, always bare, were as strong as his arms were weak, for they never touched a pole or oar.

Dirty and hungry, stuffing his hand every minute under the filth-encrusted cap to scratch away furiously, *Sangonera* enjoyed great prestige among the local kids. Tonet was the stronger, and thrashed him easily, but was recognised as his inferior, and followed all his orders. It was the prestige of one who knows how to exist on his own, without needing any support. The kids looked to him with a certain envy, seeing that he lived without fear of paternal retribution or any chores whatsoever. In addition, his mischievousness exercised a certain magic, and lads who would get a proper smacking for the most minor misdemeanour at home, felt more manly in the company of that little rogue, who acted as if the whole world was his, and knew how best to make use of it for his own ends, never seeing anything left unattended in a boat that he did not appropriate for himself.

He waged ceaseless war on the inhabitants of the air, given that catching them took less work than needed for fish in the lake. Using dark arts of his own invention he hunted the sparrows, known as *moriscos,* which infest the Albufera and are hated and feared by the farmers as an evil pest because they devour the greater part of the rice harvest.

The best time of year for him was the summer when there were lots of *fumarells*, little terns, on the lake which he used to catch in a net.

Uncle Paloma's grandson used to help in this task. They would go halves in the business, as Tonet would gravely intone, and the two would spend hours lying in wait on the shores of the lake, pulling on a string to capture the unwary birds. When they had plenty, Sangonera, an inveterate traveller, would set off down the road to Valencia with the net bag on his back packed with *fumarells* flapping their dark wings and flashing their white bellies. The little scamp would prowl the streets around the *Pescadería* fish market offering his birds, and the city children would rush to buy the *fumarells* to make them flutter around the street crossings with a bit of twine tied to their legs.

When he returned, there would be some falling out between the partners and the business would dissolve. It was impossible to settle accounts with a rogue like that. Tonet would tire of thrashing *Sangonereta* without succeeding in extracting an eighth share of the proceeds; but always credulous, and somewhat in awe of his wiles, he would soon be back looking for him in the ruined and doorless cottage where he slept on his own most of the time.

After he passed eleven, *Sangonereta* began to withdraw from the company of his little friends. His parasitic instincts drew him to frequent the church, given that this was the best way to insinuate himself into the Curate's household. In a village like El Palmar, the priest was as poor as any of the fisherfolk, but *Sangonereta* was sorely tempted by the sacramental wine in the little jugs at Mass, of which he had heard such complimentary talk in the tavern. Besides, on summer days when the lake seemed to boil under the sun, the little church seemed like an enchanted palace to him, with the dim light filtering through the green panes, its white limewashed walls and the red brick floor breathing the cool damp of the muddy soil.

Old *Paloma*, who despised the little rascal for his disinterest in using the pole, received news of this new passion with annoyed disgust. The laziest bum of the lot! How well he knew how to choose his trade!

When the priest was going off to Valencia, *Sangonereta* would carry his bundle of clothes out to the boat, wrapped in the so called *pañuelo de hierbas*, or grass hanky, and would follow along the bank bidding him farewell so emotionally that he might never have been seeing him again. He helped the priest's maid with the household chores; he fetched firewood from the Dehesa and water from the springs which rose around the lake, and purred like a well-fed cat when, alone in the silence of the tiny room that served as a sacristy, he would polish off the remains of the priest's meal. In the mornings, as he pulled the rope waking the entire village, he felt proud of his calling. The blows with which the priests enlivened his existence seemed like signs of recognition, of distinction indeed, which placed him above his erstwhile companions.

But this desire to live in the church's shade sometimes palled, giving way to a certain nostalgia for his former, wandering way of life. Then he would seek out Neleta and Tonet and together they would set off once more to play and sport along the shore towards the Dehesa which, to his innocent companions, seemed the end of the world.

One autumn afternoon, Tonet's mother sent them for firewood. Instead of getting under her feet by playing in the cottage, they could make themselves useful by fetching some logs now that winter was coming.

So, off the three went. The Dehesa was in flower and perfumed as a garden. Caressed by the still summery sunshine the bushes were covered in flowers around which softly buzzing insects fluttered and flashed like golden buttons. Twisted ancient pines swayed majestically and under their vaulted canopies the cool sweet shade formed a space like an immense cathedral. From time to time a shaft of sunlight would filter through the trunks as if a window had opened.

Every time Tonet and Neleta entered the Dehesa, they both felt overcome by the same sense of fear without knowing of what or of whom. They felt as if they were in the palace of some invisible giant who might appear at any time.

They were wandering the winding paths through the wood, sometimes suddenly hidden by bushes waving above their heads, sometimes suddenly finding themselves on the summit of an immense dune from which could be seen the great mirror of the lake lying beyond the packed columns of trees, speckled with boats as tiny as flies.

Their feet slipped on ground covered in a layer of leaf mould. At the sound of their steps or at the slightest utterance of a syllable, bushes would rustle with the mad flight of unseen animals, rabbits making for safety, while in the distance could be heard the slow tolling of cow bells from herds pastured over towards the sea.

The children seemed drunk on the scented calm of that serene afternoon. When they would go into the woods on winter days, the dry, bare bushes, the cold easterly blowing in from the sea chilling their fingers, the Dehesa's tragic appearance in the grey light of the covered sky meant they would quickly gather their bundles of brushwood and scuttle straight back to El Palmar. But that afternoon they confidently strode the same area ready to explore the whole wood, even if they should reach the end of the world.

They wandered from delight to delight. Instead of looking for firewood, Neleta, with her womanly instinct to beautify herself waved myrtle branches over her mop of hair and then wove together sprigs of mint and other perfumed flowering herbs which drove her crazy with their scent. Tonet picked woodland campanile and formed it into a crown which he placed on his little friend's unruly locks, laughing at her resemblance to the faces painted on the church altar in El Palmar. *Sangonereta*, ever the parasite, raised his snout to sniff out something to savour in all Nature's perfumed splendour. He sucked on the juicy little wild cherries, and then, with a strength that came to him only when it was his stomach calling, ripped up young palm saplings to find the *margalló*, the bitter heart in whose soft folds were enclosed the tender, sweet-tasting young leaves.

Dragon flies and butterflies fluttered in clearings called *mallaes*, low lying ground with no trees because it was flooded by the sea in winter. As they ran, the children's legs were scratched by bushes and cut by reeds as sharp as lances, but they laughed off the scrapes in their headlong rush, dazed by the beauty of the woods. On the paths they would find short, fat, brightly coloured caterpillars wriggling anxiously along. They would pick them up in their fingers, admiring these mysterious creatures whose nature they could not guess, putting them back on the ground and following them on hands and knees until they disappeared into the undergrowth. The dragonflies had them running this way and that, and they all liked the jerky flight of the commonest red ones, called *caballets*, and the *marotas*, dressed like fairies with wings of silver, green backs and chests sheathed in gold.

As they wandered aimlessly through the middle of the wood, where they had never been before, they suddenly found the look of the country changed. They were among dips and hollows so deep among the bushes as to be almost in twilight. An incessant roaring was coming ever closer. It was the sea pounding on the shore on the other side of the range of dunes ringing the horizon.

The pines were no longer straight and proud like the ones on the lake side. Their trunks were twisted, their branches almost bare and their canopies bowed to the ground. All the trees grew bent over in the same direction, as if a great invisible gale were blowing, even in the deep calm of that afternoon. The sea wind raked this side of the wood with great storms, giving it a dispiriting appearance.

The children turned back. They had heard tell of this, the most dangerous and wildest part of the Dehesa. The silence and still of the undergrowth alarmed them. This was where the great snakes slithered that were hunted by the Dehesa's keepers. This was where they pastured the great wild bulls, separated from the rest of the herd, obliging wildfowlers to keep their guns loaded with coarse salt to frighten them off without harming them.

Sangonereta, who knew the Dehesa best, was guiding his little troop back towards the lake but the tempting young palms he kept finding made him lose the path and become lost. Evening was beginning to fall and Neleta was getting scared as the woods became darker. The two boys laughed at her. The pines were like a huge house; it was getting dark inside just like in their cottages, long before sunset, while there was still an hour of daylight outside. There was no hurry, so they carried on looking for *margallós*, Sangonera's favourite palm hearts, while the little girl, dragging her feet along the path, regained her calm sucking on Tonet's gifts of tender leaves. When she found herself alone at a turn in the way, she fairly ran to catch up.

Now it really was getting dark, declared *Sangonera,* acknowledged afficionado of the Dehesa. Cowbells no longer tinkled in the distance. They had to get out of the wood, but only after picking up some firewood so as to avoid a beating when they got home. They looked for dry branches around the base of the trees and in the bushes, quickly gathering up three little bunches and tip toeing away. In a few steps they were in complete darkness. Over towards where the Albufera should be, the horizon was still marked by a glow like a great fire about to go out, but within the wood even tree trunks and bushes were scarcely distinguishable against the dark background.

Sangonereta now lost his calm demeanour, not knowing where they were heading. They were off any known path. They were deep in prickly brush which grabbed their ankles. Neleta was gasping with fear and all of a sudden gave a shout and fell headlong. She had stumbled over the stump of a pine at ground level hurting her foot in the process. *Sangonera* was all for carrying on and leaving the lazy good-for-nothing who did nothing but moan all the time. The little girl sobbed quietly, as if fearful of breaking the silence of the woods and attracting the horrible beasts which populated its dark spaces, while Tonet threatened Sangonera under his breath with a rain of kicks and punches that would be told of for generations if he did not stay with them as a guide.

They made their way slowly forward, testing the ground with each step until suddenly they weren't tripping over bushes but were on the slippery surface of a path. But at that point Tonet failed to get an answer from his companion walking in front.

-*Sangonera*! *Sangonera*!

The noise of breaking branches, of bushes pushed aside in flight, like the sound of a wild animal rushing to escape, was his only response. Tonet roared in fury. What a rotter! He was off to get out of the wood, not wanting to stay with his companion or to help Neleta.

On finding themselves alone, the two children felt any remaining confidence vanish at a stroke. Sangonera with his experience of lonely wandering had seemed their greatest source of aid. Throwing caution to the wind, the terrified Neleta now wept aloud, her sobs echoing around the silent, seemingly measureless woods. His companion's fear roused Tonet to action. He put his arm around the girl, supporting and encouraging her, asking her to try to walk and whether she would prefer to follow him if he went in front, although the poor lad didn't know where he was headed.

They stayed clinging to each for some time, she, sobbing, he, shivering at the thought of the unknown, but determined to overcome it.

Something cold and sticky whipped past, hitting them in the face, perhaps it was a bat, but the contact, though it made them shudder, shook them out of their paralysis. They pressed forward, falling and getting back up, tangling in bushes, bumping into trees, starting at the confused sounds that seemed to spur them forward. They were both thinking the same thing, but instinctively kept these thoughts to themselves so as not to let their fear grow. The idea of *Sancha* was burned into their memory. All the legends of the lake, told around the hearth on nights in the cottage, rushed in a pack into their mind, and as their hands rasped against the bark of trees, they felt they were touching the cold rough skin of enormous reptiles. The wails of coots calling in far off reed beds sounded in their ears as the cries of murdered souls. Their mad flight through the bushes, breaking branches and flattening the grass set many a mysterious creature in the dark undergrowth scampering away in a rustle of dried leaves.

They found themselves in a great clearing, a *mallada*, without any idea where they were in the endless wood. The darkness was not quite so black in this open space. Above them stretched the intense blue of the sky dusted with light like a great canvas thrown over the black masses of woodland that ringed the clearing. The two children paused in this tranquil glowing island, powerless to take another step. They shivered with fear at the deep woods surrounding them, surging shadows moving everywhere.

They sat tightly hugging each other as if the physical contact might give them strength. Neleta had stopped crying. Completely drained mentally and physically, she let her head rest on her little friend's shoulder, sighing quietly. Tonet darted glances all around, as if, even more than in the gloomy woodland, he thought he glimpsed in the clear half-light the outline of some ferocious beast ready to pounce on lost children. A cuckoo's call broke the silence; frogs in an adjacent pond, which had fallen silent at their approach, regained their confidence and restarted their croaking; big fat mosquitos constantly buzzed round their heads like black flashes in the dimness.

The two children slowly felt their own confidence return. They weren't badly off where they were;

they could spend the night right there, and as they clung together, the heat from their bodies seemed to infuse them with new hope, making them forget their fear and crazy flight through the wood.

The sky above the pines on the seaward side was just tinting with the palest white. Stars were beginning to go out, submerged in a milky tide. Still edgy in these unknown woods, the two children looked hopefully towards it, as if it were the harbinger of some being, riding to their aid on a cloud of light. The pine branches topped with leafy fronds stood out as if painted in black silhouette against this glowing background. Something brilliant began to appear above the leafy canopy, at first just a silvery rim, the merest arched line, then a dazzling semicircle and finally a huge, light honey-coloured face trailing its resplendent locks among the surrounding stars. The moon seemed to smile on the two children who gazed at it with the innocent adoration of two little savages.

The woodland was transformed by the appearance of that chubby countenance, making the reed beds on the flats gleam like sheaves of silver canes. Around the base of each tree spread a black, softly moving stain and the woods seemed to enlarge, to double in size as this second shaded canopy extended over the glowing earth.

The *buxquerots*, the wild nightingales of the lake, broke into song around the edges of the *mallada* and even the mosquitos seemed to buzz more sweetly in the light-filled space.

The two children were beginning to find their adventure quite agreeable. Neleta's foot was no longer hurting, and she talked under her breath of the odium she felt for her former companion. Her precocious womanly instincts, the cunning of the abandoned kitten, meant she was better placed than Tonet to deal with the situation. They would just stay in the woods, OK? They would think of an explanation for their adventure when they got back to the village the next day. *Sangonera* would be the one responsible. They would just spend the night there, seeing things they had never seen before; they would sleep next to each other; they would be like man and wife. Knowing no better, they shivered a little at these words, hugging each other all the tighter. They clung together as if the feeling growing between them needed the combined warmth of their bodies.

Tonet felt strangely and inexplicably embarrassed. In their playful rough and tumble, he had bumped into his little friend's body plenty of times, but never before had he felt that soft warmth which now seemed to seep into his veins and rise in a rush to his head with the same dizzying effect as the glasses of wine that his grandfather would offer him in the tavern. He stared fixedly ahead but his whole being was focussed on Neleta's head nestling on his shoulder, on the soft caress of her mouth on his neck as she breathed, like being tickled by a velvet glove. The two of them fell silent, and enchantment grew in the silence. She opened her green eyes wide, the moon reflecting in their depths like a dewdrop, as she turned to make herself more comfortable, murmuring dreamily as she cuddled into him and closed them again:

-Tonet, Tonet.

What time was it? The lad felt his own eyes closing, more from the strange drowsiness that overcame him than from sleep. Above the whisperings of the wood, he could just hear the buzzing of the cloud of mosquitos clustering around any fragment skin, however tough, left exposed by these two children of the lake. What a strange orchestra this was that sang them to sleep, wafting them over the first slow billows of their dreams. Some, screeching like strident violins, stretching out their last note seemingly forever, others, more sedate, ran up and down a short scale while the fattest, biggest ones buzzed with a deep soft hum, like double basses or the tolling of distant bells.

The sun burning their faces woke them the following morning as a barking keeper's dog bared its fangs. They were almost out of the Dehesa, and it was only a short distance back to El Palmar.

Tonet's ever caring but unhappy mother rushed at him with pole in hand to make up for her anguished night and succeeded in dealing him a couple of good blows in spite of her small build, besides which, and to take matters forward while they were waiting for Neleta's mother to get back in the "eel wagon, she also dealt her out a few slaps just so she wouldn't get lost in the woods again.

After this adventure the whole village, in silent accord knew Tonet and Neleta were betrothed and they, as if bound forever by that night of innocent togetherness in the woods sought each other out and loved each other without ever saying so, as if it were agreed that they could only ever be for one another.

This adventure marked the end of childhood for them. There was no more running about joyful and carefree, free of all obligations. Neleta followed the same way of life as her mother: she went off to Valencia every night with her basket of eels and did not come back until the following afternoon. Tonet, who was only able to see her for a moment at sundown worked all day in his father's fields or was off fishing with him and his grandfather.

Seeing his son was now a grown man, the formerly good-natured Tono was now as demanding as old *Paloma*, and Tonet was dragged out to work like an unwilling beast of burden. His father, the unflinching hero of the earth, was unbending in his determination. When the time came to plant the rice, or at harvest, the boy spent the whole day in the fields at El Saler. The rest of the year he fished the lake, sometimes with his father and sometimes with his grandfather, who took him on as crew in the boat but never ceased to curse the bitch of bad luck that had brought such rogues into the bosom of his family.

The lad also found himself compelled to work out of sheer boredom. There was no one left in the village with whom he could entertain himself during the day. Neleta was away in Valencia and his former playmates, now that they were as grown up as he was and needed to work for their daily bread, were off fishing with their fathers. *Sangonera* was still around, but after the incident in the Dehesa, he distanced himself from Tonet, remembering the beating with which his desertion that night had been rewarded.

As if this event had decided his future, the rogue

had sought refuge in the priest's house, acting as his manservant, sleeping like a dog behind the door without any thought for his father who appeared only occasionally at the abandoned cottage through whose roof the rain poured like it was in the open air.

Sangonera senior now had a mission in life; when not drunk he was completely absorbed in hunting otters on the lake, which having been the embodiment of persecution over the centuries were now reduced to a mere dozen or so.

One afternoon while he was digesting his wine on an embankment, he noticed the water swirling and boiling up great bubbles. Something was diving down there on the bottom among the nets closing off the canal, looking for the *mornells*, the long net sacks full of fish. Getting into the water with a pole someone lent him, he proceeded to rain blows on the blackish animal that was scuttling along the bottom until he succeeded in subduing and killing it.

It was the famous *llúdria*, a fabled animal that was talked of in El Palmar as if it were a fantasy, the otter that in former times used to thrive in the lake in such quantities that fishing was impossible due to the broken nets.

The old rogue was now considered the top man on the Albufera. The Palmar Fishermen's

Association was, according to its own ancient laws laid down in the Great Books looked after by its President, the Judge, obliged to pay a whole *duro* for each otter that might be presented to it. The old boy collected his prize but did not stay there. That animal was treasure and he set out to display it in the port of Catarroja and in Silla before ending up in Sueca and Cullera in his triumphal progress around the lake.

They were calling for him everywhere. There was no tavern in which he was not received with open arms. Forward, uncle *Sangonera*! Let's see the animal he's caught! After allowing himself to be feted with a number of glasses he would lovingly draw from under his cloak the poor beast, pale and stinking, to let people admire its coat and pass their hands over it, but carefully now, eh? Just to appreciate the silkiness of its fur.

Never from the moment he arrived in this world was little *Sangonereta* carried in his father's arms with such tender care as was that beast. But days went by, and people tired of the *llúdria*, nobody was giving so much as a foul glass of firewater and there was no tavern that did not quickly rid themselves of *Sangonera* like the plague, on account of the insufferable stench of the rotting corpse he carried under his cloak. But rather than abandoning it he even extracted a new type of fee, selling it in Valencia to a taxidermist, and from then on declared to all the world his new calling: to be an otter hunter.

Like someone pursuing happiness he gave himself over to finding another one. The Fishermen's Association bounty and the week of continuous free drinking when he was treated like a king were never far from his thoughts. But the second otter had no desire to be caught. He sometimes thought he had spotted it in one of the remotest drainage ditches around the lake, only for it to hide itself immediately, as if its whole family had shared the information about *Sangonera* Senior's new profession. His desperation forced him to get drunk on credit, payable on future otters that he would hunt, and he had drunk his way through two when some fishermen found him one night drowned in a canal. He had slipped in the ooze and, so drunk that he was unable to get up, had sunk into the water, forever lying in wait for his next otter.

Sangonereta's father's death meant he now took shelter permanently in the priest's house and never returned to the cottage. Priest succeeded priest in El Palmar, a punishment posting where only hopeless cases or men in disgrace went, hoping to get out again as soon as possible. On taking over the impoverished church they all took on the new *Sangonera* at the same time as an indispensable element of the establishment. He was the only one in the village who knew how to assist at Mass. He had carefully memorised all the vestments kept in the Sacristy, including the exact number of tears, repairs and moth holes. He assisted in all matters with a willingness to please and his superior never conceived an order that was not fulfilled in an instant.

He took some pride in the fact that he was the only villager that did not work a pole or spend the night in the middle of the Albufera, allowing him to look down somewhat on other people.

At dawn on Sundays, he it was who led the procession, carrying high the cross before the *Rosario del Aurora.* In two long files, men, women, and children slowly followed behind, chanting as they made their way along the single village street and then dispersing along the banks and into the isolated cottages so that the ceremony might continue. The canals glowed like sheets of dark steel in the half light of dawn, pinkly tinting the small clouds along the seaward horizon, while the *moriscos* sparrows, surged and fluttered in dense flocks from the roofs of the fish tanks responding to the melancholy chanting of the faithful with the joyful chirping of little rogues happy with their carefree life.

Christians, awake! chanted the column stretching along the village, although the funny thing about this call was that the whole population was in the procession and the only thing left to wake in the empty cottages were barking dogs and roosters, who's resounding cock-crow burst over the sad cacophony like a fanfare saluting the new light and joy of another day.

As he walked in the column, Tonet gazed in fury at his former companion, out there in front like a General, waving the cross as if it was a flag. The little sneak! He'd known how to sort out his life as he pleased all right!

He, meanwhile, was living under his father's thumb, under a man who was daily more withdrawn and less communicative, basically a good man but almost cruel with his own family in his stubborn obsession with work. These were hard times. The fields at El Saler never yielded two good harvests in a row, and the loans that Tono used to help him continue in business consumed most of his profits. The *Palomas* suffered continual bad luck in the fishing, always ending up with the worst fishing spots in the Community draw. His mother was also clearly dying, slowly fading away like a sputtering candle, as if life were draining from within her, escaping through the unhealing wounds in her tortured entrails, showing no sign of life other than the gleam of sickness in her eyes.

It was a sad life for Tonet. He no longer roused El Palmar with his pranks, the women no longer showered him in kisses, declaring him the most handsome lad in the village, he was no longer the one chosen from among his companions on the day of the Fishery Draw to plunge his hand into the leather Community Sack and draw out the lots. He was now a man. Instead of his say carrying any weight at home because he was the favoured son, they all now told him what to do, he was as worthless as la *Borda*, and at the least rebellion on his part, Tono's heavy hand would be raised against him while his grandfather looked on approvingly with a wry smile that suggested that this was the right way to bring folk up.

When his mother finally died it seemed that his grandfather's former feelings of affection for his son had been reawakened. Old *Paloma* grieved the absence of that docile soul who had silently suffered all his rages; feeling this emptiness growing around him, he clung to his grandson who, while little inclined to do as he was bid, still never dared gainsay him in his presence.

They went fishing together as in former times, they would go off occasionally to the tavern like comrades, while little *Borda* attended to the duties of the home with the prematurely grown-up demeanour one finds in such unfortunate children.

Neleta was also like one of the family. Her mother was no longer able to make the trip to market in Valencia. The damp of the Albufera seemed to have penetrated the very marrow of her bones and stiffened her frame so the poor woman was left immobile in her cottage groaning with rheumatic pain at every movement, wailing like a condemned woman, powerless to work for her daily bread. Her market colleagues used to give her something out of their own baskets by way of charity, but when her little girl felt hungry at home, she would run over to Tonet's to help la *Borda* with the household tasks with all the authority of an older sister. She was well received by Tono, who, as one engaged in a constant struggle with misery, was generously disposed to help everyone who fell.

Neleta was doing her growing up in the home of the man to whom she was betrothed. She would go there looking for something to eat, so relations with Tonet took on a character that was more fraternal than amorous.

So sure was he of her, that the lad took no particular care of his fiancée. Was he able to fall in love with someone else? Did he have the right to fall for someone else after the whole village had recognised them as betrothed? So, settled in his possession of Neleta, he paid her little attention and treated her with indifference as if they were already married, while she, in her misery, grew like a rare flower, her beauty standing in stark contrast to the scant physical attractions on offer among the other village girls; Sometimes weeks might go by without him exchanging a word with her.

Other interests were now attracting the little gent, who was becoming quite the most desirable bachelor in El Palmar. He was proud of the reputation he had acquired as a bit of a lad among his old playmates who were now all grown men like him. He had fought quite a few of them, always coming out the winner. Pole in hand he had broken some heads and one fine afternoon had charged along the bank with his great fish spear at a Catarroja boatman with a fearful reputation. His father grimaced when he heard about such adventures, but his grandfather laughed, feeling, just for a moment, at one with his grandson. The thing that old *Paloma* most applauded was that on a certain occasion he had faced up to the keepers on the Dehesa, snatching from their very noses a rabbit he had just killed. He was no worker, but he carried his blood.

The young man, still not yet eighteen, and very much the talk of the village, had his own favourite spot to which he would be off as soon as he had his father's or grandfather's boat tied up on the canal.

This was the *Cañamel* tavern, a new establishment about which tongues were wagging all over the Albufera. It was not like the other taverns, set up in a cottage, with a low smoky roof and no more ventilation than the doorway. It was purpose built, an imposing looking building among the straw thatched hovels, with blue painted stone walls, a red tiled roof and two doors, one facing the village's only street and the other on the canal side. The space between the two doors was always full of rice growers and fishermen, men who drank standing at the bar, staring hypnotically at the two rows of red barrels, or sitting on rope stools at little pine tables following the interminable games of *brisaca* and *truque.*

The luxury in this establishment filled its patrons with pride. The walls were lined to head height with tiles from Manises, above which were frescoes of a fantastic countryside, green and blue, with horses as big as rats and trees smaller than the men, while from the beams hung strings of morcillas and esparto grass sandals along with bundles of pungent yellow hemp cordage used for rigging the big lake boats.

Everyone admired the owner, *Cañamel* himself.

The money that fat slob must have! He had been in the *Guardia Civil* in Cuba and a *carabinero* in the police in Spain and, after that, had lived for many years in Algeria: he was familiar with many trades and professions and he knew so much, so much indeed, that, as *Paloma* used to put it, he would take note in his dreams of where every peseta in the place lay and would be off to collect them up the next day.

They had never drunk wine in El Palmar like his. Everything was the best in that house. The owner made his guests most welcome and creamed off his profits in a reasonable manner.

Cañamel wasn't from El Palmar, or even from Valencia. He came from some distance away where they spoke Castellano. In his youth he had been a policeman in the Albufera area and had got married to a poor ugly girl from El Palmar. Getting together some money after his adventurous life, he had given in to his wife's wishes and come back to set up in her village. The poor woman was ill and showed little sign of life; she seemed exhausted by the lifelong journeying that had made her dream of her peaceful corner of the lake.

The other publicans in the village were loud in their condemnation of *Cañamel* as they saw how he raked in the customers. The great scallywag!

For some reason he was selling his wine too cheap! But the tavern was actually the least of his concerns, his real business was elsewhere and there was indeed a reason he had come from so far away to set up there. But in the face of such murmurings, *Cañamel* just smiled sweetly. In the end they all had to live!

Cañamel's most intimate friends knew that such speculation was not without foundation. The tavern mattered little to him. His principal business took place at night after it was all closed up. Not for nothing had he patrolled the beaches as a policeman. Every month bundles would wash up on the shore, rolling about in the sand amid a swarm of black shapes that picked them up and carried them across the Dehesa to the lakeside. There, the great Albufera *laúdes*, boats that could carry a hundred sacks of rice, would be stuffed with the bundles of tobacco before setting off slowly into the darkness for the landward shore. And the following day there was neither sight nor sound of anything at all.

He would choose the men for these expeditions from among the boldest of his customers. Despite his tender years, Tonet was favoured with *Cañamel's* confidence on two or three occasions on account of his reputation as a brave lad who kept his mouth shut. A good man could earn two or three *duros* on this night shift, money which he would then restore to *Cañamel's* safekeeping by drinking in his tavern. But this unfortunate crew, talking the next day about the ups and downs of an outing in which they had been the principal protagonists would still declare admiringly:

- What guts that *Cañamel's* got, daring to put himself in harm's way with the people who are after him!

Things were going well. Everyone on the beach saw nothing thanks to the inn-keeper's skill and cunning. His old Algerian friends sent over the deliveries on time and the business rolled on so smoothly that *Cañamel,* in spite of having to generously reward the silence of those who might do him harm, swiftly prospered. Only a year after arriving in El Palmar he had already purchased rice fields and had a large bag of silver upstairs in the tavern to get people asking for loans out of trouble.

He grew rapidly in respectability. They had initially given him the nickname of *Cañamel,* or Sugarcane, on account of the soft, sweet-sounding accent in which he laboriously expressed himself in Valenciano. Later when they saw that he was rich, and without forgetting the nickname, people used to call him Paco since, according to his wife, that was what he was called in his own country, and he would fume quietly if they addressed him as Quico as they did other Franciscos in the village.

When his wife, the poor companion of his years of misfortune, finally died, her younger sister, an ill-countenanced widowed fishwife with an overbearing manner, set out to take over the tavern like the owner's wife, accompanied by her whole family. They flattered *Cañamel* with the attention and care that a rich relative inspires, talking about how difficult it was for a man on his own to run the front of house. A woman was needed out there! But *Cañamel,* who had always detested his sister-in-law on account of her foul tongue and shivered at the thought of her hoping to take her sister's place while it was still warm, threw her out the door in defiance of her scandalous proposals. He would just need a couple of old, widowed fishwives to take care of the place, who would cook the *all y pebre* for the enthusiasts who came out from Valencia and clean the bar whereon the whole village rested its elbows.

Finding himself free of obligations, *Cañamel* was against getting married again. For a man of his means, it really only made sense if he got married to some woman who had more money than him, and he would laugh out loud in the evenings listening to old *Paloma,* who was so eloquent in speaking about women.

The old boatman declared that man ought to be like the *buxquerots*, the nightingales on the lake who sing happily in the wild, but when you cage them, would rather die than be shut in.

The birds of the Albufera made comparisons easy for him. Females of every species! An evil plague! They were the most ungrateful and forgetful creatures in creation. You only had to look at the poor *collverts,* or mallards, on the lake. The drakes always flew in a pair with the ducks and hardly knew how to find their food without them. Then the shot fires, and if the duck falls dead, the drake, instead of escaping, flies round and round the spot where his companion perished until the gun ends up getting him too. But if the drake falls, the duck flies straight on without turning her head, as if nothing had happened and when she notices her companion is missing sets out to find another one. Christ! All females are the same whether feathered or dressed as shepherdesses.

Tonet used to spend the evenings playing *truque* in the tavern and could not wait for Sundays in order to pass the whole day there. He liked sitting still, having his *porrón* within easy reach, dealing the greasy cards on the cloth covering the small table and paying out in little pebbles or grains of maze representing the value of the bets. What a pity he wasn't rich like *Cañamel* so as to enjoy this lordly life always! He raged against the thought that the next day he would have to wear himself out in the boat and his passion for the easy life grew to the extent that *Cañamel* no longer sought him out for the night shift, seeing him pull a long face as he loaded the bundles and how he squabbled with his workmates to avoid the heavy work.

The only thing in which he showed any enthusiasm, and which shook him out of his lazy somnolence was a fast-approaching entertainment. On El Palmar's great fiesta in honour of the Baby Jesus, the third day of Christmas, Tonet distinguished himself above all the youth of the lakeside. When the band arrived in a huge boat from Catarroja during the evening, the young men would plunge into the canal, battling to be the one who grabbed the big bass drum. This was an honour which allowed one to parade oneself haughtily before the girls, taking charge of the enormous instrument and carrying it on one's back through the village.

Tonet jumped up to his chest in water as cold as liquid ice, beating off with his fists the foremost of the bold and clung to the boat's gunwale, making the bulky box his prize.

During the following three days of festivities there were diversions that most times ended up in blows. The dance in the plaza to the light of resinous pine tapers, where he obliged Neleta to remain seated (for she was after all his betrothed) while he danced with other girls, less good looking but better clad, and the nights of *albaes*, or serenades when the young men would go door to door until dawn singing *coplas*, escorting a skin of wine to give them strength and accompanying each song with a salvo of rockets or a volley of shots.

But once this short period was over Tonet was back to the boredom of his working life bounded by the horizon of the lake. He would escape at times, scorning his father's ire, to disembark at the port of Catarroja and wander the landward villages where he had friends from harvest time. On other occasions he took the road to El Saler and carried on to Valencia with the idea of staying in the city until hunger drove him back to his father's cottage. He had seen from up close the way some people lived without having to work and he cursed the bad luck which made him live like an amphibian in a land of reeds and mud where man must, from early childhood, encase himself in the everlasting coffin of a little boat, without which he cannot move.

A hunger for the pleasures of life rose within him, furious and overwhelming. He played on in the tavern until *Cañamel* put him out the door at midnight; he had tried every liquid drunk on the Albufera, including the pure absinthe that the city shots would bring to dilute with the stinking lake water, and on more than one night as he stretched out on his bed in the cottage his father's eyes, noting the unsteady gait and gasping breathing of the well-oiled drunk, had followed him with a severe look. His grandfather protested indignantly. It was good and healthy for him to like wine; in the end they lived day-in and day-out on the water and the good boatman had to keep his belly warm. But mixed drinks...! That was how old *Sangonera* had started!

Tonet was forgetting all those he was fond of. He beat la *Borda*, treating her as a submissive animal, and also paid little attention to Neleta, greeting her remarks with a snort of impatience. If he obeyed his father, it was so unwillingly that the great workman would pale, clenching his powerful fists as if ready to knock him off his feet. The lad scorned everyone in the village, seeing there only a miserable bunch born to hunger and fatigue, from whose ranks he had to get away at any cost. Fisherfolk coming in proudly and showing off their baskets of eels and tench made him smile. Passing the priest's house, he would see *Sangonera*, his life now dedicated to reading, passing hours on end seated in the doorway consuming religious texts and disguising his sly looks into an expression of composure. Imbecile! What would those books the vicars lent him matter?

He wanted to live, to enjoy at one stroke all of life's sweetness. One could only imagine how many people lived on the other side of the lake, in the rich villages or in the big, noisy city, who might rob him of some of those pleasures which were his by indisputable right. At harvest time, when thousands of men would come to the Albufera, attracted by the great rates offered by proprietors needing hands, Tonet would, for a short time, become reconciled to life in that part of the world. He would see new faces, make new friends and find a strange joy in these itinerants who with a sickle in their hand and a bag of clothes on their backs would go from place to place, working while there was light in the sky and getting drunk as soon as night fell.

He liked these folk and their precarious existence, and their stories amused him, more so than the local folk-tales told around the fireside. Some had been in the Americas and, forgetting the miseries of life in those remote lands, spoke of them as a paradise where everyone literally swam in gold. Others had tales of long spells in the wilds of Algeria, on the very edge of the desert, where they had hidden themselves away for a time on account of a knifing back in their home village or some robbery that had left them with a pile of enemies. As Tonet listened, he seemed to perceive, wafting through the decayed stench of the Albufera breeze, the exotic scent of those marvellous lands, and see their fabled riches glistening in the tavern's tiled walls.

This friendship with the seasonal day-labourers became close to the point that when the harvest was over, and they had settled for all their days' pay, Tonet went off with them on a veritable orgy through all the villages around the lake, a mad canter from tavern to tavern, of nightly serenades before certain inviting windows, generally ending in a brawl when, with the money running out and the wine beginning to taste rather bitter, there would be arguments about who was going to have to pay.

One of these expeditions became the stuff of legend around the Albufera. It lasted more than a week, and in the whole time, Tono never once saw his son in El Palmar. It was known that the bunch of troublemakers was roaming like wild beasts in the area around Ribera, that in Sollana they had beaten up a guard and that in Sueca two of the gang had had their heads broken in a fight at the tavern. The Guardia Civil was closing in on this pack of idiots.

One night they told Tono that his son had just

turned up in the *Cañamel* tavern with his clothes covered in mud as if he had fallen in a ditch and a gleam in his eyes after seven days of drunkenness. Off went the glum labourer, silent as always, but clenching his teeth and pursing his lips in a silent snort.

His son was drinking in the centre of the tavern with the insatiable thirst of the complete drunk, surrounded by an attentive crowd, which he kept in fits of laughter with his tales of the pranks committed on this playful outing.

With a backhander, Tono smashed the *porrón* which he was raising to his lips and knocked him head over heels. Dazed by the blow, Tonet, took a few minutes to pull himself together, but seeing his father confronting him launched forward, his glazed eyes blazing with a fearful foulness, screaming that no one hit him and got away with it, not even his own father.

It was not easy, however, to set oneself up against that big, quiet, serious man, firm in his resolve, and carrying in his arms all the strength of more than thirty years battling misery. Without even a pause for breath he contained the little whirlwind that was out to consume him with a punch that knocked him off balance, while almost at the same time he landed a kick which sent him flying into the wall sprawling on all fours on one of the card tables among some players.

The tavern's customers were all now definitely on the father's side, fearing that this big silent strongman might otherwise thrash them all in his fury. When calm was restored and they bade good night to Tono, his son was already well away. He had fled with his hands in the air, waving desperately. He'd hit him... him... who was so much feared... and in the presence of the whole of El Palmar!

Several days passed with no news of Tonet. Little by little something became known among the folk that went up to the market in Valencia. He was in the barracks at Monteolivete and would soon be embarking for Cuba. He had signed up. After fleeing to the city in desperation he had spent time in the taverns around the barracks where the overseas recruitment unit operated. The men who filled the place, volunteers awaiting embarkation and clever recruiters, had made up his mind for him.

Tono was at first inclined to oppose it. The boy was not yet twenty and thus it was illegal. He was, besides, his son, his only son. But his grandfather, tough as ever, made him hold back. This was the best thing his grandson could do. He was growing up all wrong; let him have his head and suffer for it; they would take him in hand and straighten him out! And if he died it was one rogue less; in the end they all had to die sooner or later.

The boy departed without a word in response. It was la *Borda* who, slipping away from the cottage, turned up on her own at Monteolivete to bid him a tearful farewell, deliver all his clothes and the few coins she could get hold of without Tono finding out. Never a word to Neleta; her betrothed seemed to have forgotten her.

Two years then went by without any sign of life from the lad until one day a letter arrived for his father, headlined with dramatic phrases, and couched in false sentimentalism, in which Tonet begged his father's forgiveness, and spoke of his new way of life. He was a Guardia Civil in Guantánamo and things were not going badly. A certain petulance was evident in his manner of address, suggesting a man used to roaming the country with a weapon over his shoulder inspiring terror and respect. His health was excellent, not the least sign of a problem since he had got off the boat. People from the Albufera were perfectly suited to the island climate. Brought up drinking the muddy water of that lagoon, he could go anywhere without a thought, already totally acclimatised.

Later the war broke out, and la *Borda* trembled tearfully in the corner when confused snippets of news arrived in El Palmar about the far-off fighting. Two women in the village were wearing mourning. The boys were marched off when their call-up came amid the despairing wails of families who might never see them again.

Tonet's letters however provided a calming antidote and showed him full of confidence. He was now head of a mounted guerrilla unit and seemed very happy with his life. He described his appearance in minute detail, wearing his striped jacket and wide straw sombrero, half-length patent boots, his machete slapping his thigh, his Mauser carbine across his back and a cartridge belt full of rounds for it. He had no cares, his life was his own, he was well paid, came and went as he liked, and enjoyed the freedom that came with danger. Bring on the war! he declared happily in his letters, and even at such a great distance they could make out the bragging soldier, satisfied with his posting, happy to put up with fatigue, hunger and thirst in exchange for freedom from the monotonous labour of the common man, to be able to live outside normal laws and times, to kill without fear of punishment and to feel he could take anything he laid eyes on, under the protection of the mantra "the exigencies of war".

Gradually Neleta learned more about her fiancé's adventures. Her mother had died, and she was now living with one of her aunts and made a living as a waitress at *Cañamel's* on the days when there were special customers and plenty of *paellas*.

She would turn up at the *Paloma's* cottage to ask la *Borda* if she had had a letter, listening as she read it with her eyes lowered and her lips pursed as if to focus her attention. Her feelings for Tonet seemed to have cooled after his spectacular departure, which included not the slightest backward glance at his fiancée. Her eyes would shine, and she would smile, murmuring "*Grasies*!" when, at the end of letters, the warrior would mention her name and send his regards; but she showed no desire for the lad to come back, nor get in the least excited when he would build castles in the air, and fantasise that he might even return to El Palmar wearing officer's braid.

Other matters preoccupied Neleta. She had turned into the best-looking girl in the Albufera. She was small, but with an abundance of pale fair hair framing her face like a helmet of weathered antique gold. Her skin was white, of transparent clarity threaded with tiny veins, the type of skin never seen among the women of El Palmar whose scaly epidermis, with its slightly metallic glint, suggested a distant resemblance to the tench in the lake. Her eyes were small, pallid green and shining, like two drops of the absinthe that the wildfowlers from Valencia drank.

She was spending more and more time in *Cañamel's* place, no longer just offering her services on special occasions. She now passed the whole day in the tavern, cleaning, serving glasses at the bar, keeping an eye on the hearth where the great paella pans bubbled, before strolling back ostentatiously at night to her aunt's cottage, escorted by her and making sure everyone saw her, in order that *Cañamel's* hostile relatives, who were beginning to mutter about Neleta seeing the sunrise in her boss's arms, could properly take note.

Cañamel couldn't get by without her. The old widower, who until then had lived quietly with old fish wives for servants, publicly scorning women, was unable to resist the touch of that mischievous creature who rubbed up against him with feline grace. Poor old *Cañamel* was set aflame by the green eyes of that little kitten, who managed to excite him whenever she saw him settling down, with some clever chance collision that ticked another of his secret fantasies. The old publican's words and glances ended many years of chaste behaviour. Sometimes customers would see scratches on his face, or a bruise near his eye, and laugh as the landlord scrabbled confusedly for an explanation. The girl knew well how to defend herself against *Cañamel's* irresistible advances. She got him fired up with her eyes, only to calm him down with her fingernails. Sometimes the tavern's inner rooms would resound to the crash of furniture, while the thin walls shook with furious blows, as the drinkers laughed mischievously. That would be *Cañamel* trying to stroke his little pussy cat! He 'd be back at the bar with another scratch to show for it for sure!

This struggle had to end somehow. Neleta was too determined for her not to surrender to that fat old boy, who trembled at her threats never to return to the tavern. The whole of El Palmar was touched by news of *Cañamel's* wedding, even though it was a long-awaited event. The groom's sister-in-law went from door to door pouring out bile. Women formed in groups in front of their cottages. The little dead fly! She'd known fine how to behave to hook the richest man in the Albufera! Nobody now remembered anything about her former betrothal to Tonet. Six years had passed since he left, and people practically never came back from where he'd gone.

As the owner's legitimate wife, taking possession of that inn through which passed the entire village, and where all the needy would come seeking a loan from *Cañamel*, Neleta displayed neither haughtiness, nor any desire to get her own back on the fishwives who had treated her so badly in her time serving in the bar. She treated everybody with kindness but kept the bar between her and the customers to prevent any familiarity.

She never went back now to the *Paloma's* cottage. She would talk with la *Borda* like a sister when the latter would go along to buy something and would serve old *Paloma* with wine in the biggest glass, while attempting to forget his various little debts. Tono very seldom went to the tavern, but when Neleta saw him, she would greet him respectfully, as if this silent man who kept himself to himself were like a father who might not want to recognise her but whom she secretly adored.

These were the only feelings from the past that remained alive in her. She managed her establishment as if she was never meant to do anything else; she knew how to command obedience from drinkers with a single word; with her sleeves always rolled up, her white arms seemed to attract men from all the shores of the Albufera; the tavern was doing well and she appeared each day looking fresher, more beautiful and more assured, as if suddenly endowed with all her husband's riches that people around the lake talked about so enviously.

Cañamel, on the other hand, appeared to go into a decline following his marriage. All his wife's freshness and well-being seemed to have been stolen from him. Finding himself rich and owner of the best girl in the Albufera, he felt the moment had come when, for the first time in his life, he might allow himself to feel ill. Times were not so good for the smuggling. The inexperienced young officers now in charge of the Coast Guard did not allow in any business and, as Neleta understood the business of the tavern better than *Cañamel,* he gave himself over to being ill, which, according to *Paloma*, is something the rich do to amuse themselves.

The old rogue knew better than anybody where the inn-keeper's problems came from and talked about it in mischievous terms. The beast of love had been awakened in his breast, feelings dormant for many years, during which he had felt no passion other than for making money. Neleta had the same effect on him as when she was waitressing. The two glinting green drops in her eyes, a smile, a word, their arms brushing as they filled glasses at the bar were enough to make him lose his self-control. But *Cañamel* no longer got his face scratched nor were the customers scandalised when the bar was left unattended. So thus, time passed, with *Cañamel* complaining of strange infirmities, his head aching as often as his stomach hurt, soft, fat and increasingly obese, while his manly strength faltered, as Neleta grew daily stronger as if, as the inn keeper's life evaporated, it condensed to fall on her as soft refreshing rain.

Paloma commented on the new situation in comically serious terms, suggesting that the *Cañamel* species would end up reproducing in such abundance that it would take over the whole of El Palmar. But four years went by without Neleta achieving motherhood despite her most fervent desires. She wanted a son to secure her precarious position, and as she put it, to stick one on her dead predecessor's relatives. Every six months, rumours swirled round the village that she was pregnant, and women would examine her inquisitorially as they went into the tavern, recognising the importance of this event in the struggle between the inn keeper's wife and her enemies. But the hope was always in vain.

Whenever it was thought that Neleta might be pregnant, the most atrocious gossip would begin to swirl around her. Her enemies would mention some rice grower among the men who came from the villages around la Ribera to relax in the tavern, or some wildfowler from Valencia, or even the Police Lieutenant, bored with the solitude of the Torre Nueva, who would sometimes come and tie his horse to an olive tree in front of *Cañamel's* after making it across the muddy canals.

Neleta smiled at the rumours. She did not love her husband, of that she was certain, and felt quite interested in many of the men who used to visit the tavern, but she had the prudence of the self-centred and logical woman who marries for convenience, and has no wish to upset her tranquil existence with any infidelity.

One day came news that Tono's son was in Valencia. The war had finished, and battalions of dispirited, disarmed men were disembarking in all the ports like flocks of sick sheep. They were mere ghosts of men, febrile wraiths, waxy yellow as the candles that are only seen at funerals, with the will to live burning in their deep-set eyes like a star at the bottom of a well. All were heading home, unfit for work, destined to die within the year in the bosom of families which had sent off a man and got back a shadow.

Tonet's reception in El Palmar was tinged with curiosity. He was the only man on the village to get back from "over there". But what did he look like! He was thin and wasted by the privations of the war's final days, for he was one of those who had suffered the blockade of Santiago, but otherwise he seemed strong enough, and the old fishwives rather admired his slim, scrawny frame and the martial pose he struck under the rachitic olive tree in the village square, twirling his moustache, a manly adornment in use elsewhere in El Palmar only by the Police Chief, and showing off a large collection of Panama hats, the only things he had brought back from the war. At night *Cañamel's* tavern was filled to hear his tales of things "over there".

He had forgotten about his former braggart soldier's yarns about beating up peaceful suspects and searching hovels, revolver in hand. His stories were now all about the Americans, the Yankees he had seen in Santiago, very tall lads, a bunch of toughs who ate a lot of meat and wore very small hats. That was the extent of his description of them. The enemy's enormous stature was the sole impression they had left on him. Guffaws broke the silence of the tavern when Tonet told them that one of those lads, seeing him in rags had given him some trousers before he got on the boat, but they were big, so big that they wrapped round him like a sail.

Neleta, behind the bar, gazed fixedly at him. Her eyes were expressionless, the two green drops devoid of life, but never for an instant leaving Tonet's face, as if anxious hold on to those martial features, so different from the others surrounding him, and which in no way brought to mind the lad who, ten years before, had her as his fiancée.

Cañamel, moved by patriotism and excited by the extraordinary crowd that Tonet was attracting to the tavern, clasped hands with the soldier, offered him glasses of wine and questioned him about matters in Cuba, acquainting himself with the various changes that had occurred since the far-off time when he himself had been "over there".

Tonet went everywhere accompanied by *Sangonera* who was greatly in awe of his boyhood companion. He was no longer the Sacristan and had given up on the books the priests lent him. His father's desire for the wandering life had awakened in him, and the priest had thrown him out of the Church, tired of the amusingly clumsy mistakes he was making when assisting at Mass while completely drunk. Besides, as he gravely affirmed, *Sangonera* did not agree with the way everyone laughed at what the priests got up to. So, still in the flower of his youth, but prematurely aged by constant drunkenness, broken and filthy, he lived on his wits as he had in childhood, sleeping in a cottage worse than a pigsty, and turning up in all the places where he might get a drink, though his wasted figure scarce cast a shadow on the ground.

In Tonet's company he found plenty going free, and he would be the first in a tavern to ask him to tell them about things "over there", for he knew that, as the tales went on, so the glasses would arrive.

The returning warrior appeared well satisfied with this life of relaxation and admiration. As he thought back to nights he had spent in the trenches, his stomach aching with hunger, or the terrible sea journey back in a boat full of sick flesh, littering the sea with dead bodies as it passed, El Palmar now appeared to him as a place of delights.

After a month of this pleasant life his father spoke to him one night in the silence of their cottage. What was he planning to do now? He was a grown man, and he ought to put an end to his adventuring and give some serious thought to his future. He himself had certain plans that he wanted to make his son part of as his sole heir. If they worked tirelessly with the determination of two honourable men, they even might build up a considerable fortune. A city lady, the same one as had rented him the fields at El Saler, was completely won over by his straight forwardness and his keenness for work and had just presented him with a large piece of reclaimed ground next to the lake, a polder or *tancat* of many hectares.

There was just one slight problem before they could actually work it, which was that it was covered in water, and they would have to fill the fields with a number of boatloads of earth ...a great number.

He had to either spend money or do the work himself. But there was no need to get down about it. That was how all the fields around the Albufera had been formed. Today's rich holdings were the lakebed of fifty years ago and two fit, healthy men with no fear of work could achieve miracles. This would be better than fishing in some poor area or working other people's fields.

Tonet was attracted by the novelty of the enterprise. If they had suggested to him that he farm the best and oldest of the fields around El Palmar, perhaps he would have pulled a face; but he liked battling with the lake, turning water into workable ground, taking harvests from places where the eels had wriggled among the water weed. Besides, in his superficial way of thinking, he saw only the results without focussing on the work needing done. They would be rich, and he would be able to rent out the ground and procure for himself the life of leisure he desired.

Father and son launched forth on their task, aided by la *Borda*, always excited about anything that would bring them prosperity. There is no need to mention what grandfather thought. The project made him feel the same as when his son had first set himself to till the ground. Another lot wanting to tame the Albufera, turning water into fields! But the folk carrying out this attack were his own family! The rogues!

Tonet plunged heart and soul into the endeavour, with the fleeting enthusiasm of the weak willed. His main idea was to fill up that corner of the lake in which his father sought his fortune, in one single great effort. Before dawn Tonet and la *Borda* would set off in two punts to fetch earth and carry it back later, with the trip perhaps taking an hour, to the wide expanse of still water whose edges were defined by mud dykes.

It was gruelling work, exhausting, a job for ants. Only Tono, the farmer who would have a go at anything, would take it on with only the strength of his own arms and his family to help him.

They would go to the big canals which flowed into the Albufera at the ports of Catarroja and El Saler and dredge great dollops of mud from the bottom using wide forks on long poles, lumps of dark slime that gave off an insufferable stench. They would leave these heaps from the bowels of the drainage ditches to dry on the banks, and when the sun had turned them into whitish blocks would load them into the two punts, lashed together to form a double hull. By punting together, over an hour of hard labour later, they would deliver the heap of laboriously gathered earth, and the flooded field would suck it in without any apparent result whatever, as if their cargo had just dissolved, leaving no trace behind. Fishermen would see the hard-working family glide past, two or three times every day, like water boatmen on the polished surface of the lake.

Tonet quickly tired of this gravedigger's toil. His determination did not amount to much anyway, and once its early attractions had faded, he clearly saw the monotony of the work and worked out the fearful number of months or even years that would be needed to bring the endeavour to a conclusion. He kept thinking of what it had taken to dredge up each load of earth and trembled on the edge of tears watching the water turn cloudy as they tipped it in, only to clear later, leaving the bottom looking just the same, just as deep, not even a hump visible, as if the soil had just vanished down a great hidden hole.

He began to skip work, staying in the cottage with the excuse that he was suffering a relapse of certain health problems picked up during the war, but his father and la *Borda* were hardly gone, when he would scuttle out to look for a cool corner at *Cañamel's* where he never lacked companions for a game of *truque* with a *porrón* of wine within easy reach. At most he worked two days a week.

In his detestation for the gravediggers who were destroying the lake, Paloma rejoiced at his grandson's laziness. Hee! Hee! His son was an idiot to place any trust in Tonet. He knew the lad well. A bone had stuck when he'd been born, which prevented him from bending down to any work. As a soldier he'd become tougher and there was no point in expecting anything to change. He knew the only remedy: a good beating would break him.

But since he was quite happy to see his son's business suffer difficulties, he put up with Tonet's laziness and even smiled when he saw him at *Cañamel's*.

In the village, rumours were starting to circulate about Tonet's keenness to visit the tavern. He would always sit at the bar, and he and Neleta would gaze at each other. She would talk less to Tonet than to other customers, but when not too busy, when she would be sitting doing something in front of the barrels, every time she raised her eyes, they would instinctively search out the young man. Customers also noted that every time the *Cubano* laid down his cards, his gaze would return to Neleta.

Cañamel's former sister-in-law talked about this up and down the street. They had an agreement, you only had to look at them! They were going to stick it to that idiot of an innkeeper all right! Between the two of them they were going to work their way through the fortune her poor sister had built up! But when the less credulous among them protested about the impossibility of getting together in a tavern always full of people, the harpy simply responded that they would get together outside. Neleta was capable of anything, and he, an enemy to work, had settled in the tavern, in the certainty that they would look after him there.

Ignorant of these rumours, *Cañamel* treated Tonet like his best friend. He played cards with him and would get annoyed with his wife if she did not join them. He read nothing in Neleta's glances, in those strangely glittering eyes, in the faintly ironic look with which she took these reprimands while serving her former fiancé a glass of wine.

The rumours circulating in El Palmar reached Tono's ears, and one night, taking his son outside the cottage, he spoke to him, sadly, a man tired out with battling uselessly against disgrace.

He could easily see that Tonet had no desire to help him. He was the same lazybones as in former times, born to spend his time at the bar. But he was a man now, he had been to war and his father could no longer raise his hand to him as he had done. He didn't want to work? All right, then, he would continue the operation entirely on his own, even though he worked himself to death like a dog, but always with the hope that he might leave a bit of bread to the ungrateful wretch who had abandoned him.

But what he could not so calmy watch was his son spending his days at *Cañamel's*, sitting opposite his former fiancée. There were other taverns he could go to if he wanted, and all of them without that woman.

Tonet protested vehemently at this. Lies, it was all lies! Vile insinuations from *Samaruca*, *Cañamel's* sister-in-law, who hated Neleta and never gave up on her rumour mongering. Tonet said this with all the force of the truth, swearing on his mother's memory that he had not laid a finger on Neleta, nor said the merest word to her that would bring back memories of their former betrothal.

Tono smiled sadly. He believed him and didn't doubt a word of it. But there was more to it; he was fully convinced that up to the present all the rumours were false. But he knew life. They were only glances today, but tomorrow they would fall, descend into dishonour as a result of this dangerous game of continually brushing against each other. Neleta had always seemed to him a bit of a birdbrain, and it wouldn't be her, setting the good example of modesty to him.

The brave man's attitude after this outburst was so sincere and kindly that he held Tonet's attention.

He had to remember he was the son of an honourable man, who had bad luck in business, but whom nobody in the whole Albufera could accuse of acting badly.

Neleta had a husband, and he, Tonet, was adding betrayal to the sin of looking at another man's wife. *Cañamel* was also his friend, they would spend the day together, they played cards and drank as companions, so it was cowardice to cheat on such a man, and he was liable to be paid back with a shot in the head.

His father's tone suddenly became very serious

Neleta was rich and he, his son, was poor, so people might believe that he was after her as a means of keeping himself in ease without working. This was what irritated him, what changed his sadness into anger.

He would rather see his son dead than be shamed by such dishonourable conduct. Tonet! Son! He had to think of the family, of the *Palomas*, a family as old El Palmar itself; a race of workers, unfortunate but good people, riddled with debt as a result of their bad luck, but still incapable of such a betrayal.

They were sons and daughters of the lake, content in their misery, and when they set off on their final voyage, when God should call them, they would be able to punt up to the foot of his throne and, lacking any other merit, be able to show the Lord their hands, calloused like beasts of burden but with their souls clean of any crime.

CHAPTER 4

The second Sunday in July was the most important day of the year in El Palmar. This was the day when the redolins, the fishing areas in the Albufera were allocated to the local fishermen by drawing lots in a solemn and traditional ceremony presided over by a representative of La Hacienda, a mysterious lady that no one had ever seen, but who was spoken of with superstitious respect, seeing she owned the entire lake and the endless pine forests of la Dehesa.

At six the church bell had sent the whole population scuttling into Mass. The celebrations of the birth of the Infant Jesus were pretty solemn after Christmas, but were really just entertainment, while the ceremony of drawing lots brought one's daily bread into play, and even the possibility of getting rich if the fishing was good. For this reason, Mass on that Sunday was the one heard with the greatest devotion. Womenfolk had no thought but to find their men, pushing and shoving them to fulfil their religious obligations., so the whole body of fishermen was packed, cowering, in the church, thinking more about the lake than the Mass, going over in their minds the Albufera and its canals, deciding the best spots to choose, if luck favoured them with one of the first numbers.

The little church with its lime washed walls and high windows with their green curtains, could not contain all the faithful. The double doors were wide open, and the congregation spilled outside into the square, standing bare headed in the July sun. On the altar the Niño Jesus, patron of the village, displayed his beaming smile and flowing robe, an image no more than a few inches tall but which, despite its size, could fill boats that got the best spots with eels on stormy nights as well as doing other miracles that the women of El Palmar could tell of.

Paintings that had come from former convents stood out against the white walls, great tableaux with legions of the damned, all red as if just newly cooked, and angels feathered like parrots hurrying them along with flaming swords. Above the basin of holy water, a small notice in gothic characters bore the following prayer:

"Since God's Law does not allow you to stray from the commandment to love, neither are you allowed to spit in the Lord's house".

There was none in El Palmar who did not admire these lines, written, according to Grandfather *Paloma*, by a certain priest in the far-off days when the old boatman was a lad. They had all made an effort to spell it out, letter by letter, in the endless Masses they had endured as good Christians. But while the poetry might be admired, the advice was not, and the fishermen, like true amphibians with no respect for the "Commandment to love", hoarsely coughed and spat, throughout the religious ceremony, providing a continuous soundtrack of throat-clearing, dirtying the floor, and drawing angry backward glances from the officiant.

Never had El Palmar had a priest like Father Miguel, *Pare Miquel.* They used to say that he had been sent there as a punishment, but he seemed to suffer his misfortune with relish. A tireless shot, the Mass would be scarcely finished when he would don his grass sandals and leather beret and, with his dog at his heels would either march off into the Dehesa or set off in his punt among the thick reed beds after wildfowl. As he himself used to say, one had to make the most of an unenviable position. His stipend was five *reales* a day, and, were it not for his shotgun, he would be condemned to die of hunger like his predecessors. The keepers tolerated his incursions, and his table carried assorted game every day. Women liked his energetic, strong, manly way of doing things, even using his fists as compulsion at times, while the men no less appreciated the broad-minded approach he took to the functions of his office. He was a shotgun priest. When the Mayor had to spend a night in Valencia, he left his delegated authority in don Miguel's hands, and he, happy with the change, would call the head of the Police.

- You and I are the only authorities in the village. Let's look after it.

So off they would go on their rounds all night long with their carbines on their shoulders, checking the taverns and sending people home, stopping off a few times at the Presbytery for a shot of rum, and continuing until the first light of dawn, when don Miguel would cast off his smuggler's uniform and get himself into Church to say mass for the fishermen.

While engaged on his holy Duties on a Sunday he would watch the faithful out of the corner of his eye, noting the men that kept spitting, the fishwives chatting under their breath about their neighbour's scandals and the children fighting around the door, and as he turned, rising proudly to his full height in benediction, he would cast such looks at the perpetrators that they shuddered to think what *pare Miquel* would threaten them with next. He was the one who had cuffed his ears, and sent the drunk *Sangonera* packing, having caught him red handed for the second or third time in the Sacristy with the bottle of wine. Only the priest was allowed to drink in that house. There was a streak of violence in all his holy work, and plenty of times, right in the middle of the Mass, if he found *Sangonera's* successor getting the responses wrong or being slow in taking the Gospel from one side to the other, he would land him a kick from under the lace trimming of his alb and click his tongue as if calling a dog.

His morality was very straightforward; it was based in the stomach. When the penitent confessed their sins in the confessional, their penance was always the same. What they had to do was eat more! That was why the Devil grabbed them when he saw them weak and yellowed. His motto was: More mouthfuls and less sinfuls! And if anyone pleaded poverty in response, he would get angry and start swearing, Think about it! Poor and they lived in the Albufera, the best spot in the world. There he was with his five *reales*, and he lived better than any Archbishop. They had sent him to El Palmar thinking it would make him more holy, but he would only change his job if they made him a Canon of Valencia. Why had God created woodcock, fluttering thick as flies over the Dehesa, rabbits as numerous as blades of grass, and so many wildfowl on the lake that you only had to rustle the reeds to send them up in dozens? Were they waiting for the game to drop, ready-plucked and seasoned into their pots? What they needed was more zeal for work and fear of God. There was no need for everyone to be an eel fisherman, sitting for hours in a boat like a woman, eating white flesh smelling of mud. That's why they were all mouldy sinners who gave him the creeps. Any man who is a real man, with balls, ought to get his food as he did, with a shot!

After Easter Sunday service, when the whole of El Palmar had emptied out its sack of sins in the confessional, the air of the Dehesa and the lake rang with shots, making the keepers crazy running to and fro, trying to figure out what could be driving the sudden flurry.

Mass was over, and the congregation was scattered around the little square, but the women were not going back to their cottages to prepare the midday stew. They were staying with their menfolk, facing the school where the lots would be officially verified as they were drawn, the best building in El Palmar, the only one with two storeys, a small building with the boys upstairs and the girls on the ground floor. The verification ceremony was taking place upstairs, and the Bailiff, helped by *Sangonera*, could be seen through the open windows setting up the table and Presidential throne for the gentleman coming from Valencia and the school benches for the members of the Fishermen's Association.

The village elders were clustered around the twisted, almost leafless, olive tree which was the square's sole adornment. This ancient and rachitic tree, wrenched form its mountain home to languish in the muddy soil, was the village meeting point, the place where every act of civil life's drama unfolded. Beneath its branches, deals were done, boats changed hands and eels were sold to the dealers from the city. When anyone found a *mornell* eel net, a floating pole, or any other fishing gear abandoned in the lake's waters, they would leave it at the foot of the tree and people would file past until its owner recognised it by the special mark that each fisherman would carve on the tools of his trade.

They were all talking nervously about the coming draw, in the jittery tones of people who were about to trust their whole future to chance. Whether the coming year was to be one of misery or abundance would be decided for each of them within the hour. In the little huddles the talk was of the six best *redolins*, the only spots that might make a fisherman really rich and which were allocated to the first six numbers drawn from the sack. These were spots in or near la *Sequiòta*, the route the eels took as they headed for the sea on stormy nights and could be trapped in the *redolin* nets.

Some favoured fishermen who had owned one of these spots in *la Sequiòta* had become the stuff of legend when, on a storm battered Albufera that had seen curling waves big enough to expose the muddy bottom, they had taken six hundred bushels of fish in a single night. Six hundred bushels at two *duros* each! Eyes glistened with the fire of greed, but they all talked in whispers about the fishing as they repeated these fabled numbers, because since they were children they had all accepted, and now solidly maintained, the convention of saying that the fishing was poor, in case someone from outside the Albufera might be listening and *La Hacienda*, that greedy *Grande Dame* that no one knew, might find out about it and afflict them with new taxes.

Old *Paloma* could talk of the old days, when people were not breeding like the rabbits on the Dehesa, and the Association comprised only about sixty fishermen who were in the draw. How many were there now? More than a hundred and fifty had taken part the previous year. If the population kept growing there would be more fishermen than eels, and El Palmar would lose the privilege of using its *redolins* which gave it some advantage over other fishermen on the lake.

The thought of these "others", the fishermen of Catarroja who shared the fruits of the Albufera with men from El Palmar, made old *Paloma* nervous. He hated them as much as the growers who gnawed away the margins of the lake, creating new fields. As the old boatman used to say, those people, living well away from the lake, cheek by jowl with the farm workers and working themselves on the land when the day rates were good, were no better than part-time fishermen, people that only turned to the lake when driven by hunger or when they had nothing better to do.

Deep down old *Paloma* resented the proud claim of these enemies to be considered the first people to work the lake. The fishermen of Catarroja were, according to them the original population, the people to whom the glorious King James had given the privilege of exploiting the lake after he took back Valencia, with the obligation to hand over a fifth of the catch to the crown.

"So, who were the El Palmar folk then?" the old boatman would ask with a wry smile, his temper rising in expectation of what the Catarrojans would always say in reply. According to them,

El Palmar was named as it was because, in far off times it was a palmetto-covered island. In previous centuries, people would come down from up-river at Torrente and other nearby villages, where they were involved in the broom-making trade, set up camp on the island, and after stocking up for a season with palm leaves, would then hoist sail. But little by little, a few families began to stay there. The broom makers turned themselves into fisherfolk when they realised there was more money to be made that way, and because they were cleverer and more up to date with progress elsewhere in the world as a result of their travels, they invented the *redolins*, and thus succeeded in obtaining the Royal Privilege to the prejudice of the Catarrojans, a simple people who had never been out of the Albufera.

Old *Paloma's* indignation as he would repeat these claims by the enemy was a sight to be seen. People from El Palmar, the best fishermen on the lake, descendants of some broom makers from Torrente and other places which had never seen an eel! Christ! Men got killed with a *fitora* on a canal bank for less. He was well informed and could swear it was all nonsense.

When he was a young man he had once been nominated as the Association's *Jurado* or Representative and had charge of the village's greatest treasure in his cottage, the Fishermen's

Archive, a great chest full of books, ordinances, Royal Privileges, and account books, passed down from one *Jurado* to the next, which had spent centuries going from cottage to cottage, and was always kept under a pile of cushions, in case the enemies of El Palmar might try to steal it. The old boatman did not know how to read. In his day you didn't think about such matters, and you ate better. But in the evenings a certain friend of his, a priest, had deciphered the spidery scrawl that filled the yellowing pages, and he retained a very clear memory of the contents. The most important was the Privilege from the Glorious Saint James, *Santiago Matamorros*, the Moor Slayer, for while respecting the King who had gifted the lake to the fishermen the old boatman thought little of Royalty but loved him as a Saint. Later came the concessions from Don Pedro, Doña Violante, Don Martín and Don Fernando, all monarchs, and some of them Blessed Servants of the Lord, who remembered the poor, bestowing on them the right to cut logs on the Dehesa for soaking nets and the privilege of using pine bark for dyeing the string for them. Those were far-off, different times! Kings, excellent personages who were always open-handed with the poor, were content with a fifth of the catch, unlike today when *La Hacienda* and other man-made contrivances took half a bushel of silver every three months to let them live off the lake which had belonged to his forefathers. And when anybody would say that a fifth of the catch represented much more than the famous half bushel of silver, old Paloma would scratch his head in confusion under his cap. All right: he accepted it might be more, but it wasn't paid in money and felt less.

After all this he would return to his fuming about the other people who lived around the lake. It was true that in the beginning there were no other fishermen on the lake except those that lived under the shade of Catarroja's belltower. In those days you couldn't live near the sea. Barbary pirates would arrive on the beach any time around dawn and make off with the lot, so gentlefolk had to shelter in villages so as not to find themselves wearing a chain necklace for adornment. But slowly, as security improved, true fishermen, pure fishermen, the ones who fled working on the land as they would a dishonourable call to duty, had moved to El Palmar, thus avoiding a two-hour trip every day before casting their nets. They loved the lake and thus they stayed there. It was nothing to do with being broom-makers. The El Palmar people were as ancient as anyone else; he'd heard from his grandfather plenty of times that the family originated in Catarroja and there must even still be some relatives over there, not that they wanted anything to do with them.

The proof that they were the oldest and most skilful fishermen lay in the invention of the *redolins*, a marvel that the men from Catarroja were never going to have discovered. Those poor devils fished with either nets or hooks; most days they had to cross their bellies, and no matter how good the weather, they never got themselves out of poverty. The wise Palmarians had studied the eels' habits, and finding that they made for the sea at night, and that on dark, stormy ones they would go mad, jostling their way out of the lake into the canals , they had found it more convenient to close off the ditches with barriers of submerged nets , placing alongside them the string bags, the *mornells*, and the fish would slither into the traps on their own, leaving the fisherman with nothing to do but empty the contraptions and slip them back underwater.

And what an admirable organisation it was, this Association of Fishermen of El Palmar! Old *Paloma* could get quite worked up talking about the work of his forefathers. The lake belonged to the fishermen. The whole thing belonged to everybody, not like on land where mankind had invented this nonsense of parcelling everything up, putting up boundaries and walls, saying arrogantly "This is yours, and this is mine" as if everything weren't God's and as if a man might own any more earth when dead than the clod that filled his mouth for ever.

La Albufera belonged to all the sons of El Palmar without distinction or class, the rogues that spent the day in *Cañamel's* as much as the *Alcalde*, the Mayor, who sent the eels away, far away, and was almost as rich as the pub landlord. But when it came to dividing the lake up among them all and given that some spots were better fishing than others, this annual drawing of lots had been established, so the juicy slices could be passed from hand to hand. The man who today lived in misery might tomorrow be rich; depending on your luck, this was the way that God ordained it. He who was fated to be poor, remained poor, but with the window wide open for Fortune to enter, one could feel the possibility. There he was, the oldest man in El Palmar, hoping to make his hundred if the Devil didn't get in his way. He had taken part in more than eighty draws; once he had drawn the fifth number and another tine the fourth, but never had he achieved the first; but he wasn't complaining, for he had never suffered hunger nor warmed his back at his neighbour's expense, like the folk from up country. Besides, when, the big catches in the *redolins* were finished at the end of winter, the Association would order an *arrastra*, a Sweep, in which all the fishermen in the Association took part, joining boats and nets and hands together. This common enterprise by the entire village swept the whole lakebed with a massive line of nets and the enormous catch was divided equally among everybody. That was how men ought to live, like brothers, so as to avoid turning into wild beasts. Old *Paloma* would close his discourse by saying that it was not for nothing that when He came to earth, the Lord had preached on lakes that were more or less like the Albufera and didn't surround himself with farmers but with fishermen after eels and tench.

The crowd in the square was growing bigger. The Mayor, with his assistants and the Bailiff, was on the canal bank awaiting the arrival of the boat carrying the representative of *La Hacienda* from Valencia. Personages from the surrounding area were arriving to grace the draw with their presence. The crowd parted for the Police Lieutenant galloping in, mud-stained across the ditches, from his lonely post in the Torre Nueva between the Dehesa and the sea. The current *Jurado* presented himself, followed by a lad carrying the chest with the Association's archives on his back, and *pare Miquèl*, the shotgun priest , with his cape over his shoulder, made his way from group to group assuring them that Lady Luck would turn her back on sinners.

Cañamel, not being from the village, had no right of attendance at the draw but appeared as interested as the fishermen. He never missed the ceremony, for that was where he picked up business for the whole year to make up for the drop in smuggling. The man who drew the best spot would usually be poor, owning nothing but a little punt and some nets. To make the most of la *Sequiòta*, you needed big equipment, several proper boats and paid crew, so when the poor lad, stunned by his good luck, wouldn't know where to start, he would sidle up to *Cañamel* as his guardian angel. He had everything needed; he would offer his boats, the thousand pesetas worth of string for the long barriers needed to close off the canal and the money to pay wages. In view of his esteem and affection for the lucky man, all this was the least he could do to help a friend, but since friendship was one thing and business something else, he would be happy to take half the catch in exchange for his support. In this way, the draw was almost always to Cañamel's benefit, although he did fret about the outcome, in case the first drawn numbers should go to neighbours who already had some means.

Neleta had also come along to the square for the event which was one of the village's main fiestas. She was in her Sunday best, looking like some great lady from Valencia, while la *Samaruca*, her implacable enemy, with her hostile little coven, made jokes about how high her hair was piled, her pink dress with silver-buckled belt and her "bad girl" perfume which drove the men wild and scandalised the whole of El Palmar. Since she had become rich, the vivacious blonde had taken to using striking perfumes, as if to isolate herself from the muddy stink surrounding the lake. Like all the women in the village, she seldom washed her face, so her skin was not very clean, but she was never without a generous dusting of powder, and with every step, her clothes exhaled a seductive scent of musk which made the customers' senses whirl with its heady blessing.

A wave of excitement ran through the crowd. He was here! The ceremony was going to start! Carrying his black-tasselled staff, the Mayor swept by with his minions, together with the representative of *La Hacienda*, some minor employee at whom the fishermen looked with admiration (thinking confusedly of his great power over the Albufera) mixed with hate. That little dandy was the lad who was going to make off with their half bushel of silver!

Slowly they all made their way up the school's narrow staircase which only admitted them in single file. A pair of policemen guarded the door, rifle in hand, to stop women and children getting in the way of proceedings at the meeting. From time to time the curiosity of the little ones seemed to get the better of them, but the *carabineros* just presented their rifle butts and threatened to cuff the lot of them if their chatter was disturbing the solemnity of the occasion.

The crowd upstairs was so great that fishermen with no place to sit on the benches were perching on the balconies. Some of them, the oldest, were wearing the red felt cap that old boys used in the Albufera, others covered their heads with a long-tailed, peasant handkerchief, or with straw hats. They were all wearing light colours and grass-soled sandals or barefoot, and from the packed, sweating crowd rose the cold, sticky stench of creatures living constantly in mud and water.

The President's table was placed on the teacher's dais. In the centre was the Representative of *La Hacienda*, dictating the opening titles of proceedings to his scribe and flanking him were the priest, the Mayor, the *Jurado*, the Lieutenant and other invitees, among whom figured El Palmar's doctor, a poor outcast from science who for five *reales* came by boat three times a week to cure the poor suffering from tertian fever *en bloque*.

The *Jurado* rose from his seat. He had before him the Association's account books, marvellous sets of hieroglyphics containing not a single letter, for the payees were represented by all sorts of little drawings. The old *Jurados*, not knowing how to read or write, had invented this system and thus it continued. Each page contained one fisherman's account and there was no need to write a name at the top, just the sign that each of them put on his boat and his nets for recognition. One was a cross and another a pair of scissors, while further on was a coot's beak and old *Paloma's* half-moon, so the *Jurado* could understand it and had only to glance at the hieroglyph to say this is so-and-so's account. The rest of the page was filled with lines, and more lines, each one denoting the payment of a month's tax dues. The old boatmen were loud in their support for this system. Anyone could keep an eye on his account in this way and there was no trickery like in those books full of numbers and close writing which could only be understood by gentlemen.

The *Jurado*, a sharp, shaven-headed lad with an insolent look, cleared his throat and spat a few times before speaking. The invitees on the President's dais leaned back and began talking among themselves. Initial business involved Association matters in which they could not intervene, things that needed sorting out among the fishermen themselves. The *Jurado* commenced his peroration: "*Caballers*! Gentlemen!"

He swept an imperious gaze round the meeting

to impose silence. The annoying buzz of women's chatter and the sound of children twittering away like condemned men rose from the square, and the Mayor had to send the Bailiff down to go round and impose silence so the *Jurado* could continue his speech.

Gentlemen, some things are clear. They had made him *Jurado* in order to collect dues from every one of them and to deliver to *La Hacienda*, every quarter, around one thousand five hundred pesetas, the famous half bushel of silver that the whole village talked of. All right so far, but things could not go on in this way. Many men were getting behind in their payments and the better provided fishermen were having to make up the deficit. To avoid this nonsense in future he proposed that those not up to date with their dues should not be entered in the draw.

One part of the assembly received these words with murmured satisfaction. They were those who had paid, and they could see that, with many of their colleagues excluded from the draw, their own chance of drawing one of the first numbers would be increased. But the majority of the meeting, the more miserable looking bunch, were on their feet shouting in protest and for several minutes the *Jurado* could not make himself heard.

Once silence was again established and everyone

was back in their seats a sick looking man rose, his face pallid, and an unhealthy glint in his eyes. He spoke slowly, his voice faltering, his words often cut short with a bout of shivering. He was one of those who had not paid, perhaps no one owed as much as he did. In the previous draw he had got one of the last spots and had not been able to catch enough even to feed his family. Twice in the last year he had punted all the way to Valencia with a couple of gilded white boxes in the bottom of his boat, mere trifles which he had had to take a loan for, but, well, what more could a father do for his little ones when they parted from you for ever than dress them up well? Two of his children had died of malnutrition, so *Pare Miquel* said, him over there, and then he had caught the tertian fever from labouring, and that had cost him months and months. He didn't pay because he couldn't pay. And that was the reason they were going to strip him of the chance to make a fortune? Was he not one of the Association members as had been his father and grandfather before him?

A painful silence fell, through which the sobs of the poor man could be heard, now at the end of his strength, collapsed on his seat with his head in his hands, as if ashamed of his confession.

"*No redèu, no! No, by God, no!*" shouted a voice quivering with an energy that roused everybody.

It was old *Paloma*, on his feet with his cap on his head, his eyes blazing with indignation, speaking fast with a liberal sprinkling of as many swear words and oaths as he could remember. The old boys around him were pulling his coat to call his attention to his lack of respect for the gentlemen on the President's table, but he elbowed them aside and carried on. What did such puppets matter to him, a man who had had dealings with Queens and Heroes? He was speaking because he was able to do so. Christ! He was the oldest boatman on the Albufera, and his words ought to be taken as decrees. The fathers and grandfathers of all of them were speaking through his mouth. The Albufera belonged to every one of them. Agreed? Well, he would be ashamed to take the bread out of a man's mouth whether or not he had paid *la Hacienda*. Did that lady really need every fisherman's miserable few pesetas in order to eat?

The old boy's indignation was getting the crowd worked up, although many were laughing loudly, forgetting the grievous spectacle they had all recently witnessed.

Old *Paloma* recalled that he had also once been the *Jurado*. It was good to take a firm line with the rogues who avoided working, but with poor lads who did their best but weren't able to pay through being victims of some misfortune you had to be open handed. Bastards! It wasn't as if the fishermen of El Palmar were Moors! No, all were brothers together, and the lake belonged to all of them. These class divisions into the rich and the poor were matters for landlubbers, for "labourers", among whom there were bosses and there were servants. On the Albufera all were equal. The man who couldn't pay today would still pay later, and as for those who had more having to make up for what those who had nothing, well that was how it had always been. Right? Everyone into the draw!

Tonet led the tumultuous applause for his grandfather and while Tono did not seem entirely in agreement with his father's thoughts, the whole body of poorer fishermen leapt on the old man, showing their enthusiastic support by pulling on his shirt and raining affectionate slaps on the back of his wizened neck.

Downfallen, the *Jurado* closed his books. It was the same every year, impossible to put the Association's affairs in order with seemingly forever-young old folk like that around. With a bored expression he carried on listening to the excuses of men who hadn't paid and who were getting to their feet to explain their arrears. They had people sick in the family; they had drawn a very poor spot; work had become impossible as a result of those cursed fevers which seemed to lie in wait in the reed beds at sunset to sink their claws into one's flesh; the whole miserable depressing litany of their insalubrious life on the lake was paraded before him in an endless lament.

In order to cut this otherwise interminable display short, it was agreed not to exclude anyone from the draw and the Jurado placed on the table the great leather bag of tokens.

- Hold on a minute! Came a shout from near the door.

Who was this wanting to make further annoying demands? The crowds opened up and a great guffaw of laughter greeted *Sangonera's* appearance as he slowly advanced, rubbing his drunkard's bloodshot eyes and making every effort to assume the appearance of being fit to take part in the meeting. Finding all the taverns deserted he had slipped into the school and before the draw thought it necessary to demand the floor.

- What d' you want? said the *Jurado* in ill humour, annoyed by the rogue's intervention which was really trying his patience after all the excuses from the lads who owed money.

What did he want? He wanted to know why his name had not figured in these draws over the years. He had as much right as the best of them to enjoy the privilege of having a *redoli* on the Albufera. He was the poorest of them all, but, well, hadn't he been born in El Palmar? Hadn't they baptised him in the parish of San Valero de Ruzafa? Was he not descended from fishermen? So, he ought to be in the draw!

So unexpected and grotesque did this vagabond's expectations seem, a man who never touched a net and who would rather swim a canal than pick up a pole, that the whole body of fishermen broke out in guffaws of laughter.

The *Jurado* dismissed his claims out of hand. Get out of there, good for nothing! What did it matter to the Association if his forebears had been honest fishermen, if his father had given up toiling with the pole and given himself over to leisure, since he had no more claim to be a waterman than to have been born in El Palmar? Besides, his father had never paid any dues and neither had he; the sign that *Sangoneras* had used for so many years on their fishing kit had been erased from the Association's books.

But the inebriate kept pressing on about his rights amid the crowd's growing laughter, until old *Paloma* intervened with one or two questions. Suppose in the end they let him into the draw, and he drew one of the best spots; what would he do with it? How would he work it since he was no fisherman and knew nothing of the trade? The rogue smiled slyly. The important thing was to draw the spot; the rest was his own affair. He would arrange for others to do the work for him, leaving him with the best part of the catch. His cynical smile betrayed the expression of that first man who managed to cheat his fellow into doing the work so he could live at leisure.

Sangonera's frank confession angered the fishermen. He was doing no more than speaking aloud what many of them had sometimes thought about, but these simple folk felt insulted by the rogue's cynicism, and that he personified all oppressors of the poor. Out! Out! He was pushed and shoved out the door, while the young fishermen milled about drumming the floor with their feet and pretending to fight like cats and dogs.

Don Miguel, the priest, rose indignantly to his feet, took up a fighting stance and stepped forward, his face contorted in anger. What was all this? What sort of disrespect was this they were showing the grave and important members of the President's table? If he had to come down off the dais and give some fine lad a thick lip, well, he'd know about it.

As an instant silence fell, the priest sat down,

satisfied with his power, saying under his breath to the Lieutenant,

- See? Nobody understands this flock like I do. Sometimes the shepherd has to use the crook!

But more even than *pare MIquèl's* threats, what really restored calm was seeing the *Jurado* handing over to the President the list of Association fishermen so that he could make sure they were all present. It comprised all the men of El Palmar actively engaged in fishing, and it was enough to be of age, even if still living with your father, to be included in the draw for the *redolins*.

The President read out the fishermen's names to which most men responded, "*Ave Maria Purisima!*" quite reverently, seeing that the priest was present, although some of the opposite persuasion would reply "*Avant*!" just for the pleasure of seeing him pull a face.

The Jurado emptied the greasy leather bag, almost as old as the Association itself, and the tokens rolled out onto the table, black wooden balls with a hole into which could be inserted a bit of paper with the member's name.

One by one the fishermen were called up to the President's table to receive their token and the slip bearing their name, placed there in advance, given that they did not know how to write.

The precautions that their shrewd, suspicious nature then forced these impoverished people to adopt were something to see. The least educated scuttled off in search of someone who could read in order to check that it really was their name that figured on the slip, convincing themselves only after a number of such consultations. The custom of always going by a nickname also gave them problems. Their two given names only saw the light of day on an occasion such as this and they faltered uncertainly about whether they were actually theirs.

But then came the things they had to be really careful about. They each hid what they were doing, turning towards the wall, and poking the rolled-up slip of paper into the token along with a bit of straw, a cardboard matchstick, anything that would serve for a personal indictor that their token had not been interfered with. Their distrust continued up to the very moment they deposited it back in the leather sack. They instinctively distrusted that gentleman from Valencia as country folk always do with someone in public office.

The draw was about to get underway. Taking off his biretta, the priest, don Miguel rose to his feet, and everyone did likewise. In accordance with ancient custom, they had to say the Salve Regina, for that brought good luck, so for a long moment the fishermen, caps in hand and with their eyes lowered, tunelessly intoned the prayer.

Absolute quiet. The President shook the bag to mix the tokens well, the sound shattering the silence like a distant hail shower. A child approached the dais, passed from hand to hand over the fishermen's heads, and put his hand into the sack. The suspense was immense; everyone's eyes were fixed on the wooden token from which the rolled-up bit of paper was being extracted with great difficulty.

The President read out the name, occasioning a certain amount of indecision in the assembly, used to nicknames and slow to recognise these never-used formal names. Who was the number one draw? But with a bound, Tonet was on his feet and screaming "Present!". It was old *Paloma's* grandson! What beginner's luck for the lad! He had achieved the best spot in the first draw he had ever taken part in!

People around him were enviously congratulating him but he, hardly able to believe his own good fortune just gazed at the President. Could he really pick his spot? They scarcely had to nod approval for him to blurt out his demand: he wanted la *Sequiòta*. As soon as he saw the scribe noting it down, he burst like a bolt from the room, knocking people aside and punching fists with the friends in salute.

The crowd in the square were stood waiting as silently as the upper chamber. It was customary for the first fortunate lads to go down straight away and throw their hats in the air in joy, telling everyone about their good luck. So, at the first glimpse of Tonet almost falling down the stairs, a great shout of acclamation greeted him.

- *Es El Cubano,* It's the Cuban, it's Tonet, the lad with the moustache.

Women threw themselves forward, overcome with emotion, hugging him, weeping, as if in touching him they might be blessed with some of his luck, and recalling his mother. If only the poor woman could see it, how happy she would be! Tonet, enveloped in skirts and fired up by the affectionate welcome, instinctively embraced Neleta who smiled, her green eyes shining with happiness.

The *Cubano* certainly wanted to celebrate his triumph. He sent to *Cañamel's* for cases of lemonade and beer for the ladies, and let the men drink as much as they wanted! He would pay. In a moment the square took on the appearance of an encampment. *Sangonera,* with an energy always evident when there was talk of drinking, supported what his generous friend wanted to do and fetched the hard old boards from *Cañamel's* store cupboards and went from group to group filling glasses, only stopping frequently to see to his own needs.

The fortunate few with the first drawn spots were still coming down, throwing their hats in the air, but only their own families and friends rushed to greet them. All attention was on Tonet, on the number one being so lavishly celebrated.

Fishermen were pouring out of the school. Thirty tokens had been drawn by now and only the worst *redolins* remained, the ones that hardly produced enough to feed a family and people were leaving, having no further interest in the draw.

Old *Paloma* was making his way from group to group, enjoying the congratulations. For the first time he was happy with his grandson. Hee-hee! Rogues were always the lucky ones: his father had already said as much. There he was with his eighty draws, never having got the number one, and his grandson had it the first year after getting back from distant lands. But in the end, it all fell to the family. He felt a surge of happiness thinking that for the next year he was going to be the most important fisherman on the Albufera.

Grave and self-contained as always but somewhat softened by the good fortune he went up to his son. Tono! Fortune had come knocking at his door and he had to make the most of it. He surely would help his child, who knew little of fishing matters and there would be a lot of serious business to deal with. But the old man was struck dumb at his son's cold response. Yes, that first spot was good luck if you had the tools to make the most of it. But more than a thousand pesetas would be needed for nets alone. Did they have that sort of money?

Old *Paloma* smiled, there was no lack of people who would lend it, but Tono put on a pained expression at any mention of loans. They owed plenty. What he suffered from certain Frenchmen in Catarroja was no storm in a teacup, men who sold heavy horses by instalments and advanced money to farmers. He had had to ask their help, initially in the years of bad harvests and now to push forward filling in his lagoon. He even dreamt of those velveteen clad gentlemen, muttering threats in broken Valenciano, and ready at every step to take out the terrible book in which were inscribed the loans, and the complicated system of interest payments. He had enough loans already. When a man finds himself mired in misfortune, he ought to get out of it as best he can without getting in any deeper. A farmer's debts were enough for him, and he did not want to get tangled up in new loans for the fishing. His sole desire was to get his fields above water without getting into any more difficulties.

The old boatman turned on his heel. That was his own flesh and blood…? He would rather have Tonet, with all his sloth. He was going with his grandson and the two of them would soon work out how to get round it all. Whoever owned the Sequiòta was never short of money.

Surrounded by his friends, feted by the women, and swelling with pride under Neleta's tearful gaze, Tonet felt someone touch him on the shoulder.

It was *Cañamel*, seemingly all concern for his protégé. They had to talk; there was good reason why they had always been real friends, and the tavern was like home to Tonet. There was no need to put matters off; between friends, business was always settled quickly. They stepped aside a little followed by the crowd's curious glances.

The inn keeper got straight down to it. Tonet would not have at his disposal the means to exploit the spot he had luckily drawn, wasn't that so? But here he had himself, a true friend, ready to help and join in a common enterprise. He would share everything with him.

Tonet was silent, not knowing how to reply, so taking his silence for a negative, the innkeeper returned to the charge. Were they comrades or not? Was he, like his father, thinking of going off to those foreigners in Catarroja, who sucked the life out of the poor? He was a friend: he even thought of himself as a relative because, what the Devil, he could not forget that his wife, his Neleta, had grown up in the Paloma's home, had often been fed there and loved Tonet like a brother.

The wily innkeeper made full use of these childhood memories, dwelling on the brotherly affection his wife felt for the young man, before adopting a more heroic way of resolving matters. If he had any doubts about it, he would call in Neleta to make up his mind for him. She would surely succeed in getting him back on the straight and narrow. Right? Should he call her?

Seduced by the offer, Tonet nonetheless hesitated before accepting. He feared what people would say, he thought about his father's stern advice, he looked round the watching crowd for guidance and spotted his grandfather nodding affirmatively at the back.

The old boatman guessed what *Cañamel* had been saying. He had had thought of precisely the same rich inn keeper as a source of aid. He urged his grandson on with further nods. He shouldn't turn him down: that was the man he needed.

Tonet made his decision and Neleta's husband,

seeing it in his eyes, pressed on with the terms of the deal. He would sort out everything they needed and Tonet and his grandfather would do the work. They would divide the catch. Agreed?

Agreed! The two men shook hands and set off for the tavern for a celebration meal, followed by Neleta and old *Paloma*.

News ran like wildfire round the square that the *Cubano* and *Cañamel* had joined up to work the *Sequiòta*. La *Samaruca* had to be removed thence on the Mayor's orders, and marched off to her cottage, escorted by several women, roaring like one possessed, calling loudly on her sister's name, now dead these many years, asserting ,with all the force she could command, that *Cañamel* was a shameless bastard who didn't hesitate to take his wife's lover home, just to seal a deal.

CHAPTER 5

Tonet's situation in Cañamel's establishment changed completely. He was no longer a customer but the owner's associate and companion, haughtily brushing aside the mutterings of Neleta's enemies as he entered. If he spent the entire day there, it was to discuss business matters. He would stride confidently into the inner rooms and, in demonstration that he was truly at home, would go over behind the bar to sit at Cañamel's side. On many occasions, if the latter and his wife were somewhere in the back and a customer wanted something, he would jump over amid his friends' laughter and serve it up with comic gravity, imitating his grandfather's voice and gestures.

The innkeeper was satisfied with his new colleague, an excellent lad, as he would declare to anyone in the tavern when Tonet was not there; a lad who would go far with good conduct and hard work, very far with the support of a protector like himself.

Old *Paloma* also frequented the tavern more than in the past. After some drunken scenes in the privacy of the cottage one night, the family had split apart. Tono and *la Borda* went off to their fields every morning to continue the battle with the lake, attempting to smother it under loads of earth laboriously brought from afar. Tonet and his grandfather would go down to *Cañamel's* to talk about their next project.

In reality the only ones who did any talking were the innkeeper and old *Paloma*. *Cañamel* extolled his own part in the affair, the generosity with which he had taken on the business. He was exposing his capital without knowing how the fishing would turn out and was happily making this sacrifice for half the profits. He was nothing like the foreign lenders on the landward side who only offered money against the security of a proper mortgage and rising interest rates. In this fiercely competitive trade of exploiting his fellow man, his voice shook with hatred for the newcomers. Who were these people who were gradually taking over the country? Frenchmen who came to the Valencian area with holes in their shoes and an old corduroy suit hanging off their frames. People from some part of France whose name he could not remember, but who, little by little, were becoming like the Galicians from his own country. The money they were lending was not even theirs. Capital in France generated little interest, so these Frenchies were picking it up back home at two or three per cent in order to lend money to Valencians at fifteen to twenty and make tremendous profits. They were also buying draft horses on the other side of the Pyrenees, perhaps smuggling them across, and selling them by instalments to the farmers, but arranging matters so that the buyer never actually owned the animal. It was like paying for a horse from Santiago and getting a broken nag in return. It was theft, *Paloma*, sheer robbery and unworthy of Christian folk. *Cañamel's* anger would rise as he talked about these matters with all the indignation and secret envy of the usurer who dares not, through cowardice, employ the same methods as his rivals.

The old boatman agreed with what he was saying. This was why he loved his own folk who were committed to the fishing, and this was why he got so angry when he saw his son piling up more and more debts in his attempt to become a farmer. Poor smallholders were mere slaves; they drove themselves mad working the entire year, and for whom were the fruits of their labours? Foreigners made off with their entire harvest, the Frenchman who lent them the money and the Englishman who let them have fertiliser on credit. Living a life of madness just to keep outsiders? No! As long as there were eels in the lake, the waters could go on quietly being covered by reeds and bullrushes, safe in the knowledge that it would not be he who would plough them up.

Seated together behind the counter, Tonet and Neleta gazed quietly into each other's eyes, while the old boatman and Cañamel carried on talking. The customers had become used to seeing them sitting for hours on end with their gaze locked as if devouring each other, exchanging occasional sweet nothings, but with an altogether different meaning in their looks. Women who popped in for some olive oil or wine would stop in front of them with their eyes lowered and a quizzical look on their faces, letting the last, slow, drops drip gently from the barrel into the bottle, but pricking their ears to catch some fragment of their conversation. The couple, however, just carried on murmuring together as if entirely alone, in defiance of the obvious surveillance.

Alarmed by such intimacies, old *Paloma* spoke seriously to his grandson. Was there something going on between them, as *la Samaruca* and other wagging tongues in the village would have it? Watch out, Tonet, apart from being unworthy of a family like theirs, this could lose them the business. But his grandson slapped his chest in protest with all the self-assurance of a man declaring the truth, and grandfather was convinced, although with a certain apprehension that such "friendships" turned out badly.

The tight space behind the bar was paradise for Tonet. He recalled with Neleta their times as children together; he told her about his adventures in distant lands, and, falling silent, experienced, just as he had on the night they had got lost in the woods, but more intensely now, the sweet headiness at the nearness of the body whose warmth seemed to caress him from beneath her clothes.

After dinner with *Cañamel* and his wife of an evening, Tonet would fetch an accordion from the cottage, the only thing, apart from straw hats, he had brought back from Cuba, and amaze everyone with the nasal tones of the languid *habaneras* that he coaxed from the instrument. He would sing treacly *guijaras*, which spoke of breezes, harps, and hearts as tender as guavas, in a honeyed Cuban accent that made all eyes turn to Neleta, lying back as if to unburden a soul quivering with the weight of passion.

The day following this series of serenades Neleta, dewy eyed, was at Tonet's side as he made the rounds of the groups in the tavern.

The Cuban could guess how she was feeling. She had dreamed about him, hadn't she? He had felt exactly the same back in the cottage, all through the long night, seeing her in the darkness, his hands reaching out as if he really might touch her. After confessing as much to each other they were quiet, secure in the knowledge that, while they did not quite understand it, what they shared was their moral right, certain that, whatever obstacles might be put in their way, they would, in the end, be one forever.

In the village there was no question of any further intimacy than their conversations in the tavern. During the day, people were all around them in El Palmar, and *Cañamel*, sick and constantly complaining, never left the house. Sometimes, spurred by a fleeting flash of energy, the innkeeper would whistle up *Centella*, his huge headed old hunting dog, famous throughout the lake as a scent hound, and head for the nearest reed beds with her in his punt to shoot a few waterfowl. But within an hour or two he would be back, coughing and complaining of the damp, his legs swollen, as he put it, like an elephant's and would sit groaning in a corner until Neleta had made him sip a few cups of something warm with his head and neck swathed in a collection of handkerchiefs. The contempt Neleta felt for her husband was evident in her eyes as she turned her gaze to the Cuban.

The summer was drawing to a close, and they were going to have to think seriously about preparations for the fishing. In front of their cottages the owners of other *redolins* were setting up the great nets for closing off the ditches. Old *Paloma* was getting impatient. The kit that *Cañamel* had left over from previous partnerships with other fishermen was nowhere near enough for la *Sequiòta*. They would have to buy a lot of cord and employ a great many of the women who could weave it into nets in order to make the very most of their *redolin*.

One night, Tonet and his grandfather had dinner in the tavern in order to discuss the business properly. They would have to buy the best cordage, the sort made on the shore at El Cabañal for sea fishing. With all his knowledge and experience, old *Paloma* would do the buying, but the innkeeper would go with him as he wanted to pay personally, fearful that he might be cheated if he just handed the money over to the old boy. But as a beatific glow of satiety settled upon him later, *Cañamel* began to feel somewhat fearful of the following day's journey. He would have to be up at dawn, leaving his warm bed to plunge into the damp fog, cross the lake, make his way overland to Valencia and thence to El Cabañal, before making the whole journey back again. His corpulent form, softened by inactivity, trembled at the thought of such a trip. This man, who had spent much of his life travelling the world, had sunk his roots so deep in the mud of El Palmar that the thought of a day on the move was now anguish.

His desire for a quiet day made him modify the plan. He would stay at home in charge of the establishment and Neleta would accompany old *Paloma*. Nobody like a woman to do the haggling and get things at a good price!

Neleta and the old boatman set off the following morning. Tonet would go and wait for them at the port in Catarroja at sunset to get the cordage loaded into the boat.

The sun was still high when, under full sail, Tonet guided his boat into the canal that led up through the fields towards the said port. Great *laúdes* were coming in from the threshing floors loaded with rice, and as they passed along the canal the water displaced by their wide hulls rose in a yellowish wave behind his stern, surging along the banks and muddying the clear tranquil waters of the ditches that flowed through them. Hundreds of boats were tied up along one bank of the canal, the whole fishing fleet from Catarroja which was such an object of hate to old *Paloma*.

There were black coffin-shaped hulls of various sizes, the wood worm-eaten and worn. The sharp prows of craft called *zapatos* stuck up into the air while the great barques known as *laúdes*, capable of carrying a hundred sacks of rice, sank their wide bellies deep in the water weed, their forest of simple unhewn masts and hemp cordage covering the horizon.

There remained only a narrow corridor between the fleet and the opposite bank for boats to pass down under sail, their bow waves sending a strong surge running among the moored craft.

Tonet tied up his boat opposite the port's tavern and jumped ashore. Enormous piles of rice straw were heaped around him, among which hens pecked, giving the quay the appearance of a farmyard. Carpenters were constructing boats on the bank and the echo of their hammers rang through the silence of the afternoon. The new hulls stood on trestles, their recently brushed wood fresh and yellow awaiting the application of pitch with which the shipwrights covered them. Two women were sewing in the doorway of the tavern, beyond which was the thatched roof of the public scales of the Community of Catarroja. A woman with two wicker baskets was weighing eels and tench that fishermen were unloading. As she completed the process, she would throw one eel into the large basket kept beside her, a voluntary contribution from the people of Catarroja who donated a cut from the catch to fund the festival of their patron, Saint Peter. Several carts fully laden with rice were squeaking away towards the big mills.

Not knowing quite what he was going to do, Tonet made to enter the tavern when he heard someone call him. From behind one of the great heaps of straw a hand was emerging causing the hens to scatter in fright but making signs for him to come closer.

The *Cubano* went over and found the rogue *Sangonera* lying belly up with his arms crossed behind his head as a pillow. His eyes were yellow and glistening, and flies buzzed around his face, ever more pallid and drawn with alcoholism, without him making the least effort to brush them away.

Tonet was happy with the encounter which might provide some entertainment while he waited. What was he doing there? Nothing; he was just passing the time until nightfall, waiting for the moment to go off in search of certain friends of his in Catarroja who wouldn't let him go hungry; he was relaxing, and relaxing was the best thing a man could do.

He had spotted Tonet from his hidey hole and called him, without giving up possession of this magnificent spot. His body had settled perfectly into the straw and there was no reason to lose his perfect mould. He then went on to explain why he was there. He had eaten in the tavern with some carters, excellent fellows, who had thrown him a few crusts and let him have a slug at the *porron* with each bite, while laughing at his witty remarks. But the innkeeper, typical of his whole species, had put him out the door as soon as the other customers had left, knowing he wouldn't be able to pay for anything himself. So, there he was, killing time, which is man's real enemy. Were they friends or not? Was he able to share a glass with him?

Tonet's nod put paid to his sloth and, albeit with something of an effort, he made up his mind to get to his feet. They drank in the tavern, and later, very slowly, made their way to the black-planked edge of the quay for a seat. Tonet had not seen *Sangonera* in many long days, so the wanderer told him his troubles.

There was absolutely nothing for him to do in El Palmar. Neleta, *Cañamel's* woman, a stuck-up cow who had forgotten where she came from, had barred him from the inn on the pretext that he dirtied the stools and walls with his muddy clothes. It was all a total misery in the other taverns. He could never find a drinker willing to buy him a glass, so he had been forced to quit El

Palmar and set off round the lake, as his father had done in the old days, wandering from village to village in search of generous friends.

Tonet, whose sloth had so much disgusted his own family was bold enough to offer him some advice. Why hadn't he tried working?

Sangonera made a gesture of astonishment. Him too! Even the *Cubano* was allowing himself to repeat the same thing the old boys in El Palmar had told him. Did he have much of a liking for work himself? Why wasn't he with his father, filling up his fields with earth, instead of spending the day at *Cañamel's,* lording it with Neleta at his side and drinking only the finest?

The *Cubano* smiled, not knowing quite what to reply ,but admiring, all the same, the drunkard's logic in turning round his arguments.

The man seemed soothed by the glass of wine Tonet had bought for him. The port's tranquillity, occasionally interrupted by the sounds of boatbuilder's hammers or the clucking of hens, loosened his tongue and induced him to reveal more confidences.

No, Tonet, he could not work; he would not work even if they forced him. Work was the Devil's doing, disobedience to God and the worst of sins. Only corrupted souls, those who could not come to terms with their poverty, souls gnawed by the desire to store up treasures for themselves, although it might lead to misery through constantly thinking about the morrow, could surrender themselves to work, could allow themselves to be changed from men to beasts of burden. He had reflected a lot on the matter; he knew more about it than the *Cubano* might imagine, and he did not want to lose his soul by surrendering himself to regular monotonous work in order to have a house and a family and the assurance of bread for the morrow. That was to doubt the mercy of God who never abandoned his flock, and above all he was a Christian.

Tonet laughed off these musings as the ramblings of a drunk, and dug his ragged companion on the ribs. If he was hoping this nonsense would get him another drink, he was going to be disappointed! It seemed to him that he really just didn't like work. The same thing happened to other people but more or less all of them ended up bending their shoulders to the wheel, albeit through gritted teeth.

Sangonera allowed his gaze to wander over the surface of the canal, tinged with purple in the dying light of the evening. His thoughts seemed to soar to distant heights, and he spoke slowly, in mystical tones in stark contrast to his alcohol laden breath.

Tonet knew nothing, like all the folk in El Palmar. He was able to make this declaration with the courage of the drink inside him, and with no fear that his lively minded friend would throw him head-first into the canal. Had he not just said that mankind bent their backs through gritted teeth? What did this prove if not that work was contrary to Nature and the dignity of Mankind? He knew more than was thought he did in El Palmar, more than many of the priests that he worked for like a slave. This was why he was always falling out with them. He had discovered the truth and could not live with "the blind of spirit".

While Tonet had been away wandering those lands beyond the seas, fighting battles, he was spending the afternoons at the door of the presbytery, reading the priests' books, reflecting in the silence of a village whose population had fled for the lake. He had learned almost the whole of the New Testament by heart, and still got the shivers recalling the impression the Sermon on the Mount had on him when he read it for the first time. He felt a cloud had vanished from before hie eyes, and suddenly understood why his sprit rebelled against brutalising and arduous labour. It was the flesh, it was indeed sin, that compelled men to live like beasts of burden in order to satisfy their earthly appetites. The soul protested such servitude, saying to Man: "Thou shalt not work!" and suffusing his body with the sweetly intoxicating rapture of ease, as a portent of the joy which awaits the Blessed in Heaven.

Ascolta, Tonet, ascolta, Listen Tonet, Listen, said *Sangonera* to his friend in solemn tones. He recounted his jumbled recollection of his readings of the Gospels, the precepts that remained burned on his memory. There was no need anxiously to take thought for what one should eat or how one should be clothed, for as Jesus said, the birds of the air neither sowed nor reaped but despite that, they ate; nor do the lilies of the field need to weave in order to be clothed, for they are clothed by the goodness of the Lord. He was a child of God and in Him did he trust. He did not wish to insult the Lord by working, as if he doubted God's kindness, which would surely come to his aid. Only the Gentiles or the folk of El Palmar, which was the same thing, who kept their money from the fishing without sharing it with a soul, were capable of storing up treasure for themselves, and taking thought for the morrow.

He wanted to be like the birds on the lake, the flowers which grew among the reeds, wandering, doing nothing, and with no other succour than Divine Providence. In his miserable state he never had any doubts about the morrow. "The day shall take thought for the things of itself. Sufficient unto the morrow is the evil thereof." At the moment the bitterness of the present day was quite enough for him, given the difficulty it gave him in following his intention of keeping himself pure, unsullied by any work or earthly ambition in a world where everyone fought for their existence with their fists, pestering and giving up anything to the next man just to get their hands on some of their good fortune.

Tonet was laughingly following these drunken ramblings, declaimed with rising exaltation. He muttered something about how admirable his ideas were, and suggested he abandon the lake and enter a monastery where he would at least not have to battle on in misery, but *Sangonera* protested angrily.

He had fallen out with the priest and left the presbytery for good, because it disgusted him to see, in his old bosses, a spirit contrary to that of the books they read. They were just like other people, tormented with desire for other people's wealth, always thinking about food and vestments, complaining about a decline in piety when there was no money coming in, worrying about the morrow, doubting the goodness of God, who never abandons his own. He had Faith and was living with what he was given and what he found to hand. He never lacked for a heap of straw on which to lie down at night, nor was he ever faint with hunger. In placing him by the lake, the

Lord had put within his reach all the necessities of life through which he might be an example of the true believer.

Tonet mocked *Sangonera*. Now that he was so pure, why was he getting drunk all the time? Was God telling him to go from tavern to tavern, only to crawl away later along the bank, staggering drunk? The wanderer did not, however, lose his solemn gravity. His drunkenness was causing nobody any harm and wine was a holy thing; there was a reason it was used daily in the Eucharist. The world was beautiful but viewed through a glass of wine it seemed even more inviting, clad in even brighter colours, its splendour drawing one ever closer to the warmth of its Omnipotent Creator.

Everyone had his own way of passing the time. He found no pleasure greater than the contemplation of the beauties of the Albufera. Others worshipped money, but he would weep sometimes at a sunset, that hour of twilight which was more mysterious and wonderful on the lake than anywhere inland. The beauty of the countryside entered one's very soul, and if contemplated through the lens of a few glasses of wine, had you sighing with content like a baby. He would say it again; everyone enjoyed life in his own way. *Cañamel*, for example, by piling on the ounces; he by contemplating the Albufera in such a trance that his head buzzed with *coplas*, verses far more beautiful than the ones sung in the taverns, and he was convinced that, when he was drunk, he was as good as the city gents who wrote in the papers in coming out with really notable sayings.

After a long silence, spurred on by his own verbosity, Sangonera began to offer counter arguments, only to rebut them immediately. One could say, as had a certain priest at El Palmar, that man was condemned by original sin to earn his bread by the sweat of his brow; but this was why Jesus had come into the world, to redeem man's original sin and return humanity to the life of paradise, wiped clean of any labour. But look, it was sinners who, spurred on by their own arrogance, had paid no attention to his words. Everyone wanted to live more comfortably than his neighbour and there were rich and poor, instead of there being one humanity. Those who were deaf to the Lord worked incessantly, but people were not happy, and were building for themselves a Hell on earth. They used to tell him that if people didn't work, they would live in poverty. Agreed; there would be less people in the world, but those that remained would live happily and carefree on the inexhaustible mercy of God. And this clearly had to happen, the world would not always be the same as this. Jesus had to return in order to direct man back again onto the straight and narrow way. He had dreamed of it many times, especially on the many occasions he had been ill with the tertian fever, racked with the chills, stretched out on a canal bank, or curled in a corner of his ruined cottage, he would see His robe, His stiff, tight, purple robe and he, the vagabond, would stretch out his hand to touch it, and be instantly healed.

Sangonera displayed an unbreakable faith in this Second Coming. Christ would not return to show Himself in big cities overtaken by the sin of wealth. He did not present himself the first time in the great city of Rome, but had preached in small villages, no bigger than El Palmar, and his companions were men with poles and nets, like the ones who got together in *Cañamel's*. That lake, on whose waters Jesus had walked, to the astonishment of the Apostles, was surely no larger or more beautiful than the Albufera. When the Lord returned to complete his work, it would be there among those people; He would seek the guileless, simple souls, and he, *Sangonera*, would be among them. The vagabond staggered to his feet staring into the distance in a state of exaltation composed in equal measure of inebriation and extraordinary faith, seeming to see on the canal bank, among the scattered, dying rays of the sun, the slim figure of his Beloved

Saviour, approaching without moving His feet or brushing the grasses, a mere streak of purple, the soft curls of His golden hair glinting in a cloud of light.

Tonet was no longer listening to him. The loud jingling of harness bells was heard along the Catarroja road and, behind the hut with the Public Scales, the crumpled canvas cover of a *tartana* could be seen approaching. His passengers were coming. Ever the sharp-eyed son of the lake, *Sangonera* recognised Neleta at the vehicle's window. After being thrown out of the tavern, he wanted nothing to do with the woman, and bade farewell to Tonet to return to his couch in the haystack, and lose himself in his dreams, while night fell.

The carriage stopped opposite the port's little tavern and Neleta stepped down. The *Cubano* could not hide his astonishment. What about his grandfather? She had left him behind and was heading back on her own with the load of cordage, which filled the *tartana* completely. The old man wanted to return home via El Saler, so as to have a word with a certain widow who sold *palangres*, fishing lines, at reasonable prices. He would be back in El Palmar during the evening in some boat belonging to the folk that dredged mud from the canals.

Exchanging glances, they both had the same thought. They were going to be alone together on the trip back; for the first time they were going to be able to talk, far from any prying eyes, in the deep solitude of the lake. They both paled and shivered, as if a danger they had wished for a thousand times had now suddenly and inopportunely confronted them. Their emotions were so heightened that they were in no hurry to get under way, overcome with shyness, fearful of what the people around them in the port might be saying, although they had scarcely paid them any attention.

The coachman had just finished getting the heavy bundles of cordage out of the vehicle and was heaving them into the bow of the boat where they formed a yellowish heap exuding the smell of freshly spun hemp.

Neleta paid the driver. *Salud y buen viaje!* And, cracking his whip, the man set his horse off down the Catarroja road.

The pair stood motionless for a long time on the muddy bank as if waiting for someone, not daring to get into the boat together.

Boatwrights were shouting to El *Cubano* that he had better get under way quick; the wind was going to fall light and if he was making for El

Palmar, he was going to have to pole it a good way. Visibly rattled, Neleta just smiled at the Catarroja crowd who were shouting greetings, having seen her in her tavern.

Tonet made up his mind to break the silence and addressed Neleta. Since his grandfather was no longer coming, they had to get under way as soon as possible. Those lads were right. His voice was a little hoarse, breaking with emotion, as if his feelings had him by the throat.

Neleta seated herself in the middle of the boat at the mast foot on a heap of balls of cord which gave under her weight. Tonet raised the sail and crouched at the helm as the craft gathered way with the canvas flapping against the mast in the dying gusts of the gentle breeze.

Slowly they slipped down the canal past the isolated fishermen's cottages with their garlands of nets drying on cane frames in the yards, and the old, worm-infested wooden water wheels, around which bats were starting to flutter. Fishermen on the bank were laboriously hauling in their punts by the painters tied round their waists. *Adios*! they would murmur as they passed, *Adios*! Again, silence fell, with only by the swish of the boat as it cut the water and the monotonous croaking of frogs as background. The pair sat with their eyes lowered, as if fearful to acknowledge they were alone; and if on raising their gaze their eyes met, they instantly parted again.

The mouth of the canal was widening out. The banks were lost against the water. Great lagoons ready to be filled with earth stretched away on both sides. The reeds waved gently over the flat surface like the canopy of a submerged forest in the twilight.

They were now out on the Albufera, making just a little way with the last of the dying breeze, and nothing but water all around.

The wind was now gone. The lake, flat calm without a trace of movement, took on an opalescent sheen reflecting the last of the sunlight flaring behind the distant mountains. The sky deepened to violet and over to seaward the first stars began to twinkle. Like ghosts the drooping canvas of motionless boats dotted the water's edge.

Tonet gathered the sail and, taking up the pole, began to propel the boat forward with his arms. The silence of the twilit calm was broken as Neleta got to her feet with a loud peal of laughter, intending to help her companion. She also could handle a pole. Tonet was bound to remember when they were young, their rough games, the times they would untie the punts in El Palmar without their owners noticing and run off along the canals, often with the fishermen in hot pursuit. She would take over when he got tired.

Estate quieta! Do be quiet! was his only response, as he carried on poling, short of breath from the effort.

But Neleta could not keep quiet, as if the ominous silence in which they avoided each other's glances was too much to bear, and words poured out of the young woman, as if she feared she would otherwise reveal her confused thoughts.

In the distance, the broken outline of the Dehesa stood out, like a far-off shore they might never reach. Interspersed with bursts of somewhat forced laughter, Neleta recalled for her friend the night they had spent in those woods, with all its terrors and sweet dreams, an adventure that seemed as if it had happened yesterday, so fresh was it in her mind. But her companion's silence, his eyes fixed anxiously at something in the bottom of the boat called her attention. It was then that she perceived that what Tonet was finding so appealing was her yellow shoes, small and elegant, standing out standing out against the hemp, like two pale spots, and something else besides that she had left open to view. She hastened to cover herself, and fell silent, grimly clenching her teeth and half closing her eyes, her brow furrowed in a deep frown of distress as she battled with her inner feelings.

They were making slow progress. It was hard work to cross the Albufera using only the strength of one's arms with the boat loaded. Empty punts, weighed down only by the weight of the man managing the pole, passed them close by, as swift as the *lanzaderas* the smugglers used, before losing themselves in the rapidly deepening gloom.

Tonet had been almost an hour working the heavy pole, sometimes slipping on the thick bed of shells on the bottom, and at others getting tangled in the waterweed which fishermen called "the Albufera's hair". It was obvious that he was unused to such work. Had he been on his own he would just have lain down in the bilge to wait for the wind to fill in or to be offered a tow from some other boat. But in Neleta's presence, he had too much self-respect, and he had no wish to hang around until he fell down from sheer exhaustion. Gasping for air, he emitted a snort every time he heaved back on the pole, pushing the boat forward. From time to time and without letting go he would raise an arm to wipe the sweat from his brow.

In a cooing, almost maternal tone, Neleta called softly to him. Only her shadowy outline could be seen above the heap of balls of cord in the bow. The young man desperately wanted to rest and was going to have to stop for a moment; it would make no difference if they arrived half an hour later than planned. So, she made him sit down beside her, indicating that he would be more comfortable on the pile of hemp than back in the stern. The boat lay still. As he gathered himself together, Tonet could feel the woman's soft nearness just as he had, sitting together behind the bar in the tavern.

It was now completely dark. No light was visible save the diffuse shimmering of the stars twinkling in the black depths. The deep silence was broken by mysterious noises of water disturbed by invisible wriggling creatures. Sea Bass coming in from the Mediterranean were pursuing small fry and the surface was broken by constant splashes as they desperately tried to escape. In a nearby thicket some coots let loose a cry that sounded as if they were being murdered, while reed warblers ran up and down their endless scales.

Surrounded by this silence populated with mysterious rustlings and calls, Tonet felt as if time had stood still, that he was still a little boy, and there in that clearing in the wood beside his childhood companion, the eel-wife's little daughter. He wasn't afraid now, the only thing that somewhat disturbed him was his companion's seductive warmth, the intoxicating perfume that seemed to emanate from her body and rush straight to his brain like strong liquor. Head down, not daring to raise his eyes, he circled his arm round Neleta's waist and felt, almost in the same instant a soft caress, a touch of velvet, a hand slipping over his head and a cool palm drying his brow still dripping with sweat.

He raised his gaze and saw close in the darkness two sparkling eyes fixed on his, reflecting a distant star's point of light. He felt Neleta's halo of fine fair hair tickling his temples and those powerful perfumes, which used to fill the tavern, now impregnating the very depths of his being.

Tonet! Tonet! She murmured, her voice faltering like a soft whimper. It was just as it had been in the Dehesa. But they were children no more, that innocence, in which they had clung together to restore their courage, was now gone forever and, reunited after so many years in fresh embrace, they fell back on the pile of hemp, wanting never to rise again.

The boat floated motionless in the middle of the lake, as if abandoned, without the least trace of an outline showing above its gunwales.

Some boatmen, poling across the whispering waters, sang tunelessly as they drifted past, not suspecting that lying close by on some planks in the calm of the night, lulled by the warbling of the waterbirds, Love, Ruler of the World, was gently rocking.

CHAPTER 6

This was El Palmar's great fiesta, the celebration El Niño Jesus, in December. A chill wind blew across the Albufera, numbing fishermen's fingers and freezing them to their poles. Men wore woollen caps pulled right down to their ears and were never without their yellow foul-weather gear whose loose folds rustled as they walked. Women scarcely left their cottages; the whole family would huddle round the hearth, smoking themselves quietly in a fug as dense as an eskimo's igloo.

The level of the Albufera had risen. Winter rains had swollen the lake, so fields and banks were covered in a sheet of water dotted here and there with submerged vegetation. The lake was altogether bigger. Isolated cottages which used to stand on solid ground looked as if they were floating above the water with boats tied up at their very doors. The damp slimy soil of El Palmar exuded a bitter, unbearable cold that kept people indoors. The village fishwives could not recall as cruel a winter. The usually flighty and ravenous sparrows fell from the thatch, lifeless from the cold with a sad little call, like a child's cry. Faced with the need to keep body and soul together, the keepers on the Dehesa turned a blind eye, and every morning an army of children would scatter into the woods looking for dry firewood to warm their hovels. *Cañamel's* customers huddled round the hearth, only consenting to give up their comfy grass stools next to the fire to go to the bar to refill their glasses.

El Palmar looked numb and sleepy, with neither people in the streets nor boats out on the lake. Men went out to gather the night's catch from their nets and get back quickly to the village. Their feet looked huge, wrapped in heavy cloth inside their grass sandals. Boats had a layer of rice straw in their bilges to combat the cold. At dawn on most days wide sheets of ice floated down the canal like shattered panes of glass. The weather was getting everyone down. They were children of the warm weather, used to seeing the lake boil and the fields steam with the breath of corruption under the blazing sun. As old *Paloma* declaimed, even the eels didn't feel like sticking their noses out of the mud in these dog days. To make matters worse there was often torrential rain, shutting out the lake and overflowing the ditches. Grey skies gave the Albufera a sorry look. Boats navigating through the fog had the appearance of coffins with their crews motionless in the straw, wrapped up to their eyeballs in layers of rags.

But as Christmas time approached, with the fiesta of Niño Jesus, El Palmar seemed to pull itself together, and shake off the winter glom into which it had sunk.

People had to enjoy themselves, as in every year, even if the lake froze over completely and they could walk across it, as people said happened in distant lands. More even than the desire to enjoy themselves, what really cheered them up was the thought that their joy would upset their rivals, the landlubbers, those fishermen of Catarroja who disrespected and made jokes about the Niño of El Palmar on account of how small it was. These foes, lacking both faith and good conscience, would even claim that the folk from El Palmar would immerse their Divine Patron in the ditches when the fishing was poor. Sacrilege! That was why Jesus had punished their sinful tongues and not allowed them to enjoy the Royal Privilege of using the *redolins*!

The whole of El Palmar was making preparations for the festivities. Women defied the cold and crossed the lake to go to the Christmas fair in Valencia. Their impatient throng of children would be waiting on the bank for them to return in the husband's boat, desperate to see the presents. Cardboard horses, tin swords, trumpets and drums were welcomed with whoops of joy from the little ones, while the wives showed off their more important purchases to their friends.

The Christmas festivities lasted three days, and on the second, the band from Catarroja arrived and the year's biggest eel was raffled off to help with the expenses. The third day was the Fiesta of the Niño, the icon of Baby Jesus, and the next was the festival of the Christ, all with their Masses and sermons as well as dancing at night to the sound of bombards and tambourins.

Neleta had made up her mind to enjoy the festivities this year as never before. She seemed to inhabit an eternal springtime behind the bar in the tavern. At meals, with *Cañamel* on one side and the *Cubano* on the other, everyone quietly content in the holy peace of the family, she considered herself the most blessed of women and thanked God for his goodness in letting such good people live. She was the richest and most beautiful woman in the village; her husband was content; Tonet, with his feelings now under control seemed to be falling more and more deeply in love. What more could she wish for?

She felt that the great ladies she had seen from afar on her trips to Valencia were certainly not as blessed as she was in that little square of mud surrounded by water.

Her enemies muttered. La *Samaruca* kept a close eye on her. In order to be alone without raising suspicions, she and Tonet had to invent reasons for trips to nearby villages on the lake. Neleta was the one who was sharpest at such deceptions, with a facility that made the *Cubano* rather suspect that stories about the clever tricks she had got up to with lovers before him might be true. But she appeared completely untroubled by any wagging tongues. Her enemies were now saying just the same thing as when she and Tonet had merely exchanged the odd word, so she played down the insinuations, knowing that nobody could prove she had done anything wrong and joked with Tonet in the overflowing tavern in a way that scandalised old *Paloma*. Neleta would pretend to be offended. Hadn't they grown up together? Couldn't she love Tonet like a brother, seeing how much his mother had done for her.

Cañamel backed her up, taking pride in his wife's good sense. The thing the innkeeper did not seem quite so happy with was Tonet's behaviour as a business partner. The lad had treated his good luck like a lottery win, and, like someone who isn't doing any harm and is just eating his own bread, was enjoying himself, without worrying about the fishing.

The *Sequiòta* yielded good returns. The fishing was no longer as fabulous as it used to be, but there would be nights when they might get close to a hundred boxes of eels. *Cañamel* enjoyed the satisfactions of doing good business, haggling over prices with city fishmongers, checking the weights and supervising the loading of the large baskets. In this respect the company was not doing badly, but he liked equality, that every man should do what he was supposed to without taking advantage of others.

He had promised capital and he had delivered it; all the nets were his, together with the net sacks and other gear which would make a pile as big as the tavern. But Tonet had promised to help with the work, and it could be said that he had yet to grab an eel in his fisherman's hands. He had gone out to the *redolin* on the early nights and, sitting in the boat with a cigarette in his mouth, had watched how his grandfather and the other employed fishermen emptied the huge bags into the bilges, filling the boat with eels and tench. Later he hadn't even done that. Dark stormy nights with a big swell running worried him, but that was when the big catches happened.; the work required to haul the heavy nets full of fish didn't appeal to him; the slipperiness of the eels wriggling in his hands turned his stomach, and he would rather stay behind in the tavern or sleep in the cottage. To jolt him into action by showing a good example in the face of his laziness, there were nights when *Cañamel* decided himself to go out to the *redolin*, coughing and wheezing complainingly about his aches and pains, but the bastard felt it was enough for the old boy to make this sacrifice on his own, in order that he could demonstrate his commitment to staying at home, shamelessly claiming that Neleta was afraid of being left alone in the tavern.

It was clear that old *Paloma* on his own was quite capable of taking the business forward. He had never worked with such zeal as when he found himself in charge of la *Sequiòta*, but, what the Devil, a deal was a deal, and it seemed to *Cañamel* that the lad was robbing him blind, taking advantage, given his ease with life and his complete indifference to business matters.

What luck that moustachioed buffoon had! The fear of losing la *Sequiòta* was the only thing that held *Cañamel* back.

Tonet, meanwhile, was living in the tavern as if it were his, and growing fat in the contentment of simply having to hold out his hand to get all he wanted. He was fed the best in the house, he filled his glass from every barrel, large and small, and sometimes, driven by some mad impulse, and as if to confirm his ownership, he would even touch Neleta under the counter, in *Cañamel's* presence, and just four steps from customers, some of whom could see quite well what was happening. At times he felt a mad desire to get out of El Palmar, to spend a day away from the Albufera, in the city or in one of the lakeside villages and so would plant himself in front of Neleta with the determined expression of the man in charge.

- Give me a *duro*!

A *duro*? And for what reason? Her eyes were fixed on his, fierce and commanding; she raised herself to her full height with all the haughtiness of the adulteress who has no wish to be cheated on in her turn, but seeing in the lad's looks only the desire to get away for a time, to loosen up a little from his life as the well fed cock o' the heap, Neleta would smile, satisfied, and hand over all the money he had asked, with the suggestion that he should come back soon.

Cañamel was annoyed. He could put up with it if the man had been attending to business, but no, he was making off with funds for his own purposes, asking for money as well as eating his way through half the tavern. His wife was being very kind, making up for all the gratitude she owed the *Palomas* since childhood. But with the miser's eye for detail, he went on to recount everything that Tonet had eaten and drunk in the establishment, and the prodigality with which he had shared it with his pals, all at the owner's expense. Even *Sangonera*, that pious fool thrown out of the tavern for spreading vermin all over the stools was now back under the protection of the *Cubano,* who fed him drink until he was completely gone, using the costliest bottled liquors, for the purpose, and all because he liked to hear the nonsense he had concocted in his reading as a Sacristan.

Some fine day he's going to take over my bed, the inn keeper would say complainingly to Neleta. But in her reaction to these musings, the poor fellow just could not read what was in those eyes nor see the mischievous smile that flitted behind her sly look.

As Tonet became ever more bored with spending whole days in the tavern sitting beside Neleta, looking like a lap dog waiting for his next petting, he would grab *Cañamel's* shotgun and, calling his dog, head out to the reed beds. Old Paco's gun was the best in El Palmar, a rich man's gun which Tonet thought of as his own, and with which he rarely missed. The dog was the famous *Centella,* known throughout the lake for her nose. No game ever escaped her, no matter how thick the reeds, and she could dive like an otter to retrieve an injured bird from the weedy bottom. *Cañamel* used to claim that no money in the world could buy this animal but had to admit sadly that *Centella* would now clearly rather be with Tonet, who took her shooting most days, than with her old master wrapped in sheets and blankets next to the fire. That rogue had even taken over his dog!

Keen to make the most of old Paco's superb shooting arrangements, Tonet worked his way through the store of cartridges kept in the tavern for the use of wildfowlers. Nobody in El Palmar had ever done so much shooting. Tonet's shots rang continuously around the narrow waterways, the *matas*, nearest the village, with *Centella* splashing happily through the reed beds as she warmed to her work. The fiercely keen *Cubano* could never get enough of this kind of exercise which brought back to mind his time as a soldier. He would set himself up in ambush to await the birds, using the same clever tricks and skills he had employed for concealing himself in the jungle to hunt men. *Centella* would bring the, *coots,* and mallard back to the boat with their necks limp and their plumage bloody. Later on, less common wildfowl arrived and Tonet took great satisfaction from this shooting, admiring them as they lay dead in the bottom of the bat;

the swamphen, with dark blue plumage and red beaks; the purple heron with his green and purple plumage and long narrow feathered crest; the squacco heron, the *oroval* with his sandy plumage and red crop; the white and yellow wigeon; the tufted duck, black headed with golden highlights and the *singlòt* , the glossy ibis, that resplendent brilliant-green wader.

He would get back to the tavern in the evening like a conquering hero, throwing down his game bag with its load of meat and rainbow of feathers. Old Paco should have enough there for fill the stew pot. He would generously make him a present of it, after all it was his gun! And when he would occasionally shoot a flamingo, known as a *bragat* to the Albufera folk, with its enormous feet, long neck, pink and white plumage, and looking like a mysterious Egyptian ibis, Tonet would take steps to have *Cañamel* get it dissected and stuffed in Valencia for his room, as an elegant adornment, much sought after by city gentlemen.

The innkeeper received these presents with mutters which suggested his pleasure was all relative. When would he leave that gun alone? Didn't he feel the cold in those reed beds? And since he was so fit, why didn't he help his grandfather at night with the work on the *redolin*? But the accused man just took the sick innkeeper's despairing grumbles with a smile and turned to the bar.

- Neleta, *una copa,* a glass, please.

He had done well in spending the whole day with his fingers frozen to the shotgun among the reeds in order to bring back that pile of meat. But still they muttered about him being work shy! In a joyful fit of impudence, he reached across the bar and stroked Neleta's cheeks without heeding the people present or fearing anything from her husband. Weren't they like brother and sister who'd played together as children?

Old Tono neither knew nor cared to know what his son was up to. He rose before dawn and returned home at night. Alone with la *Borda* on his flooded fields he would eat some sardines and corn bread, permitting himself no better nourishment. Returning to the cottage after nightfall he would throw himself down on his litter, faint with fatigue while his mind carried on calculating through the mists of sleep how many boatloads of earth were still needed for his fields, and how much he still had to find for his creditors, before he could think of himself as owner of those rice paddies, won with the sweat of his brow and the labour of his hands. On most nights old *Paloma* was away from the cottage fishing on la Sequiòta. Tonet never ate with the family but would finally turn up shouting and rattling impatiently at the door at the latest of hours, after *Cañamel's* tavern was locked up, rousing poor, sleepy, exhausted *Borda* to open it for him.

So that was how time went by until Palmar's season of festivities arrived. During the afternoon of the day before the Fiesta del Niño, Christmas Day, almost the whole village was crammed between the edge of the canal and *Cañamel's* back door. The band from Catarroja was expected and the village, which during the rest of the year heard no other music than the barber's guitar and Tonet's accordion, was trembling with anticipation of noise of the brass instruments and the deep rumbling of the big bass drum sounding around the line of cottages. Nobody was shivering because of the temperature. To show off their bright dresses, the women had discarded their woollen shawls and left their bare arms turning purple in the cold. The men were wearing new sashes round their waists with red or black caps still showing their shop creases. Taking advantage of their partners chatting with their pals, they scuttled off to the tavern where the drinkers' alcohol-laden breath and cigarette smoke combined with a fug smelling of wet wool and filthy sandals. People talked at the top of their voices about the band from Catarroja, swearing it was the best in the world. The fishermen from over there were a bad lot, but you had to admit that not even the king heard a band like that. The poor of the lake had to have something good for themselves. Noticing that people tying up along the bank were shouting that the band was close, all the customers rushed out in a mass and the tavern was left empty.

The tip of a great sail glided behind the reeds, and as the *laúd* carrying the band appeared in a bend of the canal, a shout broke from the crowd, fired by the sight of their red pantaloons and the white plumes waving above their helmets.

In accordance with custom and tradition the village youth proceeded to battle for the big drum. They plunged into the freezing water of the canal, like liquid ice up to their armpits, with a gay abandon that set teeth chattering among the folk watching on the bank. Old folk cried out in alarm:

- It'll be the death of you! You'll get pneumonia!

But the lads fairly hurled themselves at the boat, grabbing hold of the gunwale amid the laughter of the musicians, fighting tooth and nail for them to hand over the enormous instrument. "Give it here...to me!" until one of them, bolder than the rest and tired of asking, grabbed hold of it with such force that he almost knocked the huge drum into the water and then, throwing it over his shoulder, emerged from the ditch followed by his envious companions.

When the musicians disembarked, they formed up in front of *Cañamel's* and unwrapped and tuned their instruments while the packed crowd followed in silence, almost in veneration, watching the unfolding of an event awaited throughout the year.

Everyone felt the astonishing shock as they broke into a loud *paso doble*. Accustomed to the silence of the lake, the bellowing instruments, making the cottages' mud walls quake, were a painful assault on their ears. But once they had got over the initial surprise at the sound shattering the village's monastic tranquillity, people began to smile, lulled by music which seemed to them to come from a far-off world, a majestic and mysterious way of living that went on somewhere far beyond the Albufera's waters.

Women became all soppy and felt like crying without quite knowing why, while the men squared shoulders bent by working the boats and stepped out with a martial swagger behind the band, while girls, dewy eyed and blushing, smiled shyly at their boyfriends.

Like a gust of new life, the music swept over the

sleepy huddle, shaking them out of the torpor of living on still waters. They whooped and screamed without quite knowing why, shouting hoorahs for El Niño Jesus, running in groups in front of the band, and even the old folk got as lively and playful as the kids with cardboard swords and hobby horses who formed an escort around the bandmaster, much admiring his gold-striped uniform.

The band marched up and down El Palmar's only street several times, all along the little lanes between the cottages, out on to the canal bank and then back again along the street, keeping up the procession so that everyone should be well satisfied with the whole populace following their twists and turns and loudly joining in with the liveliest bits of the paso doble.

This musical delirium had to end sometime, and the band finally stopped in the square opposite the church. The Mayor proceeded to allocate them lodgings. Women squabbled about the importance of the various instruments, while the chap carrying the big drum set off for the best house in town preceded by its enormous box. Happy to have shown off their uniforms, the musicians now wrapped themselves in their country cloaks, cursing the cold and damp of El Palmar.

The crowd did not clear as the musicians were dispersed. At the edge of the square the tinkling rattle of a tambourin began to be heard and a few moments later a *dulzaina*, a country oboe, announced its presence with a long series of scales sounding like musical pirouettes. People broke into applause. It was *Dimoni*, the famous oboist who came every year, a good chap, as well known for his drunken capers as for his skill with the *dulzaina*. *Sangonera* was his best friend, and when the oboist would come to fiestas, the wandering rogue never left him for a moment, knowing that when it was over, they would ,as brothers, drink the money from the hat.

They were going to raffle the biggest eel of the year for funds for the fiesta. This was an ancient custom which all the fishermen respected. Any one of them who caught a big eel would keep it in his holding tank and would not dare sell it. If someone caught a bigger one, it would be kept, and the previous one's owner could dispose of it as he wanted. In this way, the Keyholders who controlled the holding tanks always had access to the biggest eel taken on the Albufera.

This year the honour of having the biggest eel was old *Paloma's*, and for good reason; he had the best fishing spot. It was one of the most satisfying experiences of the old man's life to show off the beautiful creature to the crowd in the square. He had actually caught that thing! He showed off the massive serpent, raised on trembling arms, its back green, and its belly white, thick as a man's thigh, with its slippery skin flashing fire in the light. He had to parade the appetising catch through the whole crowd to the sound of the *dulzaina*, while the Association's most respected members sold the raffle tickets from door to door.

- Here take it for a moment, said the old boatman, throwing the creature into *Sangonera's* arms.

Proud of the position of trust bestowed on him, the rogue set off with the eel in his arms followed by the dulzaina and tambourin and surrounded by the mischievous shouts of the pack of kids. Women ran to see the enormous beast up close, and to touch it with a sort of religious fervour, as if it were some mysterious lake god, with *Sangonera* driving them off shouting *Fora! Fora!* Off! Off! They were going to spoil it by touching it so much! As he arrived back at *Cañamel's*, however, he felt he had enjoyed quite enough popular adulation. Weakened by his laziness, his arms were aching and, as he suddenly remembered, the eel wasn't his anyway, so handing it over to the kids, he headed into the tavern, leaving the raffle to go ahead with the spectacular animal as the winner's trophy.

There were few people in the tavern. Neleta was behind the bar with her husband and the *Cubano*, discussing the following day's fiesta. According to tradition, the Keyholders were the men favoured with the best spots in the draw for the *redolins*, so this meant pride of place for Tonet and his associates. They had had black suits made in the city to take the front pew in the great Mass, and they were engaged in discussing preparations for the festival.

Musicians and singers were going to arrive the next day on the mail boat, along with a priest renowned for his eloquence who would preach the Christmas Day sermon and, in passing, talk up the simplicity and virtues of the fishermen of the Albufera. There was a barge over on the shore of the Dehesa loading myrtle to be scattered on the square, and, in a corner of the tavern, a firework maker was keeping an eye on several big baskets of *masclets*, iron bangers that went off like gunshots. In the small hours of the following morning, the lake was shaken by the roar of those masclets going off as if a battle had broken out in El Palmar. After that, people gathered along the canal, chomping their breakfast between two bits of bread. They were awaiting the musicians coming from Valencia, and there was much talk about how well turned out the Keyholders were. Old *Paloma's* grandson was really organising things well! It was well seen he had *Cañamel's* money within easy reach!

When the mail boat arrived, the first to set foot on land was the preacher, a rather fat priest with an imposing frown, carrying a large, red damask bag containing his vestments for the pulpit. Impelled by his former familiarity with the role of Sacristan, *Sangonera* hastened to take charge of the priestly equipage and threw it over his shoulder. Next the members of the chapel choir jumped down, well fed, long haired male singers, musicians carrying violins and flutes wrapped in green under their arms, and trebles, pallid, drawn teenagers with an aspect of well-practised mischief about them. They were all talking about the famous *all y pebre* eel stew that was made in El Palmar, as if they had made the whole trip just to eat there.

People stood where they were on the bank to let them make their way into the village. They wanted a close look at the mysterious instruments placed around the foot of the mast, which several lads were now in the process of removing. The tympani caused astonishment as they were carried ashore, with everyone discussing how these big pots, just like the ones for cooking fish, were used. The double basses were received with applause and people hurried off to the church behind the men carrying these "big fat guitars".

Mass started at ten. The mud had vanished under a thick carpet of foliage, and the square and church were fragrant with the perfumed Dehesa plants. The church was filled with candles of various sizes, and from the door appeared like a dark sky twinkling with countless stars.

Tonet had organised things well, taking an interest even in the music that would be sung at the festival. There would be none of those famous Mass Settings that sent people to sleep. That was all right for city folk used to operas. In El Palmar, as in all the Valencian villages, they wanted a setting by Mercadente.

Women sat dewy eyed, listening to the tenors intoning Neapolitan lullabies in honour of the Baby Jesus, while the men nodded their heads in time with the sensuous orchestral waltzes. That raised everyone's spirits and as Neleta said, it was worth more than a trip to the theatre and good for the soul. Meanwhile, out in the square, thunder rolled back and forth as long lines of *masclets* went off, shaking the walls of the church and often interrupting both the singers' efforts and the preacher's words.

When it was over, the congregation hung around in the square awaiting the hour for great feast to begin. At one end, the Catarroja band, rather forgotten after the splendours of the Mass, broke into their opening number. Amid this atmosphere, infused with scented plants and gun smoke, contentment descended as everyone began to think about the game stew, made from all the best birds on the Albufera, awaiting them back in their cottages.

The miseries of their former lives seemed, at that instant, to belong to a distant world to which they would never have to return. The whole of El Palmar felt it had arrived at an everlasting point of felicity and abundance as they began to comment on the preacher's grandiloquent phrases in praise of fishermen, on the half ounce of silver they had given him for the sermon, plus the ton of money the musicians had cost for sure, the gunpowder, the gold fringed hangings, now all wax stained, that adorned the church doors, and that blasted band that was now deafening them all with their martial airs.

Groups of people were congratulating the *Cubano*, stiff in his black suit, and old *Paloma,* who felt he was ruler of El Palmar for the day. Neleta swanked about among the women, her rich mantilla covering her eyes, showing off the mother-of-pearl rosary and marble-bound missal from her wedding. Nobody paid *Cañamel* any heed, despite his majestic appearance and the great gold chain sawing away at his abdomen. It seemed that it was not his money that was paying for the festival; Tonet took all the plaudits, as the owner of la *Sequiòta.* As far as most people were concerned, a man who did not belong to the Fishermen's Association deserved no respect. Deep within him, the inn keeper felt a growing hatred for the *Cubano* who, little by little, was taking over everything he owned.

This ill humour stayed with him all day. Sensing how he felt, his wife had to make a particular effort to be friendly and welcoming during the great meal laid on in honour of the preacher and musicians in the tavern's upper room. She spoke openly about her "poor Paco's" ill health, about how it often put him in a devil of a mood and begged them all to forgive him. When the mail boat took them all back to Valencia in the middle of the evening, the irritated *Cañamel,* finding himself alone with his wife, poured out all his spleen.

He was not going to put up with the *Cubano* for moment longer. It was true he got on well with the grandfather, a hard-working man who kept his promises. But that Tonet was a lazy good for nothing, who made jokes at his expense, used his money to let him live like a king, with no more to his name than his luck in the Association draw. Tonet had even denied him the small satisfaction that spending so much money on the festival might have brought. Everyone was thanking the other chap for it, as if *Cañamel* was a nobody, as if it wasn't from his pocket that the money to exploit the *redolin* was coming, and the success of the fishing was due to Tonet. He would end up throwing that rogue out of his house, even though he might be throwing out the business with him.

Alarmed at the threat, Neleta intervened. She advised him to take a dep breath; she reminded him that it was he who had sought out Tonet. The *Palomas*, besides, looked upon her as family; they had protected her in the bad times.

But with childish stubbornness, *Cañamel* repeated his threats. With old *Paloma*, fine; he was ready to go anywhere with him. But either Tonet mended his ways, or he was finished with him. Each to his own; he had no wish to part with any more of his hard-earned cash to that fine lad who knew nothing more than to abuse his generosity and his own poor grandfather. Making that money had cost him dear, and he could not abide wasting it.

The couple's discussion became so heated that Neleta broke into tears, and didn't want to go to the square where they were holding a dance.

Great wax torches used for burials in Church lit up the scene. *Dimoni* was playing old Valencian square-dances on his *dulzaina*, the *chaquera vella* or dance in the style of Torrente, and the girls of El Palmar were elegantly stepping it out, offering their hands and crossing with their partners like bewigged and powdered ladies who had dressed up as fisher girls to dance a pavane by torchlight. Then came a more spirited dance, enlivened with *coplas* where dashing couples twirled, provoking a storm of shouts and whoops when some girl, spinning like a top, revealed her stockings under the floating ring of her petticoats.

The cold caused the fiesta to peter out before midnight. Families retired to their homes, but the young folk stayed behind, the brave, merry village youth, who spent all three days of the festival in a state of continuous intoxication. They all turned up with a shotgun or blunderbuss over their shoulder, as if amusing oneself in this tiny village, where everyone knew everyone, meant you needed to have a weapon within reach.

They were getting the *albaes* organised. According to custom and tradition, they had to spend the night going door to door, singing in honour of all the women, old and young, in El Palmar, and for this task the singers had recourse to a skin of wine, and several bottles of aguardiente. Some of the band from Catarroja, good hearted chaps, had promised to accompany *Dimòni's dulzaina* with their brass, and the *albae's* serenade began to make the rounds in the cold dark night, guided by a torch from the dance.

With their weapons over their shoulders, the young men of El Palmar set off in a tight group behind the oboist and musicians who held their instruments in their cloaks to avoid the freezing touch of the metal. *Sangonera* was the final element of the assembly, loaded down with the skin of wine. He frequently felt the moment ripe for him to drop his load and prepare a glass for a "refreshment".

With a rattle of the tambourin, one of the singers would start off a *copla,* intoning the first few lines, and another would answer him to complete the verse. Generally, the last two verses were the most mischievous, so as the *dulzaina* and brass greeted the end of the *copla* with a noisy *reprise,* the young lads would break into sharp whoops and cries and flee for their lives loosing off their blunderbusses into the air.

It was the devil of a job to get any sleep that night in El Palmar. From their beds, women were able to follow the serenading parade, quivering with the noise and the firing, and were able to guess its progress from one door to another through the mortifying allegations with which they greeted each neighbour in turn.

Sangonera's wineskin did not enjoy much peace in

the course of this expedition. Glasses were passed around the groups, raising the temperature in the depths of the freezing night, and, as voices grew hoarser and hoarser, eyes sparkled more and more brightly.

In one corner two young men were struggling, hand to hand, over who ought to drink first, and, after exchanging a few blows, stepped apart, pointing their weapons at each other. Everyone else piled In, and, with a few well aimed blows, got the guns off them. The wine had got the better of them, and they had better get off to bed! And then the serenaders carried on with their singing and whooping; it was all part of the fun and happened every year.

After three hours of slow progress round the village, the whole lot of them were drunk. With his head drooping and his eyes half shut, *Dimòni* seemed to be snoring through his instrument which moaned indecisively, the notes wobbling like a bell ringer's legs. Seeing the wineskin almost empty, *Sangonera* now wanted to sing, and to a continuous accompaniment of shouts of "Get off!" and amid a chorus of whistles and whoops, was improvising incoherent *coplas* about the "rich folk" in the village.

They had no wine left, but they all had faith that on the latter half of their trip, which they would spend in front of *Cañamel's* tavern, they would get resupplied.

Near the dark and closed up tavern the serenaders came across Tonet, wrapped up to his eyes in a cloak, beneath which peeped the muzzle of a blunderbuss. Recalling what he himself had got up to on similar nights, the *Cubano* was fearful of what that loose tongued lot might indiscreetly reveal and thought to persuade them otherwise with his presence.

The assembled company, foggy with drink and fatigue, seemed newly invigorated in front of *Cañamel's* as the perfume of all those barrels came wafting through cracks in the door.

Someone broke into a song, a respectful ode to "*siñor don Paco*", coaxing him to open up, calling him "the flower of all friends" and promising him everyone's good wishes if he would only fill the wineskin. The building, however, remained wrapped in silence, not a window was touched nor did the least sound come from inside.

In the second *copla* they were still talking about "poor *Cañamel*" in familiar terms, but the singers' voices trembled on the edge of irritation which hinted at a rain of insolence to come. Tonet voiced his disquiet:

OK, lads, no nonsense now! He said to his

friends in paternal tones. But these lads were in no mood to take advice.

The third *copla* was for Neleta, the "sauciest girl in El Palmar" sympathising with her for being married to the miserly *Cañamel*, who was "no use for anything". But after this *copla*, the serenade quickly descended into a toxic flood of scandalous allusions. The assembled company was having fun. They found these *coplas* more to their taste even than the wine, and laughed out loud at this, which only goes to show how country people like to have fun at more unfortunate folk's expense. If a fisherman was robbed of a net worth a few *reales*, they'd all be furious and make common cause of it, but when someone stole another man's wife, they laughed like idiots at the joke.

Tonet was trembling with a mixture of anxiety and fury. At times he felt like running away, seeing it coming that his pals were about to go too far, but pride held him back with the false hope that his presence would put a brake on proceedings.

- Hey, watch what you're doing! He said in a low, threatening tone.

But the singers felt themselves to be the best set up lads in the village. They were little thugs who had been born while he roamed lands overseas. They were keen to show that they feared nothing of the *Cubano*, and laughed at his advice, coming up with quickly composed *coplas* that they hurled like projectiles at the tavern.

One lad, a nephew of *La Samaruca*, suddenly made Tonet's anger boil over. He came out with a *copla* about the relationship between *Cañamel* and the *Cubano*, saying that not only did they share in fishing la Sequiòta but that they also shared Neleta, and ended up saying that she would soon have the successor that she had been asking her husband for in vain.

In a single bound the *Cubano* was in the middle of the group, and in the light of the torch was seen to raise the butt of his gun and smash it into the singer's face. As the lad gathered himself and reached for his own gun, Tonet jumped back and fired almost without bothering to aim. The storm was unleashed! The bullet was lost in flight somewhere, but *Sangonera*, thinking he had heard it whistle by his nose, threw himself to the ground with a fearful scream.

- He's killed me, murderer!

In the surrounding houses, windows began to open noisily, and shadowy white figures appeared, some of them poking the muzzle of a shotgun over the sill. Tonet was instantly disarmed and impelled by a host of strong arms, cornered against a wall, struggling like a madman to get his hand on the knife he kept in his sash.

- Let go of me! he screamed, foaming at the mouth in rage! Let go of me! I'm going to kill that bastard!

The Mayor and his night patrol, who were following the serenaders closely in anticipation of trouble, got in among the combatants. With his leather cap and carrying his rifle, *pare Miquèl* began to dispense blows with the butt, content that the exercise of authority permitted him to do so with impunity.

The Police Chief led Tonet off towards his cottage under threat from his Mauser, and they took la *Samaruca's* nephew into a house to wash off the blood from the rifle blow.

Sangonera played his part. He continued to writhe about on the ground, bellowing to everyone that he was dead. To revive him they gave him the last of the wine from skin, and the rogue, happy to take this type of medicine, swore he was completely done in and just couldn't get up until our energetic priest, guessing what he was up to, dispensed him two therapeutic kicks which instantly got him to his feet.

The Mayor ordered the serenaders to be on their way, they had already done enough singing at *Cañamel's*, and he wanted him disturbed no further, out of the kind of respect for him that country people always feel for the rich.

Somewhat deflated, the serenaders made off. *Dimòni's dulzaina* ran up and down the scales in vain, for the singers, with the wineskin now dry, found their throats suddenly blocked up.

Windows were being closed and the street was deserted, but as they retired, the last of the curious thought they heard the sound of voices from the tavern's upper floor, the crash of furniture and something like a woman's distant wail cut by the low growl of a furious voice. The next day all talk in El Palmar was of the goings on during the serenades in front of *Cañamel's* place.

Tonet did not dare to turn up there. He feared to confront the unfortunate situation that his friends' stupidity had placed him in. He spent the morning wandering the church square not bold enough to go any nearer, just watching the door of the packed tavern. It was the last day of revelry and merry making in the village. They were celebrating the Fiesta of the Christ and the band would take the boat for Catarroja in the afternoon, leaving the village once again sunk in monastic tranquillity for a whole year.

Tonet ate in the cottage with his father and la *Borda* who, through gritted teeth, had suspended their tough battle with the waters so as not to give the neighbours anything else to talk about. Tono decided it was best not to know anything about what had happened the previous night. His demeanour, graver than ever, clearly signalled this was what he wanted. Besides, he had used the time to make good some things that needed repairing in the cottage, for this hard-working soul could not rest for a moment.

But la *Borda* needed to know; you could read it in her innocent eyes which seemed to accentuate her ugliness, in the softly compassionate look she fixed on Tonet, shuddering at the danger he had confronted the previous night. As soon as the two young folk were alone, she blurted out:

- Sir, if father knew what happened… the shame would kill him!

Old *Paloma* did not turn up at the cottage, he was doubtless eating with *Cañamel*. Tonet met him in the square during the evening, His rugged features registered no emotion, but he spoke bluntly to his grandson, advising him to come to the tavern. Old Paco had something to say to him.

Tonet put off the visit for a little while. He stayed in the square watching the band form up for the last time to play what people called the "Passacaglia of the Eels". The musicians would be disappointed if they returned from El Palmar without taking back some fish for their families.

Every year before leaving they would go round the village intoning this final paso doble, and children with wicker baskets would go in front of the big drum gathering whatever the people wanted to give them; eels, tench, and mullet not to mention the sought-after sea bass, the *lubina*, that the Keyholders kept for the bandmaster.

The band commenced playing, walking slowly, so that the fishwives could hand over their offerings, and this was the moment Tonet made up his mind to enter *Cañamel's*.

- *Buenas tardes, caballers!* Good afternoon, gentlemen! He announced loudly, stiffening his courage.

Neleta, behind the bar, darted him a glance whose meaning was unclear, but lowered her head so that he would not see her deeply sunken eyes, red rimmed with weeping. *Cañamel* responded from the back of the establishment, majestically pointing him to the door into the inner rooms.

- Go on, go on, we have to talk.

The two men went into the *estudi*, next to the kitchen which was sometimes used as a bedroom for wildfowlers from Valencia.

Cañamel did not even give his colleague time to sit down. He was livid with rage, his piggy eyes more deeply sunk than ever in puffy folds of flesh and his short stubby nose quivering with a nervous tic. Old Paco got straight to the question. "That Stuff" had all to stop; they could neither carry on as business partners nor be friends, and as Tonet tried to protest, the fat old innkeeper, who was experiencing a fleeting surge of heady energy, perhaps for the last time in his life, stopped him with a look. Nothing to be said, it was useless. He was resolved to bring it to an end and even old *Paloma* knew the reason why. They had started the business with an agreement that he would provide the money and the *Cubano* the labour. His money had not been lacking, but what he had never seen from his associate was any effort on his part. He just lorded it about, while his poor grandfather worked himself to death. But, If only that were all! He had set himself up in that place as if it were his own property. He appeared to be the owner of the tavern. He ate and drank of the best and made free use of the till as if he was the master, he allowed himself liberties which he would rather forget, he took over his dog and his gun, and according to what people were now saying...even his wife!

- Lies, all lies! Cried Tonet with all the conviction of the guilty man.

Cañamel looked back at him in a way that put him on his guard, suddenly fearful. Yes, it was certainly a lie. He also believed it was, and it was a good thing for Tonet and Neleta that he did; because if he should ever, even remotely, suspect that the porkies those idiots had been singing about the night before might be true, he was the very man to wring Neleta's neck and put a bullet between Tonet's eyes. So, what did he think of it all now? Old Paco was a kind man, but despite his infirmity, he was quite man enough when it came to someone touching what was his.

Trembling in silent fury the old inn keeper advanced like a sick old horse, but one of a powerful breed, who can rear on his hind legs right up to the last. Tonet could only gaze at the old adventurer in admiration, a man grown fat and soft in his sickness but who still could summon the energy he had had as an unscrupulous warrior.

The distant echo of the brass band making its way round the village resonated round the silent room. *Cañamel* had more to say, his words accompanied by the approaching music.

Yes, it was all lies but, no, he wasn't there to be made a joke of by people. Besides it weighed on him seeing Tonet always in the tavern enjoying those "brotherly intimacies" with Neleta. He wanted no more of this false brotherly nonsense in his home. He agreed with old *Paloma*. In future it would be the two of them on their own that would carry on the business on la *Sequiòta*, and the grandfather already well understood that he would pay out his grandson from his share. Tonet had no agreement with *Cañamel*. He was the owner of *la Sequiòta*, according to the draw, but should old Paco take back his nets and his capital and Tonet fall out with his grandfather, then we would see how he could sort it all out on his own!

Tonet offered neither protest nor resistance. Whatever his grandfather had agreed was all right with him.

The band was back in front of the tavern. It stopped, the musical din making the walls shake.

Cañamel raised his voice to make himself heard. Now that the matter of the business was settled, the two of them still had to talk man to man. He, with all the authority of the husband who doesn't want people to laugh at him, but also a man who well knew how to eject a troublesome customer when it was needed, ordered Tonet to never come near the tavern again. Was that completely understood? Their friendship was over! It was absolutely the right thing to do in order to avoid any future muttering or further falsehoods. The door of that establishment must henceforth for the *Cubano* be as far above him, as unattainable as ...as the *Miguelete* of Valencia. And while the trombones roared away outside the door, *Cañamel* raised his almost spherical figure on tiptoes and lifted his arm to illustrate the enormous, indeed immeasurable, distance which must, in future, stand between the *Cubano* and he and his wife.

CHAPTER 7

Tonet realised how much he loved Neleta a couple of days after he left the tavern. Perhaps the loss of the relaxed and happy way of life he had enjoyed, that abundance into which he could sink as into a wave of felicity, contributed to his despair. But more than that, he missed the enchantment of those secret trysts about which the whole village could only guess, secrets that could be revealed at any moment, the dangerously addictive bliss of risky caresses with the husband and customers so close.

Now an outcast from *Cañamel's*, he knew not where to turn. He tried to strike up acquaintances in El Palmar's other taverns, miserable hovels with no more to them than a little barrel where the only customers of an afternoon would be lads weighed down with debt who couldn't get into Cañamel's. Like some great potentate finding himself by mistake in a seedy dive, Tonet fled such encounters.

He spent the days wandering around the village outskirts. When tired of this, he would venture to El Saler, to El Perelló or to Catarroja's docks, anywhere to kill time. Despite his aversion to work, he would pole away for hours in his punt in order to see a friend, with no other aim than to smoke a cigarette with him.

The situation obliged him to live in his father's cottage, anxiously keeping an eye on Tono, who sometimes would fix him with a stare that seemed to suggest that he well knew everything that had happened. Driven by sheer boredom, Tonet suddenly changed tack. It would be better to lend his poor father a hand than roam the Albufera from one end to the other like a caged animal. And so, with the fleeting burst of enthusiasm that lazy folk can summon when they make up their minds to work, he was off the very next day, dredging mud from the ditches as in the old days.

In a show of gratitude for this act of repentance, Tono stopped frowning and actually addressed a few words to his son. He knew everything. Things were turning out just as he had said. Tonet had not behaved like a *Paloma,* and it hurt his father to hear what was being said about him. It wounded him deeply to see his son living at the old innkeeper's expense and stealing his wife as well.

- Lies, lies, protested the *Cubano* with all the forcefulness of the guilty, They're vile, wicked stories!

All right, that was better. Old Tono was happy for it to be like that. The important thing was to have escaped the dangerous situation. Now to get on with the work, to be an honourable man and help his father with the task of filling in his ponds. When they were all turned into fields, and people in El Palmar saw the *Palomas* bringing in plenty of sacks of rice, Tonet would soon find another lady friend. He'd be able to choose from all the girls in the surrounding villages. Nobody said no to a rich man!

Cheered by his father's words Tonet plunged into the work with a vengeance. Poor *Borda* wore herself out trying to keep up with him, even more than when she was with Tono. The *Cubano* always seemed to feel she wasn't working hard enough, and was demanding and brutal with the poor girl, loading her up like a beast of burden, although it was he who first began to show signs of fatigue. Gasping for breath under the weight of baskets of earth and continual work with the pole, poor *Borda* still had a smile on her face and when, aching in every bone, she prepared the meal of an evening, she would gaze in gratitude at her Tonet, the prodigal son who had made his father suffer so much, but whose good behaviour was now allowing the hard-working man to bask quietly with confidence in the future.

But while the *Cubano* seemed to have the wind in his sails, it never blew the same two days running, He could be blown about by furious storms of activity but then quickly beset by the calms of overwhelming and complete laziness. After a month of continuous work Tonet got tired, as in former times. Large parts of the fields were already covered, but there remained some deep holes which made them despair, bottomless pits through which the defeated waters seemed to surge back, slowly gnawing away at the earth accumulated at the cost of so much work. Faced with the size of the undertaking, the *Cubano* felt dejected and a little fearful. He was now used to the abundance of *Cañamel's* tavern and compared it unfavourably with la *Borda's* measly stews, the meagre, thin wine, the tough corn bread, and mouldy sardines that were his father's only sustenance.

His grandfather, who carried on frequenting *Cañamel's* as if nothing had happened, irritated him by his diffidence. He ate there twice a day and got on perfectly well with the innkeeper who seemed happy with the energy with which the old man worked *la Sequiòta*. And to hell with his grandson! Not even exchanging a word when he saw him at night in the cottage, as if he did not even exist, as if he wasn't the real owner of *la Sequiòta*!

Cañamel and his grandfather might have an agreement to work it, but they would be disappointed. Perhaps all the innkeeper's blustering was really designed just to get rid of him half-way through, so there would be more profits for them. And so it was, that with the countryman's cold, fierce wiliness, which takes account neither of feelings nor of family in matters of money, Tonet confronted Old *Paloma* one night as he was setting out for a trip to the *redolin*. He was the owner of the *Sequiòta*, the real owner, and he hadn't seen a penny for a very long time. He was well aware that the fishing was not as good as in other years, but the business was carrying on and grandfather and old Paco were tucking away the *duros* into their belts. He had learned all this from the eel buyers. All right! He wanted the books opened, to be given his share, or if not, he would take over the *redolin* and look for some less greedy partners.

With all the despotic authority that he used to believe gave him absolute rights over the whole family, for just a few moments old *Paloma* felt obliged to smash his grandson's head open with the end of his pole. But he then suddenly thought on the blacks that the *Cubano* had killed "over there" and, hold on! you didn't hit a man like that even if he was family. Besides, his threat to take back the *redolin* filled him with dismay. Old *Paloma* took the moral high ground. If he wasn't giving him money, it was because he knew him too well, and money in a young lad's hands was the road to perdition. He would just drink it, or be off playing cards with those rogues shuffling the deck in the shadows of some bar in El Saler; he would prefer to keep an eye on it himself, so by this reasoning he was really doing Tonet a favour. In the end, when he died, who would all his stuff be for, if not for his grandson?

But Tonet was not to be fobbed off with mere hopes. He wanted what was due to him or he would take back control of the *redolin*. After more than three days of hard bargaining, the old boatman was forced to delve into his money belt and, with a pained expression, haul out a wrap of *duros*. He could take them, mean-spirited Judas, and when he had spent them in a few days let him come back for more. Let's get grandfather completely cleaned out! He now saw very clearly what old age held in store for him, working like a slave so his lord and master could be provided with an easy life. And with that he left Tonet alone, as if the slender feelings he still might have for him were now lost forever.

Finding himself with money in his pocket, the *Cubano* did not return to his father's cottage. He wanted to spend his leisure in shooting, living a soldier's life, earning his daily bread with gunpowder, so he started by buying a shotgun somewhat better than the venerable weapons that were kept in the cottage. *Sangonera*, who had been thrown out of Cañamel's the day following Tonet's expulsion, wandered around with him, now that he could see he was fed up with the life of heavy labour at his father's place and at complete leisure.

The *Cubano* readily fell in with the rogue. He made good company and could even be useful to him. He had somewhere to live, and although it was worse than a dog kennel, it would still provide them some shelter.

Tonet would be the shot and *Sangonera* his retriever. Everything would belong to them equally, both food and wine. Was the rogue agreed? *Sangonera* indicated he was quite happy. He could also contribute to the common good. He had the golden touch for lifting *mornells* out of the canals and taking some fish before slipping the nets back into the water. He wasn't like certain unscrupulous thieves, who, as Palmar fishermen used to say, not only robbed them of their souls but also their bodies, meaning the entire net bags. Tonet would find the meat and he the fish. Deal done!

From then on it was only occasionally that old *Paloma's* grandson would be seen around the village with his shotgun over his shoulder, whistling comically to *Sangonera,* following in his footsteps, head down and carefully checking all around to see if there might be something they could make use of within reach of his talons.

They would spend weeks on end in la Dehesa, living like cavemen. Tonet had often thought, in the midst of his tranquil sojourn in El Palmar, of the soldier's life of limitless freedom albeit one full of danger, where, with death ever before his eyes, he sees neither barriers nor obstacles in his path, and rifle in hand, satisfies his desires without recognising any law but that of necessity.

Habits acquired during his years of jungle warfare were now revived in la Dehesa, just a few steps from groups of people where The Law and Authority held sway. He and his companion would fashion shelters from dry branches anywhere in the woods. When hungry, they would kill a couple of rabbits or a brace of wood pigeons fluttering above the tree tops, and when they needed money for cartridges or wine Tonet would shoulder his shotgun, and in a morning would succeed in bagging a clutch of game that his vagabond pal could sell in El Saler or in Catarroja port, returning with a skin of wine to hide in the bushes.

Tonet's shotgun, blasting away across the whole Dehesa, was something of a challenge to the keepers who had to stir themselves from their peaceful and isolated existence.

Sangonera would be as alert as a guard dog when Tonet was shooting, and when the rogue's sharp eyes spotted their foes approaching, he would whistle his companion to take cover. On several occasions old *Paloma's* grandson found himself face to face with his pursuers and gallantly defended his wish to live in la Dehesa. One day a keeper fired at him and seconds later, by way of a threatening response, heard a round whistle past his head. Lame suggestions didn't count for much with an old soldier. He was a lost soul who feared neither God nor the Devil. He shot as well as his grandfather and when he sent a round near your head it was because his simply wanted to give you a warning. To get rid of him for good you would have to kill him. The keepers, who had numerous family with them in their huts, ended up in an unspoken compromise with the bold shot, and when his gun blasted off, they would pretend not to have heard it properly, and charge off in the opposite direction.

Sangonera, who had been beaten and kicked out from everywhere around, felt strong and proud under Tonet's protection, and would gaze around insolently at folk when he went in to El Saler, like a yapping puppy who trusts in the protection of his master. In return for this protection, he honed his skills as a guard dog, and when the occasional pair of Guardia Civil came down from la Huerta de Ruzafa, *Sangonera* could sense their presence as if he could smell them.

-*Els tricornios*, those lads in tricorn hats, he would say to his companion, they're already here.

On days when yellow webbing and patent tricorns appeared on the Dehesa, Tonet and *Sangonera* would take refuge on the Albufera. Safe in one of old *Paloma's* punts, they would glide among the thickets downing birds which the vagabond, quite used to plunging up to his neck in water in the depths of winter, would retrieve.

Tonet was living just a few steps away from his father, but, fearing his sad frowning countenance he avoided seeing him. *La Borda* would come in cautiously to change Tonet's clothes and lend a hand in a way that only a woman knows how. Worn out by the day's labours, the poor girl would mend his rags by the light of a taper as the two scruffs sat nearby, never uttering a single word of reproach, daring to dart only an occasional pitying glance at her brother.

When the two companions in arms spent the night alone, with no let-up in their drinking, they would tell each other their most intimate thoughts. Used now to continuous intoxication thanks to *Sangonera's* good example, Tonet could not bear the weight of his secret and told his comrade all about his love trysts with Neleta.

At first the rogue was inclined to object. That was not a good thing to do! "Thou shalt not covet thy neighbour's wife". But then finding himself out of favour with Tonet and with all the former sacristan's rough casuistry, he was immediately able to find excuses and justification for the moral failure. The truth was that they had a certain right to love each other. To have "known" each other after Neleta's marriage would have been an enormous sin. But they had "known" each other since childhood, had been sweethearts, so it was *Cañamel's* fault for sticking his nose in where nobody asked him and upsetting their relationship. He well deserved what had happened. As he recalled the times when the fat old chap had thrown him out of the tavern, he smiled with satisfaction at his matrimonial misfortune and considered himself avenged.

Later, when there remained no more wine in the skin and the taper was beginning to sputter,

Sangonera, his eyes half closed with drink was rambling incoherently about his beliefs.

Tonet nodded off without listening, used to this stream of consciousness, while the cottage's straw roofing, stirred by the gusts of wind allowed the rain to filter through.

Sangonera never tired of talking. Why was he so unfortunate? What was the reason for Tonet's suffering, bored and self-absorbed now that he could not go near Neleta! Because the whole thing was unfair, because, in their greed for money, people persisted in living contrary to God's commands.

Sidling up to Tonet, he woke him up speaking in a mysterious voice of the dawning realisation of all his hopes. Good times were coming. "He" was already in the world. He had seen "Him" as he could now see Tonet, and "He" had touched him, a poor sinner, with his cool, divine hand. For the umpteenth time he went back over the story of his mysterious encounter on the shores of the Albufera. He was making his way back from El Saler with a packet of cartridges for Tonet when, on the track that bordered the lake, he suddenly felt a surge of emotion as if something was coming towards him that robbed him of all his strength. He legs gave way under him and he fell to the ground, overcome by drowsiness, wanting to vanish and never to wake again.

- It's because you were drunk, Tonet would say when they got to this point.

But *Sangonera* would not have it. No, he was not drunk. He had consumed very little that day. The proof was that he remained fully aware of his surroundings, although his body refused to obey him.

It was at the close of evening and the Albufera was a deep purple, the sky reddening in bloody waves, and against this background *Sangonera* saw a man come towards him on the track and stop when he got next to him.

The rogue shuddered as he recalled it. The soft sad eyes, the parted beard, the long hair. How was he dressed? He remembered only a white robe, something like a very long blouse or tunic, and on his back, which seemed bowed by the weight, some enormous contraption that *Sangonera* could not quite make out. Perhaps it was the instrument of torture with which he would newly redeem Mankind. The figure bent over him with all the fading twilight concentrated in his eyes. He stretched out His hand and stroked *Sangonera's* brow with His fingers, a touch that sent shivers from the roots of his hair to the tips of his toes. He murmured some strange incomprehensible words in a soft musical voice and passed smiling on His way, leaving Sangonera, overcome with emotion, to fall into a deep slumber from which he awoke hours later in the depths of the dark night.

He had seen no more, but it was Him, of that he was sure. He was returned to the world to save his creation, as he had promised Mankind; once again He was searching out the poor, the simple, the miserable fisherfolk of the lake. *Sangonera* was to be one of the Elect: there was a reason for that touch of His hand. So, with fervour and faith, the vagabond announced his intention to abandon his friend as soon as the sweet vision reappeared.

Annoyed to have had his sleep disturbed, Tonet grumbled threateningly in a surly voice. Would he please shut up? He had told him plenty of times that that was no more than a drunken dream. To sum up, and in short, which is how things ought to be done, he ought to have realised that the mysterious stranger was a certain Italian traveller who spent two days in El Palmar sharpening knives and scissors and carried the tools of his trade on his back.

Sangonera kept his counsel, fearful of his protector's hand, but his faith was deeply insulted and silently rebelled at Tonet's vulgar explanation. He would see Him again! He knew for certain he would hear again that strange, sweet language, feel that cool hand on his brow, and see that soft smile, and was saddened only by the possibility that the encounter might again happen at the end of an evening when he had quenched his thirst too often and found his legs giving way.

This was how the two companions spent the winter, *Sangonera* nursing the most impassioned hopes and Tonet thinking of Neleta, whom he never saw, since on his rare trips to El Palmar the young man would stop at the Church Square, not daring to go any closer to *Cañamel's*.

This absence, stretching over months and months, made his recollection of past happiness grow, enlarge out of all proportion to reality. Neleta's image was everywhere before him. He saw her in the woods where they had got lost as children, on the lake where they gave themselves to each other in the sweet mystery of the night. He could not move in that circle of water and mud which circumscribed his life without encountering something which brought her to mind. Toughened as he was by his life as an outcast, the spur of abstinence meant that Tonet often spent nights tossing and turning in restless agitation when *Sangonera* would hear him cry out for Neleta like a roaring bull.

One day, driven by this maddening passion, he

knew he just had to see her. The increasingly sickly *Cañamel* had gone to the city, and at midday, when the customers would all be at home and he would be able to find Neleta alone behind the bar, the *Cubano* strode resolutely into the tavern.

Seeing him in the doorway, she gave a cry as if he had come back from the dead. A flash of joy passed across her face, but her eyes immediately darkened as reason flooded back and she lowered her head with an unapproachable expression of fury.

- Go away, away, she murmured, do you want to lose me?

He, lose her? The idea caused him such a pang of grief that he dared make no reply. Instinctively he stepped back, and immediately regretting his weakness, was out into the square and away from the tavern.

He made no attempt to return. When his stifled passion made him think of her, he only had to remember that look to be overcome with a cold shiver. It was all over between them. *Cañamel*, the old butt of their jokes, was now an insuperable obstacle.

The hatred he felt for the husband drove him to seek out his grandfather, thinking that anything he could get out of him would be all the less for Neleta's husband. Money! He wanted money! They were getting rich from *la Sequiòta* and had forgotten about him, the owner. These demands resulted in angry discussions between grandfather and grandson which miraculously did not end in blows on the canal bank. Other boatmen were astonished at the patience old *Paloma* displayed in bringing his grandson round. It was a poor year, la *Sequiòta* was not producing the results they had hoped. Besides, *Cañamel* was ill and proving intractable. There were times when old *Paloma* himself wished the year was over, and it was time for a new draw, so that the business which was giving him so much grief could go to the devil. His old way of doing it was fine: let every man fish for himself; Companies! As much trouble as women!

When Tonet did succeed in dragging a few *duros* out of his grandfather, he would whistle cheerily for *Sangonera,* and they would make their way from tavern to tavern all the way to Valencia to spend several days of dissipation in dives in the slums, until their rapidly emptying pockets obliged them to return to the Albufera.

He had learned during his discussions with his grandfather of *Cañamel's* illness. No one talked of anything else in El Palmar given that the innkeeper was the most important figure in the village and that, in times of need, almost everyone had sought his support. *Cañamel's* health problems were now becoming more serious. It wasn't just hypochondria as everyone had thought at the beginning. His health was broken, but when they saw him getting fatter every day, more swollen , overflowing with flesh, people declared gravely that he was going to die of an excess of health and good living.

He was complaining more and more without being able to say exactly what was wrong. The rheumatism, which was the product of a life lived amid that marshy terrain, combined with his inactivity, and was spreading throughout his body, playing hide and seek with the poultices and other home remedies that chased it around but could never quite catch up with its wild capers. In the morning the old man would be complaining of his head and in the afternoon about his stomach or his swollen hands and feet. The nights were terrible, and more than once he was out of bed in the middle of winter, opening windows and saying he was suffocating indoors and couldn't get enough air into his lungs there.

There was one moment when he thought he had got to the bottom his problem. He had it now! And he knew exactly what was gnawing away at him! When he ate a lot his difficulty with breathing increased and he felt very nauseated. His problem was in his stomach, so he began to self-medicate, turning to old *Paloma* as a sage in such matters. As the old boatman declared, what he had was too much of a good thing, the sickness that came from eating and drinking too much. Abundance was the enemy!

La *Samaruca*, his awful sister-in-law had become a little closer since he had thrown Tonet out. Finally, as the cruel harpy put it, and at last, her brother-in-law had felt embarrassed.

She would step out to meet him when *Cañamel* was going to go out for a stroll through the village. She would call him from outside the tavern, for she did not dare confront Neleta in her own home, knowing she would be shown the door, and by claiming an exaggerated interest, learned about her brother-in-law's health from these encounters, and sympathised with all the crazy things he had had to put up with. He ought to have remained single after the death of his "dearly departed". He had wanted to play the lad by getting married to a girl and had got the lot: loss of face and loss of health. He would get out of these rash decisions and let's be thankful it hadn't cost him his life!

When *Cañamel* spoke to her about his problem being in his stomach the malicious woman fixed him with a look of astonishment, as if a thought had just crossed her mind that left her somewhat shaken. Was it really his stomach that was the problem? Mightn't they have slipped him something to finish him off? The old innkeeper saw then in the wicked woman's evil glance a glint of suspicion so obvious, so driven by hatred of Neleta, that it infuriated him to the point of almost hitting her. Out, out, you evil creature! That's what his "dear departed", who feared her sister like the Devil, used to say. Turning his back on la *Samaruca*, he resolved never to see her again.

To suspect Neleta of such a horrible thing! His wife had never been so kind and caring to him. If old Paco retained any trace of rancour over the time when Tonet had made himself master of the tavern with the silent aid of his wife, it had vanished in the face of Neleta's behaviour, who put all the place's business worries out of her mind in order to concentrate on her husband.

She had no confidence in the knowledge of the visiting doctor, a taciturn tradesman scientist who came twice a week to El Palmar, suggesting quinine for everything as if he had no idea of any other medication, and as her husband's infirmity increased, she dressed him like a baby, putting on each article amid complaints and protests from the arthritic patient and took him off to Valencia for the top doctors there to examine. She spoke on his behalf, advising him like a mother that he had to do everything that these gentlemen asked of him.

Their answer was always the same. It was just a touch of rheumatism, but severe rheumatism that wasn't affecting just one particular part, but had spread throughout his body, and resulted from his over-active life of wandering as a youth and his sedentary life of inactivity now. He had to stir himself, to work, take plenty of exercise and above all stop having too much of everything. And no more drinking, for you could see he was a professional landlord used to drinking with his customers. And no more of abusing himself in other ways too. At this the doctors, not daring to put things any more clearly in the presence of his wife, would lower their voices and finish off the consultation with a meaningful wink.

They returned to the Albufera, fired up with renewed energy after hearing the doctors. He was ready to do anything: he really wanted to stir himself and get off this weight that was enveloping his body and stifling his breathing; he would take the waters as they recommended; Neleta knew better than he did, and he would do as she told him and astonish those learned gentlemen with his self-control. But he had barely set foot inside the tavern when all his iron resolve evaporated. He was clutched in the sweet embrace of complete inertia, hardly daring move a muscle without a supreme effort and much complaining. He would spend his days beside the hearth, gazing emptily at the fire and downing glass after glass at the urging of his friends. He wasn't going to die from just one more! If Neleta gave him a severe look, scolding him like a child, he would make his humble apologies. He couldn't show disrespect to his customers; you had to look after them, business before health!

With his willpower gone and his body racked with pain, as his debility increased his carnal appetites seemed to grow, and ceaselessly tormented him like jabs of fire. He found certain relief in trying to have sex with Neleta. It was a lash that shook him to the very core of his being but through which he seemed to find some calm. She would tell him off; he was killing himself. He ought to remember what the doctors had said. But old Paco would excuse himself with the same answer as when drinking. One more time wouldn't kill him. So, she would give in, resigned to it, even as her cat's eyes glinted with an evil secret, as if within the depths of her soul she enjoyed a perverse appetite for love-making with this sick man as a means of accelerating his death.

As he surrendered to his carnal instincts, Cañamel would roar. It was his only pleasure, his constant thought amidst the painful immobility of rheumatism. He would feel he was suffocating when he lay down in bed at night and would have to see in the dawn sitting up, wheezing painfully on a wicker chair by the window. He felt better during the day and when he grew tired of toasting his toes at the fire, he would shakily make his way into the back rooms.

- Neleta! Nelta! He would call anxiously, in a voice that his wife recognised as a plea.

And Neleta would put on a resigned expression and go back with him, leaving the bar to her aunt, out of sight for more than an hour while the customers smiled knowingly, living as they did cheek by jowl with the owner and his wife.

With the end of their rights over the *redolin* in sight, old *Paloma* was becoming daily less respectful to his colleague and used to say that *Cañamel* chased his wife around the tavern like a bitch in heat.

Samaruca claimed that they were murdering her brother-in-law. That Neleta was a criminal and her aunt a witch. Between the two of them they must have given old Paco something that had addled his brain, perhaps those "follow-me powders" that certain women knew how to make to prevent their men straying. And that is how the poor old chap seemed, following her about with his tongue hanging out, but his thirst never satisfied, one more scrap of health dropping off him every day. And there was no justice in the world that this crime went unpunished!

The state old Paco was in rather justified the rumours. Customers would see him motionless by the hearth, even at the height of summer, seeking the heat of the fire on which the paellas bubbled. Flies buzzed about his head without him making the least effort to brush them off. He was wrapped in a cloak on the sunniest of days, whimpering like a baby, complaining of feeling sore with the cold. His lips were turning blue, his puffy, floppy cheeks took on a pale, waxy hue and his bulging eyes were deeply sunk and rimmed in black. He was become an enormous, fat, trembling, phantasm, whose presence made the customers feel awful. Now that his business dealings with *Cañamel* in the *redolin* were finished, old *Paloma* was not going into the tavern. He said openly that the wine was less to his taste when he looked at that groaning bundle of pains. As the old chap now had money of his own, he was frequenting a little tavern to which his friends had followed him and the crowd in *Cañamel's* was correspondingly much diminished.

Neleta advised her husband to go to the baths that the doctors had recommended. Her aunt would go with him.

- Next month, replied the sick man, later, later.

And he stayed motionless in the little wicker chair with no willpower to separate from his wife or get himself out of the corner in which his entire existence now seemed stuck.

His ankles were beginning to swell, assuming monstrous dimensions. Neleta had been waiting for this. This was the "malleolar swelling" (the exact phrase, she well remembered the name) which a doctor had told her about on her last visit to Valencia.

This manifestation of his illness did, however, shake *Cañamel* out of his stupor. He quite well knew what this was: the cursed damp of El Palmar that crept in through your feet when you stayed still. He did what Neleta told him when she ordered him to take himself off to a different place. Like all the richer people in El Palmar, he had a little rented house in Ruzafa for times of illness. There he could make use of the doctors and pharmacies in Valencia. *Cañamel* set out on the trip accompanied by his wife's aunt and was away for a fortnight. But the swelling had hardly started to go down when old Paco was wanting to get back, declaring that he was now well, He could not live without Neleta. In Ruzafa he felt the cold touch of death when he called for his wife and her wrinkled, scowling aunt appeared, looking like an old eel.

Old habits began to reassert themselves and, like a continuous background lament, *Cañamel's* faint moaning was once more heard in the tavern.

At the start of autumn, he was back in Ruzafa in an even worse state. The swelling had spread up his enormous legs, already disfigured with arthritis, and now real elephant's feet which he dragged about with difficulty, supporting himself on the nearest thing available and letting out a groan every time his foot struck the ground.

Neleta accompanied her husband to the mail boat. Her aunt had gone on ahead in the morning's "eel wagon" to get the little house in Ruzafa ready.

That night, as she settled down to sleep after closing up the tavern, Neleta thought she heard from the canal side a low whistle that she recognised from childhood. She half opened a window and looked out. He was out there, slinking by like a dejected dog in the vague hope that they would open up for him. Neleta closed the window and went back to bed. What Tonet was suggesting was madness. She was not stupid enough to compromise her future in a bout of juvenile passion. As her old enemy, la *Samaruca* used to say, she knew better than any old woman.

Flattered however by Tonet's passionate approach, by the fact that he had run to her as soon as he thought she was on her own, she fell asleep thinking of her lover. She had to let time pass. Their former happiness would bloom again, perhaps when they least expected it.

Tonet's circumstances had undergone another change. Once again, he was being a good boy, living with his father and working on the fields, which were almost covered with earth, thanks to Tono's tenacity.

The *Cubano's* sojourns in la Dehesa were at an end. The Guardia Civil from la Huerta de Ruzafa were patrolling the woods frequently. These moustachioed, hard-faced soldiers had made abundantly clear to him their determination to reply with a Mauser round to the first shotgun blast fired among the pine trees. The *Cubano* took the warning to heart. These lads in their yellow webbing were not like the keepers on the Dehesa; they would leave him tied to the foot of a tree and all that the incident would cost them would be a report on a scrap of paper. He sent *Sangonera* on his way and the vagabond returned to his wandering life, crowning himself with garlands of flowers from the bank when he was drunk and seeking the mystic apparition by the lake that had made such an impression on him.

For his part, Tonet hung up his shotgun in his father's place and swore everlasting repentance to him. He wanted them to see him as a properly serious person. He would be kind and respectful to Tono, as he had been to his father before him. His crazy escapades were finished for good. Completely won over, his father embraced him as he had never once done since he returned from Cuba and, together they hurled themselves into covering their fields with earth with all the ardour of the man who sees his work nearing completion.

Sorrow infused Tonet with renewed strength, stiffening his resolve. Impelled by the passion gnawing at his entrails, he had spent several nights roaming around the tavern, knowing that Neleta was on her own. He had seen the window quietly half open and then close again. There was no doubt she had recognised him, but despite this remained silent and unapproachable. He ought to hope for nothing. The only thing left for him was the love of his family. He began to grow closer to Tono and la *Borda*, becoming part of their hopes and dreams, sharing their problems and their misery, and admiring the simplicity of their way of life, for he now scarcely ever drank and would spend the evenings telling his father of his adventures as a soldier. La *Borda* was radiant with happiness, and every time she chatted with a neighbour, it was to heap praises on her brother's head. Poor Tonet! How kind he was, and how happy his father was now.

Suddenly one day Neleta left the tavern for Ruzafa. Such was her haste that she could not wait for the mail boat but summoned old *Paloma* to take her to El Saler in his punt, or to Catarroja or to anywhere on the landward side from where she could get to Ruzafa.

Cañamel was very ill. He was dying. But this was not the most important thing for Neleta. Her aunt had arrived during the morning with news that left her speechless behind the bar. La *Samaruca* had been four days in Ruzafa. She had installed herself in the house like a close relative and the poor aunt had not dared protest. In addition, she had brought a nephew with her that she loved like a son, and who lived with her: the same man Tonet had struck, the night of the *albaes*. The old nurse had at first kept quiet, like the kindly, simple woman she was. They were relatives of *Cañamel's,* and she was not so hard-hearted as to deprive a sick man of such visitors. But later on, she had overheard some of the conversations between *Cañamel* and his sister-in-law. The witch was making every effort to convince him that nobody loved him like she and her nephew did. They spoke about Neleta, telling him that no sooner had he left on his trip than old Paloma's grandson was in the tavern every night. And in addition (and here the old woman faltered with fear) the previous day two gentlemen had turned up, brought along by la *Samaruca* and her nephew, one of whom questioned *Cañamel* in a quiet voice while the other wrote it all down. It must have been something to do with a Will.

Faced with this news, Neleta showed what she was made of. The soft, lilting tones, so sweetly inflected, in which she usually spoke, turned harsh; the clear reflections in her eyes glinted like talc and a wave of greenish pallor swept across her skin.

- *Recordons*! Watch out! She screamed like one of the boatmen who thronged the tavern.

Was this what she had married *Cañamel* for? Was this why she had put up with never ending illness, and made such efforts to appear sweet and caring? Erect within her throbbed the immense strength of the selfish country girl who places self-interest above love.

He first reaction was to want to punch her aunt, who was telling her all this so late in the day, when there was perhaps nothing that could be done about it. But such an explosion of anger would have been a waste of time, and instead she sprinted for old Paloma's boat, in such a hurry that she seized a pole herself to get them out of the canal and the sail set as soon as possible.

She swept like a hurricane into the little house in Ruzafa, half-way though the afternoon. Seeing her, la *Samaruca* paled and instinctively backed towards the door, but hardly had time to take a step when she was struck by a slap from Neleta, and the two women silently grappled each other by the hair, in wordless rage, twisting and turning from one side of the room to the other, bumping off the walls and sending furniture flying, their clenched fists sunk in each other's manes like two cows yoked together, unable to move apart.

La *Samaruca* was strong and somewhat feared among the womenfolk in El Palmar, but Neleta's sweet little smile and musical voice concealed the striking power of a viper and she bit her enemy in the face with a fury that drew blood.

- What's this? moaned *Cañamel's* voice from the next room, alarmed by the din, what's happening?

The doctor who was with him emerged from the bedroom and assisted by la *Samaruca's* nephew, managed to separate the women after a great effort, and not without receiving a few scratches in the process. Neighbours were piling up in the doorway, admiring the silent rage with which the women were fighting, and praising the little blondie, who was in tears of frustration at not being able to "get more off her chest".

Cañamel's sister-in-law fled, followed by her nephew; the door was closed, and Neleta, her hair awry and her pale complexion red with scratches, entered her husband's bedroom after first rinsing the other woman's blood from her teeth.

Cañamel was a ruin of a man. The monstruous swelling of his legs, oedema as the doctor called it, now extended all the way up to his abdomen and his lips had a bluish, cadaveric tint.

Slumped in the wicker chair with his head sunk into his shoulders, he seemed even more enormous, emerging from his apoplectic stupor only with the greatest effort. He did not ask the cause of all the noise, as if he had instantly forgotten about it, and only when he saw his wife, did he make a feeble effort to smile as he murmured:

- I'm ill, very ill.

He could not be moved. Whenever he tried to lie down, he felt he couldn't breathe, and she had to rush to sit him up, as if his last moment had come. Neleta made her preparations for a long stay. La *Samaruca* wouldn't be making a fool of her anymore. She wasn't going to take her eyes off her husband until she got him back safe and well to the village.

But even she had to shake her head in disbelief at any thought that *Cañamel* might be able to return to the Albufera. The doctors did not conceal their conclusion that his condition was terminal. He was going to die of rheumatic heart disease, of "asystole". There was no cure; the heart would simply cease functioning at the moment least expected and put an end to his life.

Neleta was not for abandoning her husband. She couldn't get those gentlemen, who had written those papers in his presence, out of her mind. *Cañamel's* drowsiness infuriated her; she wanted to know what he had dictated under la *Samaruca's* cursed influence and would shake him in an attempt to rouse him from his stupor.

But when old Paco did momentarily come to himself, he always answered the same way. He had organised everything well. If she was good, if she loved him as she had so often sworn she would, she had nothing to fear.

Cañamel died two days later, sitting, bloated in his wicker chair with his legs livid, of cardiac asthma.

Neleta scarcely shed a tear. Something else was on her mind. When the body had been despatched to the cemetery and she found herself free of the prodigious condolences of the people of Ruzafa, her only thought was to find that *notario* who had drafted the Will and acquaint herself with her husband's wishes.

She had not long to wait to get what she wanted. Just as he had assured her in his final moments, *Cañamel* had known how to sort things out all right.

He named Neleta as sole heir to his property with no other bequests or legacies. But he ordained that if she married again, or if, by her conduct, she demonstrated that she was maintaining an amorous relationship with any man, then any liquid assets should pass to his sister-in-law and the relatives of his first wife.

CHAPTER 8

Nobody knew how Tonet made his appearance back in the tavern of the now departed Cañamel. The regulars spotted him one morning, seated at a little table, playing truque with Sangonera and some other unemployed lads in the village, and no one was very surprised. It was natural for Tonet to frequent the establishment of which Neleta was now the sole owner.

The *Cubano* was back spending all his time there, once again leaving his father, who had really believed him totally changed, completely in the lurch. But this time there were none of those little shared intimacies between him and the landlady, that suspicious outward show of "brotherly love", that had scandalised El Palmar. Clad in full mourning, Neleta was ensconced behind the bar, now looking even more beautiful with her air of authority. She seemed to have grown now that she was rich and free. She joked less with the regulars, appeared prim and tetchy, and took the jokes that customers were used to throw at her with a fierce frown and pursed lips. With her sleeves rolled up, a drinker only had to brush his arm against hers as he took his glass for her to show her claws and threaten him with the door.

The number of customers was increasing, now that the bloated spectre of the suffering *Cañamel* had disappeared. The wine the widow served seemed better, and the smaller establishments in El Palmar began to lose customers.

Tonet, dared not look directly at Neleta for fear of what people would say. La *Samaruca* was already saying plenty, now that she saw him back in the tavern! So, he sat in his corner, playing cards and drinking, as Cañamel used to do in the old days, and seemed completely kept at a distance by the woman to whom everyone's eyes turned, more than they did to him.

Shrewd as ever, old *Paloma* understood his grandson's situation. He was always there so as not to give any offence to the widow, who wanted to keep him within sight and impose her complete authority upon him. Tonet, was just "on duty" as the old chap used to say, and although he might from time to time feel like getting out into the reed beds to fire off a few shots, he was keeping calm and staying silent, no doubt fearing Neleta's recriminations when they were alone.

She had suffered a lot at the end, having to put up with the demands of the ailing *Cañamel*, and now that she was rich and free, she was making up for it by making Tonet feel the weight of her authority.

Taken aback by the speed with which death had sorted everything out for him, the poor lad was even beginning to doubt whether it really was a good thing being back at *Cañamel's* without having to worry about the annoyed landlord suddenly turning up. But looking round the abundance, which was now entirely Neleta's, he did as he was bid by the widow. She was keeping a close eye on him, treating him with tough love like a strict mother.

- No more drinking! she would say to Tonet when, at *Sangonera's* urging, he would dare to ask for a couple more glasses at the bar.

Old *Paloma's* grandson, obedient as a child, would deny himself and stay quietly in his seat, respected by everyone, for nobody was ignorant of his relationship with the place's owner.

The regulars who had witnessed their intimacies when *Cañamel* was around, found it completely logical that they should have reached such an understanding. Hadn't they been sweethearts? Hadn't they been in love to the point of exciting the jealousy of easy-going old Paco? They would get married now, as soon as the months of waiting that the Law required of a widow had passed, and the *Cubano* would then assume all the airs of the legitimate owner, behind that bar which he had already crossed as a lover.

The only people who did not accept this solution were la *Samaruca* and her relatives. Neleta would not get married, of that they were certain. That honey-tongued little bitch was too much of a lady to do things as God ordained. Rather than pass on to the first wife's relatives what was very much theirs, she would prefer to mess around with the *Cubano*. That was nothing new for her. Poor *Cañamel* had seen much worse before he died!

Spurred on by the Will, which offered them the possibility of becoming rich, and by the conviction that Neleta wasn't going to make it any easier for them by getting married, la *Samaruca* and her people set up a strict surveillance operation around the lovers.

When the tavern was closing up towards midnight, the great fat *Samaruca*, bundled up in her shawl would keep an eye on the regulars as they came out, watching for Tonet among them.

She spotted *Sangonera*, staggering unsteadily towards his hovel. His drinking companions followed joking behind, asking if he had seen the Italian knife-grinder again. Completely drunk, he retained his calm. Sinners! It seemed impossible that, being Christians, they would make jokes about That Meeting! He was still to come, to whom all things were possible, and their punishment would be not to recognise Him, not to follow Him, to deprive themselves of the bliss reserved for the Chosen Ones!

Sometimes when he stood alone in front of his cottage, la *Samaruca* would suddenly confront him, arising out of the darkness like a witch. Where was Tonet? At this the vagabond would only smile mischievously, divining the fat lady's ill intentions. Some little questions for him, eh? Spreading his fingers in a vague gesture that seemed to suggest that he was trying to encompass the whole of the Albufera he would reply:

- Tonet…?..is…everywhere!

La *Samaruca* was relentless in her enquiries. She was there at the *Paloma's* cottage before daybreak, so that when la *Borda* opened the door she would strike up a conversation with her, at the same time darting enquiring glances into the house to see if Tonet was inside.

Neleta's implacable enemy became convinced that the young man was staying the night in the tavern. What a scandal, seeing it was only a few months since *Cañamel* had died! But what really most irritated her about this brazen love affair was that the old landlord's Last Will and Testament was not being complied with, and half his worldly goods still remained in his widow's hands instead of being passed on to his first wife's relatives. La *Samaruca* made trips to Valencia and got to know people who had the Law at their fingertips and then entered a period of furious activity, lying in wait for nights on end around the tavern together with relatives to act as witnesses. She was waiting for Tonet to emerge from the place before dawn in order to provide proof of his relationship with the widow. But the tavern doors were never opened all night long; the place remained dark and silent, as if everyone within slept the sleep of the saints. When the tavern was opened up in the morning, Neleta would be there behind the bar, calm, smiling, coolly looking everyone in the eye, like a woman with nothing to reproach herself for. Some time later, Tonet would appear as if by magic, without the regulars being able to tell for sure whether he had come in from the street or from the canal side.

It was difficult to catch the pair *in flagrante*! Faced

with Neleta's guile, la *Samaruca* was beginning to lose hope. To avoid leaks, Neleta had got rid of the tavern's maid and replaced her with her aunt, that witless old woman who, out of respect not untinged with fear for her niece's violent nature and the wealth of her widowhood, resignedly accepted everything that happened.

Don Miguel, the priest, aware of La *Samaruca's* shadowy machinations, got hold of Tonet more than once to lecture him about the need to avoid a scandal. They ought to get married; the testamentary issues could come out any day when they least expected it and would be the talk of the whole Albufera. Even though Neleta would lose one part of her inheritance, would it not be better to live as God ordained without all this subterfuge and lying? The *Cubano* shrugged his shoulders. He wanted marriage, but it was for her to resolve the issue. Neleta was the only woman in El Palmar who, while, as ever, all sweetness, would stand her ground with the plain-speaking vicar. She was predictably annoyed, therefore, to hear herself reprimanded by him. It was all lying! She had no need for anyone else. She did not need men. One male servant was needed in the tavern, and she had Tonet, the companion of her childhood. Was she not able to choose, in an establishment like hers, full of "interested parties", the man who best deserved her trust? She knew fine that all this was just vile insinuations by *la Samaruca* to get her to hands on her "dearly departed's" rice fields, half of the fortune, to the creation of which she had contributed as a devoted and hard-working wife. But what a cheek that witch had, waiting around for the inheritance! The Albufera would dry out first!

Neleta's innate greediness as a poor country girl simmered under the surface as a spirit capable of the very pinnacle of fury. The buried instincts of so many generations of impoverished fishermen, gnawed by misery, were being awakened, men who had only been able to gaze in envy at the wealth of people who possessed land and who sold wine to the poor, slowly piling up the money. She recalled her famished childhood, her days abandoned, alone, when she would huddle in the *Paloma's* door, hoping Tonet's mother would take pity on her, the effort she had had to make to secure her husband, and then to put up with him during his illness; and now that she found herself the richest woman in El Palmar, would she, for the sake of a few scruples, have to share her fortune with people who had always sought to do her harm? She felt herself capable of doing anything, even breaking the law, before she let her enemies have a penny. She turned bright red with anger at the thought that even a fraction of the rice fields she had looked after so passionately might possibly become la *Samaruca's* and clenched her fists in the same furious rage as had made her hurl herself on her opponent in Ruzafa.

The possession of wealth was changing her. She loved Tonet dearly, but in choosing between him and her worldly goods would not hesitate to sacrifice her lover. If she abandoned Tonet, he would come back more or less straight away, for his life was for ever linked to hers; but if she let go of the tiniest part of her inheritance, she would never see it again.

This was why the proposals he timidly put to her during nights in the silence of the tavern's upper room so annoyed her.

The life of constant running away and forever hiding was weighing heavily on the *Cubano*. He wanted to be the legal owner of the tavern, to reveal his new situation to the whole village, to get even with people who had shown him little respect. And besides (and this was something he carefully concealed) once he was Neleta's husband, her overbearing attitude to him, the despotic behaviour of a rich lady who abused her position and could show her lover the door, would all be less of a problem. Given she loved him, why weren't they getting married?

But when Tonet would say this to her in the

darkness of the bedroom, the bed's straw paillasse would rustle with Neleta's impatient tossing and turning. Her voice would become hoarse with fury. Him too? No, my boy, she knew what she needed to do, and she wasn't asking for any advice. They were all right as they were. Was he short of anything? Wasn't he able to make use of it all as if he owned it? What was the point of giving don Miguel the pleasure of marrying them so that after the ceremony they could leave half her fortune in la *Samaruca's* filthy hands? She would let her arm be carved off before she would carve up her inheritance! Besides, she knew what the world was like; she used to get away from the lake and would take a trip to the city, where gentlemen admired her sauciness, and it was no secret to her that what seemed like a fortune in El Palmar, beyond the Albufera represented merely genteel poverty. She had the aspirations of an ambitious woman. She wouldn't be filling glasses and dealing with drunks forever; she wanted to end her days in an apartment in Valencia like a lady, living off her rents. She would lend out money better than *Cañamel* had; she would organise it so that her fortune would produce endlessly generous returns, and when she was truly rich, she might perhaps then decide to give in to la *Samaruca* by handing over to her what by then she would regard as a mere trifle. When that time came, and if he carried on behaving well and doing what he was told without any nonsense, then he would be able to talk to her of marriage. But for the present, *No, recordons,* Watch out! Nothing about wedding stuff nor about handing over money to anyone; she'd be split from stem to stern like a kipper first.

So fired up was she as she put it like this, that Tonet dared make no reply. Besides, the lad, who aspired like a bully to lord it over the whole village, felt completely under Neleta's thumb and was even a little afraid of her, realising that he was not now so sure of her affections as he had been at the beginning.

It wasn't that Neleta was tired of their lovemaking. She did love him; but her wealth gave her great superiority over him. Besides, being alone with each other during the interminable winter nights in the closed-up tavern without running any risk at all had dowsed all the dangerous excitement, the quivering sexual thrill, which used to sweep her off her feet when *Cañamel* had been around and they would snatch a kiss behind closed doors, or have a quick encounter in the fields around El Palmar, always at risk of being discovered.

After four months of this quasi-matrimonial bliss, with nothing to stop them but la *Samaruca's* easily fooled spy system, the moment came when Tonet believed that he might just achieve his desire to get married. Neleta was grave and preoccupied. The vertical crease in her brow indicated the turmoil in her mind. She would quarrel with Tonet on the slightest pretext, hurl insults, push him away and bewail ever falling in love with him, cursing the moment of weakness that made her open her arms to him; but next, spurred by the lusts of the flesh, she would take him back, surrendering herself completely, as if the overpowering problems she was struggling with were completely beyond her control.

Her nervy and constantly changing mood had turned their nights of lovemaking into explosive encounters, in which caresses alternated with rejection and recrimination, and it took very little for them both to feel like biting their lips, the very lips that moments before had been made for kissing. Finally, one night, choking with rage, Neleta revealed what she had been hiding about her situation. She had kept quiet up till then, in disbelief at her bad luck; but now after checking for two months in a row,she was sure. She was going to have a baby. While she carried on weeping and wailing, Tonet was floored but at the same time happy. While Cañamel had been alive this could have happened without causing any problem. But the Devil, who was as usual, roaming about, had doubtless thought it best to raise these difficulties at the most inopportune moment, at the very time she was obsessed with keeping their love secret, so as not to give any comfort to her enemies.

Once the initial surprise had passed, Tonet timidly asked her what she planned to do. She guessed her lover's inner thoughts from the tremor in his voice and broke into a cackle of ironic laughter which clearly showed her mettle. Ha! So, he thought that this would make her get married? He didn't know her! He could be sure she would kill herself before giving way to her enemies. What was hers, was hers, very much so, and she would defend it. Tonet wasn't going to get himself married because of this, for there's an answer to everything in this world!

This explosion of rage ripped through the dirty little trick that Nature had allowed itself to play on them, a little surprise, just when they thought themselves more secure. But with its passing, Neleta and Tonet carried on with their life as if nothing had happened, avoiding mention of the problem growing between them, becoming more reconciled to it, calm because its final end was still far off and vaguely trusting in some kind of unexpected event that might save them.

Without saying anything to her lover Neleta was seeking some means of unburdening herself of this new life she felt lurking in her entrails, like a hidden threat to her greedy ambitions. Alarmed by what she had been told in confidence, her aunt told her about some potent remedies. She remembered conversations with old women in El Palmar when they would bewail the rapidity with which impoverished families were growing. As suggested by her niece she went up to Ruzafa, or even as far as the city to consult the quacks who enjoyed some dark infamy in the lower strata of society and came back with strange remedies made from revolting ingredients that turned your stomach.

On many nights Tonet would discover stinking pessaries hidden within Neleta's body, in which the landlady was placing great faith, and poultices of woodland herbs which suffused their lovemaking with an air of magic.

But over the course of time, all the remedies proved useless. The months were going by and the ever more desperate Neleta was becoming convinced of the futility of her efforts.

As her aunt used to say, that hidden soul was well bedded in, and Neleta was battling in vain to get it out of her innards.

The lovers' night-time discussions were stormy affairs. It seemed as if *Cañamel* was getting his own back, rising like a spectre between them to make them bump off each other.

Neleta wept in desperation, holding Tonet responsible for her misfortune. He was to blame; it was his fault that her whole future was threatened. And when she tired of insulting the *Cubano*, she would tetchily fix her angry gaze on her belly, which, now freed from the constraints to which she daily submitted it to frustrate the curiosity of strangers, seemed to grow nightly into an ever more monstrous swelling. Neleta hated the being hidden within with uncontrollable fury as it moved among her entrails and would beat it savagely with her closed fist as if she wanted to knock it out as it lay in its warm wrapping.

Tonet hated it as well, seeing it as a threat. Having picked up something of Neleta's avarice, the thought of losing part of the inheritance that he now considered his was quite terrifying.

All the remedies that he had heard of in the confused ramblings of other boatmen he passed on to his lover. They included brutal interventions, offenses against Nature which made your hair stand on end, or ridiculous cures that made you smile, but Neleta's blooming health made a joke of them all. That little body, so delicate in appearance, was strong and solid and continued quietly carrying out the most sacred role in Nature, without their evil desires being able to impede or change the course of the holy task of bearing new life.

The months went by. Neleta was having to make the most supreme efforts and suffer the toils of agony in order to conceal her state from the village. In the morning she tightened up her corset in the cruellest manner, making Tonet tremble, sometimes not having the strength herself to contain her overflowing motherhood.

- Pull, pull. She would say having offered her lover the strings of her corset with a stern expression, gritting her teeth to hold back her painful gasps.

Tonet would haul on the strings, a cold sweat breaking out on his brow, shaken by little woman's sheer willpower as she groaned in silence and gulped back her tears of distress.

She made up her face and used plenty of cheap perfume in order to turn up in the tavern as calm and beautiful as ever without anyone being able to read in her looks any of the signs of her state of health. La *Samaruca*, still sniffing around the place like a gundog, sensed something was afoot as she darted quick glances through the door in passing. The other women, with all the experience of their sex, also wondered what was going on in the tavern.

An atmosphere of watchfulness and suspicion seemed to be gathering around Neleta. There was a lot of muttering in cottage doors. La *Samaruca* and her relatives argued with women who didn't like what they were saying. Gossips who would usually send their kids to the tavern for wine or olive oil went along themselves to plant themselves at the bar, looking for some pretext to make the landlady get up off her chair and serve them, while they followed her every move voraciously, taking in the details of her tightly bound shape.

- Oh yes, she is! Some would declare triumphantly in conference with their neighbours.
- Oh, no she's not! shouted back others. It's all lies.

And Neleta, who could guess the cause of all these comings and goings, welcomed the curious with a joking smile. Aha! What could be biting them that they couldn't pass without looking in? It seemed someone in the place had won the lottery!

But her insolent good humour, the bold front she put on to pique the womenfolk's curiosity, evaporated at night, at the end of another day of suffocating confinement and forced cheerfulness. As the whalebone corset dropped off her, so her brave face also fell, like a soldier who has done more than his duty in some heroic endeavour and now can do no more. She was overcome with despair as her swollen figure burst free and she realised she would have to suffer the same torture all over again the following day in order to keep her condition hidden.

She couldn't do it anymore. So strong in many ways, she finally had to admit it to Tonet in the depths of a night that was no longer one of lovemaking but rather of anxiety and shared distress. Curse her strong constitution! How she envied those frail, weak, sickly women whose bellies never seemed able to carry a new life!

In these moments of depression, she would talk of running away, of leaving the tavern in her aunt's hands to hide away in some lonely corner of the city until she could get out of the hole she was in. But a moment's thought made her realise the futility of flight. The spectre of la *Samaruca* rose before her. Running away would simply confirm what had, up till then, been mere suspicions. Where could she possibly go without *Cañamel's* terrible sister-in-law following her?

It was, besides, the end of summer. They were about to begin harvesting her rice fields and everyone's curiosity would be aroused by the absence of a woman who looked after her interests with such jealous care, unless there was a very good explanation.

She would stay where she was. She would confront the danger face to face; by staying put, they would be less vigilant. She was terrified when she thought about the actual birth, a pain-filled mystery, seeming to her even more beyond comprehension, wrapped as it was in the shadows of the unknown, and attempted to take her mind off her fear by immersing herself in the operational details of the harvest, such as haggling with the labourers about their rates. She quarrelled with Tonet, who would go off on his own account to keep an eye on the day labourers, but always taking with him in the punt his shotgun and the faithful *Centella*, so that he spent more time shooting than counting bushels of rice.

Some afternoons she would leave the tavern in the care of her aunt and set off for the threshing floor, a patch of hard beaten mud in the midst of the watery fields. Such outings were a balm for her painful condition.

Hidden among the baskets she would cast aside her corset with a distressed look and sit down next to Tonet on the huge pile of sharp smelling rice straw. Below her the horses plodded round and round in the monotonous task of threshing, and beyond them stretched the immense green surface of the Albufera reflecting the blue and red mountains that ringed the horizon.

These tranquil afternoons calmed the two lovers' fears and worries. They felt happier than in the closed-up bedchamber whose darkness was populated with unseen terrors. The lake was smiling sweetly as it delivered the annual harvest from its entrails; the singing of the threshers and the crews on the great boats loaded with rice seemed to be lulling the motherly Albufera to sleep after her effort, which secured the lives of her sons and daughters living on her shores.

The serenity of the afternoon also soothed Neleta's irritation and infused her with new confidence. She counted off the passing months on her fingers and checked the expected end of gestation which tallied with what was going on inside her. There was very little time now before the grievous event which could change the course of her life. It would happen the following month, November, perhaps during the great annual shoots on the Albufera to celebrate St Martin and St Katherine's days. As she reckoned it up, she realised that it was not yet a year since Cañamel had died, and without seeming to realise how wrong her instinct was to have things turn out always to her own benefit, bewailed the fact that she had not surrendered to Tonet months earlier. Had she done so she would have been able to show herself in public without worries, simply attributing the paternity of the new being to her husband.

The possibility that Death might intervene in her affairs renewed her spirits. Who could know whether, after all these frights, her baby might be stillborn? It wouldn't be the first! Taken in by this rather faint hope the lovers began to talk about the baby being dead as a sure thing, inevitable, and Neleta monitored foetal movement closely, appearing quite happy when the hidden being showed no signs of life. It would be dead! There was no doubt about it. The good luck which she had always enjoyed was not going to desert her now!

The end of the harvest took her mind off these preoccupations. The sacks of rice were piling up in the tavern. The harvest filled all the building's inner rooms, piled up next to the bar, displaced regulars from their usual seats and even took up space in the corners of Neleta's bedroom. She looked approvingly at the wealth enclosed withing the bulging sacks, intoxicated by the pungent rice dust. To think that half that treasure might have been la *Samaruca's*! It was only when she remembered this that Neleta felt her strength return, powered by her anger. She was suffering plenty as a result of keeping her pregnancy a secret, but she would die before allowing any of this to be taken away.

She really needed all the strength she could get. Her situation was worsening. Her feet were swelling, she felt an overwhelming urge not to move, just to stay in bed, but despite this she was down at the bar every day, for any suggestion that she was ill would revive suspicion. She moved slowly when customers obliged her to get up, and her forced smile through painfully clenched teeth made Tonet shudder. Her tightly constricted frame seemed ready to erupt out its strong whalebone binding.

- I can't do it anymore! She moaned in desperation throwing herself on all fours on the bed.

In the silence of their bedchamber the words the two lovers exchanged were mingled with terror, as if they could see rising between them the threatening ghost of their sin. What if the child was not stillborn? Neleta was sure of it. She could feel it rumbling around her insides with a vigour that put paid to all her criminal plans.

Unable to own up to her wrongdoing and jeopardise her fortune, her womanly wiles suffused her with all the bold resolution of a major criminal.

There was no point in taking the newborn to

some village around the Albufera in search of some trustworthy woman to bring it up. They would be forever in fear of the foster mother's indiscretion, their enemies' wiliness and even a mistake on their part as they began to develop feelings for the little one which would lead to them being discovered. Looking around the sacks of rice piled around her bedroom, Neleta reasoned it all out with terrifying coldness. Nor was there any point in thinking about some hide-out in Valencia. Once on the trail, la *Samaruca* would seek them out in Hell itself.

As her gaze seemed to wander in pain and anguish at the dangers of the situation, Neleta fixed her green eyes on her lover. Come what may, they had to abandon the newborn. They had to make up their minds and do it. Real men stepped up to the plate in dangerous times. They would take it to the city during the night and leave it in the street, in a church porch, anywhere. Valencia was a big place ...and who could tell who the parents were!

Having suggested a crime, this tough little lady now proceeded to find excuses for her evil doing. Being abandoned might turn out to be a stroke of luck for the little one. If it died, so much the better, and if it was saved, who knew whose hands it might fall into! Riches perhaps awaited it; stranger stories had been known. She fell to recalling childhood fables about kings' sons or shepherdesses' bastards abandoned in the forest who, instead of being eaten by wolves, grew up to be powerful men.

Tonet listened in terror. He tried to put up some resistance, but, weak willed as ever, Neleta's glance stilled him with one fearful look. Besides, he too was feeling the gnawing of greed. Everything that Neleta owned he considered his, and he was angered by the idea of sharing his lover's inheritance with her rivals. He closed his eyes in indecision, trusting in the future. It wasn't something to completely lose hope over, it could still be sorted out. Good luck would perhaps resolve the conflict at the last minute.

He relaxed in a brief moment of calm, letting his mind empty for a minute of Neleta's criminal suggestions.

He was bound to her for ever; she was all he had, and the tavern was the only home he now knew. He had broken with his father with whom, aware of the rumours in the village about his affair with the landlady, and seeing that weeks and months were passing without him spending a single night in the family cottage, he had had a brief and painful meeting. What Tonet was doing was bringing dishonour down on the *Paloma* family and he could not abide to have as his son a man who was living openly off a woman who was not his wife. Since he chose this life of dishonour, to live apart from his family and to help them in nothing...why should they have anything to do with him? He would now have no father and would only be allowed to meet him again when he had recovered his honour. After this Tono continued covering his fields with earth with the loyal aid of La *Borda*. Now the great project was reaching its conclusion he felt depressed, asking himself who would ever thank him for all the effort, and only carried on with the undertaking through sheer grit as a working man.

The time for the great shoots was approaching, St Martin' day and St Katherine's day, El Saler's fiestas.

Wherever boatmen met, all the talk was of the great number of birds on the lake that year. The gamekeepers, who kept an eye from afar on the areas and patches of brush where the flocks gathered, noticed how they had grown rapidly. They formed great black stains on the surface. When a boat passed close by, they took to the air in arrow formation to settle back down a short distance away like a cloud of locusts, hypnotised by the sheen on the lake and unable to flee the waters in which death awaited them.

The news had spread throughout the province.

and guns would be more numerous than in other years.

The great shoots on the Albufera threw every keen gun in Valencia into a turmoil. They were very old gatherings, whose origin was known to old *Paloma* from the days when he had kept the records as a *Jurado*, as he told his friends in the tavern. When the Albufera belonged to the Kings of Aragon, and only kings were allowed to hunt there, King Martin wished to bestow a fiesta on the citizens of Valencia and chose his Saint's Day. Later the shoot was repeated in the same way on St Katherine's day. Everyone had an equal right to take part in these two shoots, using crossbows and taking innumerable birds from the reed beds, and the privilege, which became a tradition, carried on every year across the centuries. Nowadays the two days of free shooting were preceded by two days when the Albufera's leaseholders accepted payment for the choice of the best spots, which attracted shots from every town in the province.

Both boats and boatmen to carry the shots were becoming scarce. Old *Paloma*, who was well known over many years to the aficionados, was at a loss how to satisfy all the demand. He himself had a longstanding contract with a rich gentleman who paid magnificently for his experience of all matters to do with the Albufera.

This, however, did not stop shots pestering the patriarch of the boatmen, and old *Paloma* was searching high and low for punts and men for all those who were writing to him from Valencia.

The evening before the shoot, Tonet saw his grandfather come into the tavern. There were going to be more guns than birds that year on the Albufera, and he still did not know where he was going to get boatmen. All of them from El Saler, from Catarroja and even from El Palmar were signed up; and now an old customer, to whom nobody could say no, was asking him to arrange a punt and a man for a friend of his, who was shooting for the first time on the Albufera. Would Tonet like to be that man and get his grandfather out a difficult situation?

The *Cubano* declined. Neleta was bad. During the morning she had abandoned the bar, unable to bear the pains. The much-feared moment would be upon them very soon, and he needed to be there in the tavern.

But his curt refusal was interpreted as disrespect by the old man who became very angry. Just because he was a rich man now, he was allowing himself to disrespect his poor grandfather, leaving him to look ridiculous. He had put up with everything so far; he had had to suffer his laziness when they were working the *redolin*, he had averted his gaze from his conduct with the landlady which brought little honour to the family, but to leave him in a difficulty which he considered a matter of honour? Christ! What would his city friends say of him when they found that on the Albufera, where they thought he was the Boss, he couldn't find a man to look after them. His disappointment was so obvious, so visible that Tonet had a change of heart. To deny his help on the great shoots was, for old *Paloma,* an insult to his prestige, and, at the same time, something of a betrayal of that land of reeds and mud where he had been born.

Resignedly, the *Cubano* assented to his grandfather's request. He thought, too, that Neleta would be able to wait. False contractions had been alarming her for some time, and today's crisis would be just the same as the others.

Tonet arrived in El Saler as night was falling. As a boatman, he ought to be at the *Demaná* with his shot to witness the distribution of pegs.

The hamlet of El Saler, now far from the lake, at the end of a canal, at the Valencia end, presented an extraordinary appearance on the occasion of the great shoot.

In the part of the canal which they called the port, the black punts bumped in dozens, leaving not an inch free, making their thin gunwales creak and scrape against each other, trembling under the weight of the huge wooden buckets which had to be set up next day on stakes driven into the bottom mud. The guns would use these buckets as hides when shooting.

Various good looking, city girls had set up tables between the houses in El Saler, selling toasted chickpeas and musty nougat by the light of candles protected by paper shades. In the house doorways, village women were boiling up their coffee makers, offering cups with "a touch" of liquor in which there was more rum than coffee. An extraordinary mix of people thronged the village, increasing by the minute with the arrival of carriages and coaches from the city. They were the bourgeoisie of Valencia, clad in high gaiters and wide brimmed hats like Boer commandos in the Transvaal, proudly swaggering about in their multi-pocketed shirts, whistling to their dogs and proudly showing off the modern shotgun in its yellow sleeve hanging from their shoulder; there were also well-off tradesmen from towns up country, with flowing cloaks and cartridge belts over their waistbands, some with a large hanky folded like a mitre and others wearing it like a turban, or yet again letting it hang in a long tail down the back of their necks, each displaying by their head covering which corner of the province of Valencia they came from.

The shotgun seemed to be a great leveller. Shots treated each other as companions in arms, all worked-up at the thought of the following day's fiesta, chatting away about English powder, Belgian guns, the superiority of centre-fire weapons, quivering, luxuriating in the wild ambience of the bazaar, as if they could already sense the heady whiff of gun smoke in their words. Their enormous, silent dogs cast around instinctively, always alert, going from group to group sniffing hands until dropping motionless at their master's side. In all the cottages, now turned into hostelries, women were cooking dinner, bustling about with all the energy demanded by these days of celebration which sustained them through the greater part of the year.

Tonet spotted the building called *La Casa de los Infantes*, a stone-built ground floor with a high, tiled roof, dotted with several skylights, a great eighteenth century townhouse, now slowly crumbling, since wildfowlers of the Blood Royal were no longer coming to the Albufera, and currently occupied by a tavern. Opposite, stood the *Casa de la Demaná* a two-storey building which looked huge among the humble cottages, exhibiting several curved iron grills on its peeling walls and a bell on the roof used to call the wildfowlers to the distribution of pegs.

Tonet entered, casting a glance around the ground floor where the ceremony would take place. A huge lantern dispensed a muddy light upon a table and chairs for the Albufera lease holders, their dais being separated from the rest of the room by an iron railing.

Old *Paloma* was there in his position as Most Venerable Boatman, exchanging pleasantries with well-known shots, wildfowling fanatics he had known around the lake for half a century. These were the Aristocracy of the Shotgun. There were rich men and poor men among them; some were big property owners, and others city butchers or modest tradesmen from nearby towns. They neither saw nor wanted to see each other for the rest of the year, but on meeting on the Albufera every Saturday on small shoots, or when they got together on the big ones, they would greet each other like brothers, offering tobacco, lending cartridges, and listening, wide eyed, to the tales of fantastic shoots that took place up in the hills during the winter. Their shared enthusiasms, and a liking for a tall tale welded them into a band of brothers. Almost all of them bore tell-tale signs of the risks associated with this passion which had taken over their lives. Some, feverishly illustrating a tale with gestures, exhibited hands missing fingers after a gun had exploded; others had cheeks furrowed by the scar of a flash burn. The oldest veterans, hobbling around stiffly, dragging arthritic limbs after spending a dissolute youth, could not stay quietly at home for the big shoots and, despite all their aches and pains, would come along to bewail the lack of style among these new shots.

The meeting broke up as boatmen were arriving to announce that dinner was ready, and they left in groups to distribute themselves around the brightly lit cottages marked by the red stains cast before their doorways on the muddy ground. A strong smell of alcohol perfused the environment.

The wildfowlers were apprehensive of the Albufera water and could not drink it, like local people, for fear of catching something, so they brought with them a prodigious load of absinthe and rum, which strongly perfumed the air as they cracked open the bottles.

Seeing El Saler in such a state of excitement, looking as if an army was encamped within, Tonet recalled the stories his grandfather had told him, about orgies organised in former times by rich shots from the city, with women running about naked, pursued by the dogs, about the fortunes that had been lost in those miserable hovels during long nights at gaming tables between the shoots, about the crazy pleasures of a bourgeoisie become *nouveau riches* who, as soon as they were out of sight of their families in this wild corner of the world, and fired up by the sight of blood and the scent of gun smoke, found the human beast reborn.

Old *Paloma* was looking for Tonet to introduce him to his gun. He was a fat gentleman of kindly and peaceable appearance, a city industrialist who, after a life devoted to work, thought the time had come to enjoy himself like rich people did and was now copying the pleasurable tastes of his new friends. He seemed uncomfortable with all his terrifying kit, weighed down by shooting bags, his gun, and high boots, all new and recently purchased. But as his gaze fell on the cartridge belt slung like a bandolier across his chest his face broke into a grin beneath his broad felt hat, as he thought how much he resembled one of those heroic Boers whose pictures he had so much admired in the newspapers. He was shooting on the lake for the first time and was putting all his trust in his boatman to choose his peg when his number was called.

The three of them dined in a cottage with other guns. The after-dinner chat was a noisy affair on evenings like that. The rum was measured out by the glass, and village folk were clustered round the tables like hungry dogs, laughing at the gentlemen's jokes, accepting everything they were offered, each one just drinking what the guns thought was good for them.

Tonet scarcely ate a thing, hearing the shouting and laughter of the crowd as if he were dreaming the raucous protests which greeted the outrageous claims of the guns about their shooting. He could not get Neleta out of his mind, picturing her, curled up in pain in the tavern's upper room, rolling around the floor, stifling her groans, unable to relieve her suffering by crying out.

Outside the cottage, the bell on the Casa de la Demaná rang out in the wavering chime of a hermitage.

- That's two, said old Paloma, who was paying close attention to the number of strokes, more fearful of being late than missing Mass.

When the bell chimed for the third time the guns and their boatmen left the table and headed for the place where the pegs were given out.

The light from the great overhead lamp had been increased by two oil lamps placed on the table on the dais. Behind the railing were the Albufera's lease holders and behind them, all the way to the back wall, guns with lifetime shooting rights on the lake, who were all there in their own right. On the other side of the rail, filling the door and spilling out of the building were the boatmen and the less well-off guns, the little people who came along to the shoots. A stench of damp cloaks, mud-stained trousers, cheap liquor, and tobacco rose in waves from the men crammed against the rail. The guns' waterproof jackets squeaked against each other with a sound that set your teeth on edge. The white facades of the cottages opposite could just be made out as vague splodges in the great dark gap of the open door.

In spite of the size of the crowd, nothing broke the silence that seemed to seize each one as he stepped over the portal. You could feel the same speechless anxiety that reigns in courts when a man's fate hangs in the balance, or in a draw when fortunes are decided. If anyone spoke it was in a low voice, a timid whisper like at a sick bed.

The Senior Leaseholder rose to his feet:

- Gentlemen…

The silence became even more profound. He was going to proceed with the allocation of pegs.

At both ends of the table, erect as heralds of the Lake Authority, stood the two most senior Keepers of the Albufera, two slim, brown gentlemen, sinuous in their movements and prominent in the jaw, two jacketed eels, who seemed to have spent their lives at the bottom of the lake, appearing only for the purpose of presenting themselves at such great shooting occasions.

One Keeper was going down a list to check if all the pegs would be taken up on the following day's shoot.

- Number One...Number Two...

He went down them in order, according to the amount that was paid annually and their seniority. As the boatmen heard their master's number, they answered for them

- Present, present...

After checking the list came the solemn moment, *la Demaná*, the request that each boatman, by agreement with his gun or in his own expert opinion, was making for a peg in the shoot.

- Number three! Said one of the Keepers.

And immediately the man who held the said number shouted out the name of his chosen spot, carried on the tip of his tongue. "Lord's grove", "Rotting boat", "Antina's corner". The silly names of the Albufera's nooks and crannies sounded round the room, places called things as boatmen saw fit, many of them names that could not be repeated without making ladies blush, or which turned the stomach if brought up at the table, despite which they all rang out in this solemn company without raising the slightest grin.

When the second Keeper, who had a voice like a bugle, heard the choice made by each boatman he would raise his head and, with his eyes closed and his hands gripping the rail, emit an ear-splitting cry that ripped through the silence of the night:

> - Number three goes to Lord's grove.... Number four goes to San Roc corner... Number five to the barber's...

The allocation of pegs lasted almost an hour and while the Keepers slowly sang them out, a lad inscribed them in a book on the table.

With the allocation of pegs finished, they proceeded to the issuing of "perambulatory" Shooting Permits to the little people, permits which only cost a couple of *duros,* and with which the workmen in their little punts could go wherever they wanted on the Albufera, within a certain distance of the pegs, picking off birds that escaped the guns of the wealthy.

The better-off guns were shaking hands and saying goodnight. Some were planning to sleep in El Saler and make their way to their peg at daybreak, others, perhaps keener, were heading out straight away on to the lake to keep a personal eye on the installation of the enormous tank within which they had to spend the day. “Let’s go! Good luck and enjoy yourself!”, they shouted, calling to their personal boatman to make sure the preparations were all going to plan.

Tonet was no longer in El Saler. In the silence of the *Demaná* ceremony, he had been seized with anguish. He could not get the tortured image of Neleta out of his mind, writhing in torment on the floor, alone over there in El Palmar with no one to comfort her under the threatening and watchful gaze of her enemies.

He couldn’t stand the pain and left the *Casa de la Demaná* with the intention of heading back straight away to El Palmar, even though that would mean falling out with his grandfather. Near the tavern, the *Casa de los Infantes*, he heard someone calling him. It was *Sangonera*, hungry and thirsty after having done the rounds of the wealthy guns’ tables without gleaning anything but the most insignificant scraps. The boatmen had eaten everything.

Tonet suddenly thought he might get the rogue to substitute for him, but the son of the lake shrank from the suggestion that he might crew a boat, even more than if the priest had invited him to give the Sunday sermon. He didn’t do that sort of thing; and besides he didn’t like poling for anyone. Tonet well knew what he thought; work was the Devil's business.

But Tonet, in turmoil and impatient to be off, was in no mood to listen to *Sangonera's* nonsense. No objections or he would relieve his hunger and thirst by kicking him straight into the canal. Helping each other out of a mess was what friends were for. He was quite capable of managing somebody else's punt when it came to getting his hands on the nets in the *redolins* and stealing the eels! In addition, if he was hungry, he would have the time of his life with the load of provisions that gentleman had brought from Valencia. Seeing *Sangonera* hesitate at the thought of stuffing himself, a few good punches settled the matter and sent him staggering towards the wildfowler's boat to have the necessary preparations explained to him. When his master turned up, he could say that Tonet was sick and had chosen him as a substitute.

Before the somewhat confused *Sangonera* had stopped babbling, Tonet had jumped into his little punt and set off poling like a madman.

It was long trip. He had to cross the whole length of the Albufera to reach El Palmar and there was no wind, but Tonet was driven by fear and uncertainty, and the punt flew like a shuttle through the dark tissue of the water dotted with starry points of light.

It was after midnight when he reached El Palmar. He was exhausted, his arms aching with the desperate effort, and all he wanted was to find the tavern quiet and to fall like a log into his bed. Tying up his boat in front to the house he saw it was closed and silent like all the others in the village, but the cracks in the door showed as streaks of reddish light.

Neleta's aunt opened it, gesturing out of the corner of her eye, as she recognised him, to alert him to some men seated at the hearth. They were farmers from around Sueca who had come up for the shoot, long standing customers with fields near El Saler who could not easily be got rid of without arousing suspicion. They had dined in the tavern and were dropping off to sleep around the fire in order to be in their punts an hour before daybreak and scatter across the lake waiting for birds that escaped untouched from the good pegs.

Tonet bade them all good evening, and after exchanging a few words on the following day's fiesta, went up to Neleta's bedroom.

She was in her nightgown, pale, her features contorted, both hands pressed against her sides with an expression of madness in her eyes. The pain was making her throw caution to the wind and she was emitting roars that terrified her aunt.

- They're going to hear you, exclaimed the old woman.

Making a supreme effort to control the suffering, Neleta stuffed her fists in her mouth or chewed on the bedclothes to stifle her groans.

At her urging, Tonet went back down to the tavern. He wasn't going to do any good staying up there, but being with those men, distracting them in conversation might prevent them hearing something that aroused their suspicions.

Tonet passed more than an hour, warming himself in a corner of the fireplace, chatting with the famers about the recent harvest and the magnificent shooting that was in preparation. There was one moment when conversation was cut short. Everyone heard a wild inhuman cry rip through the air, a scream like some woman being murdered. But Tonet's calm reaction settled them:

- The mistress is a little unwell, he said.

So, they carried on talking, paying no attention to the old woman's steps hurrying about above them and making the ceiling shake. After half an hour or so, when Tonet felt they had all forgotten about the incident, he went back up to the bedroom. Some of the farmers already had their heads down, overcome by sleep.

Upstairs, he found Neleta stretched out on the bed, white, pallid and still, showing no sign of life apart from the shine in her eyes.

- Tonet, Tonet, she said weakly.

Her lover could tell from her voice and look everything that she wanted to say to him. It was an order, an unbreakable mandate. Despite her weakened state, the fierce resolution which had frightened Tonet on so many occasions, was back after the crisis which had just consumed her. Neleta spoke slowly, in a feeble voice like a distant whisper. She had come through the most difficult part. It was now up to him. Let's see if he had the courage.

Her aunt, trembling and hiding her head, not thinking about what she was doing, handed Tonet a bundle of cloths within which wriggled a tiny creature, dirty, foul smelling, and purplish in colour.

Seeing the newborn near her, Neleta put on an expression of terror. She did not want to see it, she was afraid of looking at it, afraid of her own feelings, terrified that if she and the baby exchanged glances, even for an instant, her motherly instincts would be reborn, and she would lose the resolve to let him be taken from her.

Tonet, take it away, now...!

Tonet gave a few hurried instructions to the old woman and went back down to take his leave of the farmers, finding them all asleep. Once he was outside the tavern on the canal side, the old woman handed the wriggling bundle over to him through a lower floor window.

When the window was closed and Tonet was left alone in the blackness of the night, he felt his courage suddenly evaporate. The bundle of rags and soft flesh that he was carrying under his arm filled him with dread. It seemed that in that instant a strange nervous excitement had put him on the alert and sharpened all his senses. He could hear every sound in the village, down to the most insignificant, and it seemed to him that the stars had turned blood red. The wind shook the dwarf olive tree next to the tavern, and the rustling of the leaves set Tonet off at a run as if the whole village was waking up and setting off after him to ask what he was carrying under his arm. He felt sure that la *Samaruca* and her relatives, alerted by Neleta's daytime absence, were patrolling around the place as usual, and that the fierce witch was going to suddenly appear on the canal bank. What a scandal if they were to surprise him with that bundle! What a desperate state Neleta would be in then!

He threw the cloth-wrapped bundle into the bottom of the punt, setting of a wail that mixed desperation and rage, and, seizing the pole, cleared the canal at a mad pace. Spurred on by the new-born's cries he poled furiously, terrified that lights would start going on at windows and curious voices start to ask where he was going.

He quickly left the dwellings of El Palmar behind and was out onto the Albufera. The quiet of the lake, the glow of the calm and starry night, seemed to renew his spirits. Above was the dark blue of the heavens and below the silvery blue of the water, stirred deep down by mysterious movements that made the stars' reflections glitter against the background. Birds twittered in the reed beds and the surface surged with the whispered splash of fish being chased. From time to time the furious cry of a new-born child emerged from this background.

Exhausted by a night continuously on the move, Tonet carried on poling, driving has little craft towards El Saler. His strength was spent, and his senses dulled by fatigue, but his mind, sharpened and alert to danger, was a whirl of activity.

He was already a good way from El Palmar, but it would take more than hour yet to reach El Saler. From there to the city would mean another two long hours of walking. Tonet looked at the sky; it must be three o'clock. Within two hours it would be daybreak, and the sun would already be on the horizon when he got to Valencia. He also thought with a sudden start about the long walk through the market gardens at Ruzafa, always under the watchful eye of the Guardia Civil, about the Consumer Protection checks at the city gates where they would want to examine the package under his arm, about the people who were usually up before dawn and would meet him on the way and recognise him. And all with that desperate wailing going on, becoming stronger by the minute, and posing a threat to him even here, alone in the middle of the Albufera.

Stretching before him Tonet could see only an endless, infinite road and felt his strength failing. He would never make it before dawn to the deserted city streets, to those church portals where children were left like an embarrassing bundle of rags. It was all too easy back in El Palmar, in the silent solitude of that bedroom to say: "Tonet, do this!" but you then had to confront a reality filled with impassable barriers.

Even out there on the lake, danger was growing by the minute. At other times he could have made his way from one shore to the other without meeting anybody: but on that particular night, the Albufera was full of people. In every reed bed and thicket, the work of invisible men could be seen, getting things ready for the shoot.

An entire population was on the move in the darkness, coming and going in their little boats. The sound of mallets driving in the stakes for the guns' pegs sounded across the silence of the Albufera, which reflected noise over tremendous distances, and handfuls of burning dry vegetation glittered like red stars on the surface, by whose light, boatmen were completing their preparations. How was he going to make it through these people who knew him, to the accompaniment of this neonatal cry, an incomprehensible sound in the middle of the lake? He crossed paths with a boat some way away, but still within hailing distance. There could be no doubt about it, they had been taken aback by that sound:

- *Compañero*, shouted a faraway voice, what've you got there?

Tonet made no reply but his determination to continue with the voyage deserted him and, throwing down the pole, he sat down at the end of the punt. He just wanted to stay where he was, even though the dawn would reveal all. He was too frightened to do anything else and gave up, like a straggler who throws himself to the ground, completely spent, knowing his hour has come. He realised he was totally powerless to carry out his promise. Let them find him, let everyone find out what had happened, let Neleta lose her inheritance...he could do no more!

But scarcely had he reached this desperate conclusion than his mind began to churn with an idea that seemed so hot it burned at the touch. At first it was a tiny flicker, then a glowing ember, and then it flared into a blaze until finally breaking into a great conflagration that filled his whole head, threatening to burst it wide open like an explosion, while a cold sweat broke on his brow, like the icy breath of this swarm of evil thoughts.

What was the point of going any further? What Neleta wanted was for the evidence of her problem to disappear, so as not to lose any part of her fortune, to just get rid of it, since having it around was going to compromise the happiness of both of them, and for that purpose there was nowhere like the Albufera, which had often taken to oblivion men pursued by the law, thus sparing them more searching examination.

He shuddered to think that the lake would leave no trace of that frail, newly born being, but would the little one be any more likely to survive if he were to abandon him in some city byway? "The dead to not return to accuse the living". As Tonet thought along these lines he felt, growing within him, the hardness of heart of the older *Palomas*, the cruel coldness of his grandfather, who could see his children die without shedding a tear, in the selfish belief that death is a blessing in a poor family, for it means more bread for those that survive.

In a moment of clarity, Tonet felt truly ashamed of his evil intentions, of the indifference with which he had come to view the death of the tiny being lying, now silent, at his feet, wearied by his furious crying. He had looked at him for a moment, but the sight had induced no emotional response. He recalled the purplish face, the pointed head, the staring eyes the oversize mouth, opening and closing, stretching seemingly from ear to ear, a ridiculous head, an ugly head, which left him cold, without the least trace of feeling. This, however, was his son...!

In explanation of this coldness, Tonet recalled what he had so often heard from his grandfather. Only mothers felt an immense, instinctive tenderness towards their children from the moment they were born. Fathers feel no immediate love for them, time has to pass, and it is only as the child grows that they feel themselves bonded, as a result of continuous contact, in a relationship of deep love and affection.

He was thinking about Neleta's wealth, on keeping that inheritance intact which he considered his own. He was hardening his heart, this lazy man, who suddenly found all the problems of his existence resolved, and his selfish self was asking whether it was sensible to risk his good fortune to keep alive this tiny, ugly little being which was no different from any other new-born child, and which aroused in him not the slightest feeling.

Nothing bad would happen to his parents if he were to disappear, but if he lived, they would have to hand over to people they hated half the bread they were putting in their mouths. Tonet, cursed his lack of resolve, unable to see, like most criminals, that he was mixing up cruelty and courage, and stayed stuck on the little boat's stern as time ticked by.

It was becoming less dark, and it was obvious that dawn was approaching. Skeins of birds slid across the grey dawn sky like glinting coloured drops. The first gunshots rang out, far off towards El Saler. The tiny child began crying again, nearly dead with hunger and the cold of the early morning.

- *Cubano*, is that you? Tonet thought he heard called from a boat in the distance.

Fear of being recognised brought him to his feet with the pole in his hand. A glint of fire lit his eyes, like the fire that sometimes would light Neleta's green gaze.

The punt shot deep into the reed beds following the watery leads between the stems. He went haphazardly, from one clump to the next, not really knowing where he would end up, but redoubling his efforts like one pursued. The bow of his punt split and buckled the stems, and tall grasses parted to allow the little craft through, as his frenzied work on the pole sent it slithering across almost-dry patches and over the densely matted, tangled roots of the reeds.

He was in full flight, but from whom he did not know, as if his own criminal thoughts were rowing up behind him in pursuit. Several times he bent down, extending a hand to that bundle of rags from which now emanated screams of rage, only to withdraw it immediately. And when, nearing his wits' end, he got the punt tangled in some roots, like a skipper trying to lighten ship by jettisoning the heavy ballast, he just grabbed the bundle and hurled it with all his might over his head and beyond the surrounding thickets.

With a crash of splintering stems the bundle disappeared among the reeds. The rags fluttered for an instant in the half-light of dawn like a white bird dropping dead in the mysterious depths of the clump.

And now the poor man really did feel the need to get away, as if someone was within touching distance. He poled dementedly through the reeds until he found an open lead, and then followed its twists and turns among the tall stems until, finally, slipping out onto the wide Albufera in the empty punt, and he could take a deep breath, and contemplate the wide blue band of dawn on the horizon.

He then threw himself down into the bilge and slept the deep sleep of complete exhaustion, the sleep of the dead, which follows any emotional crisis and always supervenes immediately after a crime.

CHAPTER 9

The day began with various setbacks for the gun entrusted to Sangonera's skill. In setting up the peg before dawn the prudent burgher had to beg the assistance of some passing boatmen, who had a good laugh, seeing the famous rogue's new calling.

Well accustomed to the task, they quickly drove three stakes deep into the slimy bottom of the lake and set on them the enormous tank that was to serve as a hide for the gun. They then surrounded the peg with stems, to fool any trusting birds that came near, thinking it was a clump of reeds in the middle of the water. To aid the deception, decoys floated around the peg, several dozen ducks and coots carved in cork, bobbing on the gently undulating surface. From a distance it gave the impression of a flock of birds swimming quietly near the reeds.

Happy to have got out of doing any actual work, *Sangonera*, invited his master to take occupation of the peg. He would take himself off a little way in the punt so as not to alarm any game, but when he dropped a few coots, the gun had only to give a shout and he would be there to pick them up off the water.

- There you are! Good luck, don Joaquin!

The vagabond spoke so humbly, and showed himself so willing to be useful, that the kindly gun felt all his irritation over the earlier nonsense evaporate. He was fine: he would call him as soon as he had dropped a bird. So as not to get bored while he was waiting, he could have the occasional dip into the various dishes among the provisions. His lady wife had supplied him with enough for a trip round the world.

He indicated three enormous, carefully stoppered pots, an elephant's sufficiency of bread, a basket of fruit and a huge leather flask of wine. *Sangonera's* jaw trembled with emotion at finding entrusted to his care that treasure trove, which had been sitting there, tempting him in the bow, since the previous evening.

Tonet hadn't been kidding when he said how well the customer looked after himself. Many thanks, don Joaquin! Since he was kind enough to invite him to have a dunk, he would indeed allow himself a little *sucaeta*, just to pass the time, just a little sip, nothing more.

So, pushing off a little way from the peg, he set himself up within calling distance of his gun and curled up in the bottom of the punt.

The sun had risen, and shots were ringing our all over the Albufera, echoing and re-echoing across the lake. As soon as skeins of birds were spotted against the grey sky, they had to beat their way higher, alarmed by the thundering burst of shots, and it only needed them to drop a little lower, fluttering down in search of the water for an immediate cloud of lead to envelop them.

Finding himself alone on his peg, don Joaquin could not help feeling something a little like fear. There he was, isolated in the middle of the Albufera, inside a heavy bucket, with nothing holding him up but a few stakes, terrified to move, with the thought lurking at the back of his mind that that whole elaborate coffin could come crashing down, entombing him in the mud. Soft little wavelets lapped the wooden edge, level with the man's beard, and the continuous chap-chap sound was giving him shivers. If that lot sank, thought don Joaquin, no matter how quick his boatman got there, he would already be on the bottom, with all the weight of his shotgun, cartridges, and those huge boots (which were pinching him insufferably), now deeply sunk in the rice straw with which the bucket was stuffed. His legs were burning, while his hands were stiff with the dawn cold and the icy touch of his gun. And this was having fun! He was finding very few fun moments in such a costly pleasure.

And the birds! Where were all those birds that his friends were downing by the dozen? There was one moment when, turning quickly on his revolving seat, he raised his gun quivering with excitement. They were already right there, swimming around the peg without a care in the world. While he had been thinking to himself, half asleep in the chill of the dawn, dozens had arrived, escaping the distant shots, and were swimming around him now, confident of having found a safe refuge! He just needed to fire, without taking aim, he was sure to hit something. But just as he was making ready, he suddenly recognised the decoys, the whole flock of cork birds that, for want of experience, had completely slipped his mind, and he lowered his weapon, looking around, fearful of encountering the amused glances of his friends.

He resumed his watch. What the devil were those other guns firing at since shots never ceased disturbing the peace of the lake? Shortly after sunrise, don Joaquin could at last fire his virgin weapon. Three birds passed almost level with the surface. In a tremble, the novice shot fired. Those birds seemed enormous to him, monsters, veritable eagles, grown huge in his excited eyes. The first shot made them quicken their wing beats but was immediately followed by a second and a coot, folding its wings fell in a tumble to lie still on the water.

Don Joaquin was on his feet with such a jolt that he set the peg shaking. He felt at that moment above all other men: he felt so proud of himself, sensing within him a hero's hitherto unsuspected savagery.

- *Sangonera*! Boatman! he shouted in a voice trembling with emotion. Got one... I just got one!

His reply was an almost unintelligible roar from a mouth full of food, stuffed full, a mouth that could scarcely utter a word. That was fine! He would go and pick them up when there were a few more.

Content with this feat, the great hunter settled back, hidden behind his curtain of stems, feeling he could clear the lake of birds on his own. He spent the whole morning firing away, more and more intoxicated by the heady whiff of gunpowder and the pleasure of destruction. He fired again and again with no heed for range, greeting every bird that came within sight with shot, even when it was flying as high as the clouds. Christ! That was real fun! Firing away blindly like this, some shot occasionally caught unfortunate birds which fell, victims of fate and inexperience, after having escaped the guns of better shots unharmed.

Sangonera, meanwhile, was keeping well hidden in the bottom of the boat. What a day! The Archbishop of Valencia was no better off in his palace than he was in that little punt, sitting on the straw with a hunk of bread in his hand and a pot of stew gripped between his legs. Let there be no more talking about the "abundance" to be had a *Cañamel's* place! Only the poor would be dazzled by that miserable spread! City gents were the ones who knew how to look after themselves!

He had started by making a minute examination of the three pots, carefully stoppered, with thick cloths tied around the tops. What would this first one be like? He picked one at random and, on opening it, his nostrils dilated in pleasure at the bouquet of cod in tomato sauce. That had to be tasted! The cod was crumbled into a luscious red tomato sauce, so smooth and appealing that, as the first mouthful slid down, *Sangonera* felt his gullet bathed in a nectar sweeter than the contents of those little flasks of holy wine which used to tempt him sorely in his days as a Sacristan. That would do fine! There was no reason to try anything else! He meant to respect the mystery surrounding the other pots, not to dispel the excitement awakened by their stoppered tops, beneath which, doubtless, lay extraordinary discoveries. Now, where were we…? Placing the delightfully scented pot between his knees, he began to sup, appreciatively, calmly, like a man with all the day before him who knows that he will never lack for something to do. He supped slowly, but with such skill that every time his hand, fitted with a large hunk of bread, made its way into the depths, the level in the pot dropped significantly. The enormous mouthful filled his maw, swelling his cheeks, as his jaw worked with the strength and regularity of a mill wheel, while his eyes, fixed on the pot, explored the depths, calculating exactly how many more trips his hand would have to make to transport the entire contents to his mouth.

From time to time, he would haul himself out of this reverie. Christ! An honourable working man ought not to forget his duties amidst his pleasures. He would look out from the boat and, spotting some birds approaching, would blurt out a few words of advice:

- Don Joaquin! Over…from El Palmar! Don Joaquin! Over… from El Saler!

After alerting his gun to where the birds were coming from, he felt fatigued by so much effort, and took a hearty pull on the wineskin before resuming his silent dialogue with the pot.

His master had downed some three coots when *Sangonera* laid aside the now almost empty vessel. A few shreds remained stuck to the earthenware sides at the bottom. The rogue felt the prickings of conscience. What would be left for his master if he ate everything? He ought to content himself with just a taste, so stowing the carefully re-stoppered pot back under the bow his curiosity impelled him to open the second.

Lord! What a surprise! Back bacon, pork sausages, the best of charcuterie, all cold but with a fatty bouquet that sent the vagabond into ecstasies. How long had it been since his stomach, used to the tasteless white flesh of eels, had felt the weight of all these goodies produced up country? Sangonera felt he would be failing in respect for his master, were he to hold back from this second pot. It would be equivalent to saying that he, a starving vagabond, wasn't moved by gratitude for the good things that were served in don Joaquin's house. One little taste more or less wasn't going to annoy his gun!

So, he settled down once more in the bottom of the boat, cross-legged with the pot between his knees. As he tasted the first mouthfuls, *Sangonera* shuddered with pleasure, closing his eyes to better appreciate their slow descent into his stomach. What a day, Lord, what a great day! It seemed that, for the first time ever, he was spending the whole morning chewing. He now looked back disdainfully to the first pot, stowed under the bow. That dish had been fine as an amusement, something to tickle the stomach and get the jaws into practice. But this was the good stuff, *morcillas* (black pudding), *longanizas* (country sausages) and the appetising *lomo* (back bacon) which melted in the mouth, dispensing so much flavour that you were looking for another bit and then another without ever having enough.

Noticing how quickly the second pot was emptying Sangonera felt compelled to be of service to his master, to carry out his duties to the letter, so, with his jaws still working, he gazed around, emitting shouts that were more or less roars.

- Over… El Saler side. Over … El Palmar!

Purely in order to avoid getting food stuck in his throat, he made pretty continuous use of the wineskin. He drank and drank of that wine, so much better than Neleta's, and the red flood seemed to excite his appetite, opening new routes into the bottomless pit of his stomach. His eyes glittered with joyous intoxication, his rapidly colouring face began to take on a tint of violet, noisy burps shook his frame from head to foot, and, beaming with pleasure, he patted his swollen belly.

- How's it goin', eh? How're ya doin'? he asked his stomach, patting it like an old friend.

He was drunker and happier than he had ever been, with the intoxication of a man who had eaten well and was drinking to help his digestion, not the sad, gloomy type of drunkenness that used to take hold of him, when he would sink glass after glass on an empty stomach, after coming across folk on the lake side who were always happy to share a drink, but never offered him so much as a bit of bread.

He immersed himself, smiling, in his drunkenness, not that this stopped him continuing with his eating. The Albufera was bathed in a rosy glow, the luminous blue sky seemed riven with a beaming smile just like the one that had touched his cheek one night on a track through the Dehesa. The only patch of black before him, gloomy as an empty tomb, was the mouth of the pot between his knees. He had consumed everything. Not even a scrap of sausage remained.

For a moment his own gluttony horrified him, but then his appetite made him laugh and to get over his embarrassment he took a long pull on the wineskin.

He laughed fit to burst, thinking about what they would say in El Palmar when his feats became known, and, from a desire to complete the venture by sampling all of don Joaquin's fare, he took the top off the third pot.

Lord! Two fine capons neatly trussed lay between the earthenware sides, their skin golden and dripping fat; two of the Lord's most adorable creatures, headless, with drumsticks trussed tight to the body by several turns of well toasted string and the breasts pert and white as a girl's. He was no man if he didn't try his hand at that, even if it meant don Joaquin having a go at him with his gun! How long was it since he had tasted such delicacies! He hadn't actually tasted meat since the days when he used to act as Tonet's gundog, and they used to do a bit of poaching on the Dehesa. But thinking of the meagre, stringy meat of those wildfowl, his pleasure mounted as he devoured the capons' soft white flesh and golden skin, which crunched between his teeth, while fat poured from the corners of his mouth.

He ate robotically, his mind fixed on swallowing over and over, keeping an anxious eye on what was left in the bottom of pot, as if he was on a bet. From time to time, he was seized by fits of childishness, drunken pranks, making a racket and playing games. He would grab apples from the basket of fruit and hurl them at birds flying in the distance, as if there was any chance of reaching that far.

He felt great affection for don Joaquin, on account of the happiness he had brought him; he wanted to hold him close and embrace him; with calm insolence he talked familiarly with him, using the baby form of his name, and without so much as a bird in sight kept up a continual roar of:

- Chimo! Chimo! Fire...they're in range!

His gun spun vainly round and round, looking everywhere. Not a bird to be seen! What did that fool want? What he ought to be doing was coming over to pick up the dead birds floating around the peg. But *Sangonera* had curled up again in the bottom of the boat without paying any attention to what was ordered. There was still time! He would do it later! Plenty of kills was what he wanted. In his enthusiasm to try everything he now uncorked the bottles, enjoying both the rum and the absinthe in quick succession, while, now at the height of the day, the sun began to go dark in his eyes, and his legs seemed to have become nailed to the boat's planking, lacking the strength to move.

At noon, don Joaquin, hungry and anxious to get out of the bucket which kept him immobilised called to the boatman. Vainly his voice resounded in the silence.

- *Sangonera*! *Sangonera*!

Sticking his head over the gunwale the rogue looked straight at him, muttering over and over about coming straight away, but remaining motionless, as if it weren't actually him being called. When his master, red faced from the effort of so much shouting, threatened him with his gun, he made an effort, staggered to his feet, searched the whole boat for the pole which he had in his hand, and eventually began to edge slowly closer. When don Joaquin was able to jump into the punt, he could finally move his legs, stiff after so many hours standing. On his orders, his boatman began to pick the dead birds, but was groping around, as if he couldn't see them, leaning forward so far that several times he would have fallen in the water if his master had not held on to him.

- You rogue! exclaimed his gun, are you drunk?

He soon had his explanation as he examined his provisions, while a silly looking *Sangonera* looked on. The empty pots, the flaccid and wrinkled wineskin, the opened bottles, just a few hunks of bread and a fruit basket that could be up ended into the lake without any chance of something falling out of it.

Don Joaquin felt a strong desire to take the butt of his gun to the boatman, but once the thought had passed, he was left looking at him in astonishment. Had he finished everything off, all on his own? Well, the idler certainly had a way of taking a sip or two! Where had he put so much stuff? Could the human stomach really contain…?

But as he listened to the furious gun calling him a shameless rogue, *Sangonera* could only reply in a whining voice:

- Aye, don Joaquin, I'm bad, very bad!

And yes, he certainly did feel bad. You only had to look at his yellow face, his eyes vainly battling to stay open, his legs which could no longer keep him upright.

The furious shot was on the point of hitting *Sangonera* when the lad collapsed into the bottom of the punt, sinking his nails into his waistband as if he wanted to tear his belly open. He curled into a ball convulsed by agonising spasms that clenched his teeth and glazed his eyes.

He groaned, next arching himself back, fighting to rid himself of the huge load of food which now threatened to suffocate him. His passenger did not know what to do, once more regretting his tiresome trip to the Albufera. After half an hour of cursing and swearing, when he thought that he was condemned to take the pole himself and set off for El Saler, some of the farmers shooting on their own around the lake finally took pity on his cries.

They recognised *Sangonera* and guessed the cause of his illness. This was a potentially fatal obstruction that could put paid to the rogue for good. As part of the brotherhood of country folk who feel moved to lend their aid to even the humblest of men, they loaded *Sangonera* into their boat in order to take him over to El Palmar, while one of them remained with the gun, content to act as his boatman instead of shooting himself.

In mid-afternoon the women of El Palmar found the rogue dropped on the canal bank as still as a bundle of rags.

- *Pillo*! The scoundrel, *Alguna borrachera!* Some binge! they all cried.

But the good lads, who then had the charity to carry him like a corpse on their shoulders to his miserable hovel, shook their heads sadly. This wasn't just drunkenness, and if the rogue managed to get out of this, he could well claim to have nine lives. They told the tale of portentous consumption which had brought him to the point of death, at which the folk of El Palmar could not but laugh in astonishment, while at the same time being unable hide their sense of pride, content that it was one of their own who had shown the size of his stomach.

Poor *Sangonera*! News of his problem spread throughout the village, and women went in groups to the door of his cottage, crowding into the entrance which everyone had previously shunned. Laid out on the straw, looking up, glassy eyed, at the roof with a waxy pallor, *Sangonera* roared and shook with pain as if his guts were bursting. From every orifice streamed a nauseating mix of liquid excretions and semi-digested food.

- How're ya doin', *Sangonera*? they ventured from the door.

The sick man's only reply was a painful groan as he rolled over, turning his back on them, upset by the whole village parading through.

Other women, keener to do something, came in, and getting down on their knees beside him, prodded his abdomen, wanting to know where it hurt him. They discussed between them the most appropriate medications, recalling those which had proved successful in their own families, and then sought out certain old wives, well regarded for their home remedies, who enjoyed more respect than El Palmar's poor doctor. Some came along with poultices of herbs, carefully and secretly kept in their cottages, while others came with a pot of warm water, suggesting that the sick man should down it in one. They were unanimous in their opinion. The unhappy man had food "stuck" in the stomach entrance and had to "unplug" it. Lord, what a pity for the poor man! His father dead from alcohol poisoning and him "kicking the bucket" from an obstruction. What a family!

Nothing demonstrated to *Sangonera* the gravity of his situation so much as these womanly concerns. He saw it in the generally sympathetic atmosphere, and realised how much danger he was in when he reflected on the fact that he was being looked after by the same women who, just the day before, had made a joke of him and given their husbands and sons a telling off for keeping him company.

- Poor chap, poor chap, they all murmured.

With the courage and resolve of which only women are capable in the face of adversity, they clustered round, skipping over the foul emanations that bubbled from his mouth. They knew what it was all about: he had a "knot" in his guts and with motherly care they coaxed cuddled and finally persuaded him to relax his tightly clenched jaws, open his mouth and gulp down all sorts of liquid miracles which shortly poured back over his nurses' feet.

As night fell, they left him: they had the evening meal to cook back at home. The sick man was all alone in the depths of the hovel, motionless under the reddish glow of a candle the women stuck in a crack. Village dogs poked their noses round the door, looking long and hard at the sick man with their fathomless eyes before slinking off with a gloomy growl.

It was the men who went along through the night to visit the cottage. The issue was much talked about in *Cañamel's* and boatmen, astonished at *Sangonera's* feat of consumption wanted to see him for the last time.

They clustered unsteadily around the doorway, for many of them were drunk after eating with their guns.

- *Sangonera*, old son! How are you?

They pulled back quickly, however, struck in the face by the stench of the disgusting filth in which the sick man writhed. Some of the more lively went straight up to him with a rough joke and an invitation to have one last drink in *Cañamel's*; but the sick man could only reply with a soft groan closing his eyes as he sank back, vomiting, shaking, semi-conscious. By midnight the vagabond was completely alone.

Tonet had no wish to see his former companion. He had got back to the tavern after sleeping long in the boat, a deep and troubled sleep, punctuated at intervals by terrible nightmares amid a lullaby of shots from the guns which rolled round his sleeping brain like continuous thunder.

Going in, he was surprised to see Neleta seated in front of the barrels, waxy pale, but otherwise unconcerned, as if she had passed a quiet night. Tonet could only stand amazed at his lover's strength of will.

They exchanged a deep and knowing look, like two criminals who realise they are bound ever tighter together by complicity.

After a long pause, she plucked up courage to ask him a question. She wanted to know how the delivery had gone and he answered, with his head to one side and his eyes lowered, as if the whole village was looking at him. Fine...he had left it in a safe place, nobody would find it. Following these few, hastily exchanged words they both fell silent and pensive, she behind the bar and he seated in the door, with his back to Neleta, avoiding eye contact. They both seemed numb, as if a huge weight had dropped on their heads. They were afraid to speak to each other, for the sound of each other's voice revived thoughts of the previous night.

They had emerged from a very difficult situation and were no longer in any danger. Neleta, lively as ever, was astonished at the ease with which everything had resolved itself. Weak and ill as she was, she still found strength to stay at her post; nobody else could suspect what had happened through the night, and yet the two lovers themselves felt suddenly parted. Something they shared had broken and could never be mended. The space that scarcely glimpsed little soul had left when it vanished, was growing immeasurably larger, pushing the two unhappy beings apart. Both were thinking that in future there would be nothing between them but the occasional exchange of glances as they recalled their old crime. For Tonet there was the spectre of an even greater worry; that she did not know the child's real fate.

As night fell, the tavern was filled with boatmen and guns heading back to their fields around la Ribera, showing off the bundles of dead birds strung up by their beaks. What a great shoot! They were all drinking, talking about the luck some particular shots had had, and about *Sangonera's* prodigious feat. Tonet went from group to group, wanting to take his mind off things, drinking and chatting with them all. His plan to forget everything by getting drunk, made him drink and drink with forced gaiety, and his friends rejoiced in the *Cubano's* good humour. Never had they seen him so happy.

Old *Paloma* came into the tavern and fixed his searching gaze on Neleta.

- My Queen, how pale, are you ill?

Neleta talked in vague terms of a headache that had stopped her sleeping, while the old boy winked slyly, connecting the "bad night" with his grandson's escape. He faced him later. He had put him in a ridiculous position with that Valencian gentleman. His conduct was not worthy of an Albufera boatman. When he was younger, he would have handed out more than one beating for less. It would only occur to a stupid oaf like him to pass *Sangonera* off as a "boatman", a man who had stuffed himself fit to burst as soon as he was left on his own.

Tonet made his excuses. There was still time for him to be of some use to that gentleman. It would be the fiesta of St Katherine in a couple of weeks, and Tonet was going to offer to be his boatman. With his anger cooled by his grandson's excuses, Old *Paloma* said he had already invited don Joaquín to a shoot in the El Palmar reed beds. He would be coming the following week and he and Tonet would act as boatmen for him. You had to keep the Valencian gentlemen happy so the Albufera would always have its *aficionados*, otherwise what would become of the lake folk?

Tonet got drunk that night, and instead of going up to Neleta's bedroom, stayed snoring by the hearth. Neither of them wanted to see the other, but rather to avoid each other's company, finding a certain relief in being alone. They were terrified of finding themselves in the same room, fearful of recalling that little soul, a memory which stood between them like the cry of a life at once snuffed out.

The following day Tonet got drunk again. He didn't want to be left alone with his thoughts, needing to tame them with alcohol in order to keep them quietly asleep.

Fresh news reached the tavern concerning *Sangonera's* situation. He was dying and nothing could be done. The men had gone back to their duties and women who went to the cottage recognised the futility of their ministrations. The older ones had their own explanation for the problem. The mass of food blocking the entrance to his stomach was rotting, you only had to look at how his stomach was swelling.

The doctor from Sollana arrived on one of his weekly visits, and they took him to *Sangonera's* cottage. This tradesman of science shook his head. There was nothing more he could do. It was a fatal appendicitis, the consequence of an astonishing feat of self-abuse which left the doctor in disbelief. Throughout the village they repeated the bit about "appendicitis", as the womenfolk took pleasure in pronouncing what was, for them, such a strange word.

Don Miguel, the priest felt the moment had come to make his entry into the renegade's cottage. No one knew how to see people off promptly and frankly as he did.

- What, are you a Christian? He boomed from the door.

Sangonera was astonished, of course he was a Christian! As if scandalised by the very thought he looked up at the cottage ceiling, gazing in expectation and rapture at the patch of blue sky showing through holes in the roof.

Good! Right, just between men then, no more lies, continued the priest, he ought to confess himself because he was going to die. No ifs and buts, with that gun-toting priest there was no beating about the bush with his faithful.

An expression of terror passed across the vagabond's eyes. His misery-filled existence seemed at that moment to hold all the enchantment of limitless freedom. He beheld the lake of sparkling water, the rustling Dehesa with its perfumed thickets full of wildflowers and even the bar at *Cañamel's* at which he had day-dreamed, contemplating a rose-tinted life through the glass. And he was going to leave it all behind! Tears began to brim his glassy eyes. There was nothing for it. The time had come for him to die. In another world he would see better that heavenly smile, immense in its mercy, which had caressed him one night by the lake.

Suddenly calm amid his bouts of nausea and clenched teeth, he softly confessed to the priest all his petty pilfering from the fishermen, episodes so great in number that he could not recall them except as whole. Together with his sins, he confessed his hopes, his faith in Christ who would come again to save the poor, his mysterious encounter one night on the lake side. But the priest rudely interrupted him.

.

- *Sangonera*, less of the nonsense. You're raving! The truth...tell the truth.

He had already told the truth. His sin consisted

entirely in avoiding work because of his belief that it was against God's will. Just once had he agreed to be like other people, to hire out his labour to other men and come in contact with wealth and all its comforts and, oh boy, wasn't he just paying for it now with his life!

The women of El Palmar were truly moved by the vagabond's final moments. He had lived like a heretic since fleeing the church, but he was dying as a Christian. His illness did not permit him to receive the Lord' body, and he stained the priest's vestments with vomit as he was administered the Final Sacrament.

The only people who then entered the cottage were some dedicated old women who shrouded all those who died in the village as an act of self-denial. The stench in the hovel was insufferable. People talked in mystery and wonder of *Sangonera's* final hours. Since the previous day it was not food that he had vomited up but something worse, and the womenfolk passing by could only hold their noses and imagine him stretched out on the straw surrounded in filth.

He died on the third day of his illness, his belly swollen, his face contorted and fists clenched in suffering, and his mouth stretched wide from ear to ear in a final convulsive rictus.

El Palmar's better-off women who frequented

the presbytery were deeply moved with commiseration for the unhappy man who had been reconciled with God after a dog's life. They wanted his final journey to be one of dignity and set off for Valencia to make preparations for his burial, spending in the process more than *Sangonera* had ever seen when he was alive.

They dressed him in a religious habit, placed him in a silver-striped, white coffin and the whole village paraded before the vagabond's body.

His former companions rubbed their drink-reddened eyes and stifled their laughter on seeing their old buddy looking so clean in a bachelor's coffin, dressed as a friar. Even in death he seemed a bit of a joke. Farewell *Sangonera*! The *mornells* wouldn't be getting emptied any more before their owners could get to them, he wouldn't be dressing himself up in flowers along the canal banks like a drunk heathen. He had lived a free and happy life without the fatigue of hard labour and, even in the grip of death, had known how to set off for the next world using the best that wealth could supply, and at someone else's expense.

At midnight they placed the coffin in the "eel-wagon" amid the baskets of fish and the Sacristan of El Palmar with three friends, conducted the body to the cemetery, stopping off at every tavern on the way.

Tonet did not pay much attention to his friend's death. He was living in a haze, constantly drinking, a silent drunk. Fear stifled any desire to speak, for he feared to say too much.

- *Sangonera's* dead! Your old pal! They would say to him in the tavern.

His answer was just a groan, drinking and falling asleep at the same time, while his companions conveniently attributed his silence to grief for his dead comrade.

Neleta, pale and sad, as if a ghost were passing every few moments before her eyes, attempted to stop her lover drinking.

- No more drink, Tonet, she would say quietly.

But she was startled by the dismissive look of silent fury which was the drunk's only reply. She could see that any control she had had over him had vanished. Sometimes she even discerned a glint of hatred in his eyes, the bitterness of a slave resolved to strike and annihilate his former oppressor.

He paid no attention to Neleta, filling his glass at will, from every barrel in the place. When sleep overcame him, he would drop anywhere into a corner, and lie there, dead to the world, while *la*

Centella, with a dog's tender instincts, licked his face and hands.

Tonet couldn't bear his waking thoughts. As soon as the drunkenness began to wear off, he would feel really terrible, deeply troubled. He started in alarm at the shadows people cast on the floor as they entered the tavern, as if fearful of some apparition that shattered his dreams with a shudder of terror. He needed to get drunk again, to avoid emerging from this state of intoxication, which anesthetised his soul and blunted his feelings.

Through the veils of alcohol that enshrouded his thought processes, everything seemed diffuse, faraway, and indistinct. He began to feel that many years had passed since that night on the lake, the last of his life as a man, the first of a life of shadows, through which he groped his way with a mind obscured by alcohol. The memory of that night made him shudder whenever intoxication began to fade. Only while drunk could he bear it, make it seem less clear, like those distant little embarrassments which seem to cause less hurt as they become lost in the mists of time.

With this binge in full swing, his grandfather unexpectedly came to see him. Old *Paloma* was awaiting the arrival the following day of don

Joaquín for a shoot in the reed beds. Was his grandson going to keep his word? Neleta insisted he accept. He wasn't feeling well, but it would do him good to take his mind off things, and it was over a week since he had been out of the tavern. The *Cubano* felt attracted by the prospect of a day of excitement. His enthusiasm as a shot bounced back. Was he going to stay off the lake for ever?

He spent the rest of the day filling cartridges and cleaning the departed *Cañamel's* magnificent shotgun, and, absorbed in this work, drank less. La *Centella*, leapt around him barking joyously to see the preparations.

Old *Paloma* presented himself the following morning, bringing in the punt don Joaquín and all his splendid shooting kit.

The old boy was impatient and urged his grandson to get a move on. He only wanted to stay long enough for the gentleman to get a mouthful and then get straight to the reed beds. They had to make the most of the morning.

With little delay they were off, Tonet leading, with *Centella* on the bow of his punt like a mascot and, right behind, old *Paloma's* boat, where don Joaquín was looking with amazement at the old boy's gun, that famous and much-mended weapon which had accounted for so many wildfowl on the lake.

The two boats slid out onto the Albufera. Tonet, noticing his grandfather poling to the left wanted to know where they were heading. The old boy was astonished at the very question. They were going to the Bolodró, the biggest thicket near the village. That was where there were more swamphens and moorhens than anywhere else. Tonet wanted to go further on, to the thickets in the middle of the lake, so a lively discussion broke out between the two boatmen. But the old boy ended up getting his way, and Tonet had finally to follow him, ill humouredly and resignedly putting his back into it.

The two punts slipped into a narrow lead between the tall beds. Clumps of bullrushes grew among the reeds, stems and rushes jumbled together and trails of blue and white campanile formed a web of garlands above this watery jungle. The tangle of roots gave an appearance of solidity to the masses of stems. The bottom showed through the clear water of the lead where strange vegetation reached up to the surface, meaning you never quite knew whether the boats were floating, or were actually slipping across green meadows covered with thin glass.

Deep was the silence in this corner of the Albufera which seemed even further from civilisation in daylight. The only noise was the occasional bird chirping in the thicket, or some bubbling on the water, suggesting the presence of mysterious creatures hidden in the slimy bottom.

Don Joaquín was getting his gun ready hoping some birds would cross from one side of the thicket to the other.

- Tonet, take a turn round the outside, ordered the old boy.

The *Cubano* quickly positioned his punt in order to go round the outside of the thicket, shaking the stems so as to alarm the birds and make them head from one side of the clump to the other. It took him more than ten minutes to make his way all around the edge.

When he got back to his grandfather's side don Joaquín was already blasting away at alarmed and frightened birds who were changing roost and fluttering across the open lead.
Wildfowl were showing over stretch of water that lay open to the sky. They hesitated to risk it for just a moment and then, some flying and others swimming, crossed the lead, just as the shot swept through them.

It was straightforward in this enclosed space, but don Joaquín basked in the glory of being a great shot, seeing how easy it was to down the game. La *Centella* launched herself off the punt to reach the still fluttering birds and retrieve them with a triumphant expression to her gun's hand. Nor was old *Paloma's* gun inactive. The old boy was fully engaged in supporting his customer's efforts while complimenting his shooting as usual. Whenever he saw a bird on the point of getting away, he would fire, making the good burgher think it was he who had brought it down.

A nice duck paddled past and, as don Joaquín and old *Paloma* fired almost simultaneously, disappeared into the reeds.

- That's a runner, shouted the old boatman.

The gun was clearly a bit upset. What a pity! It would die among the reeds without them being able to retrieve it.

- Find, *Centella*, find, shouted Tonet to his dog.

Centella threw herself off the punt and launched into the reeds with much crashing of stems as she shouldered her way through.

Tonet smiled, certain of the outcome; his dog would retrieve the bird. But his grandfather was less certain. Those birds could get hit at one end of the Albufera, and if they made it to the reeds, turn up dead at the other. That bitch besides, was an antique like him. In the old days, when *Cañamel* had bought her, she was really worth something, but now you couldn't trust her nose.

Tonet, not thinking much of his grandfather's opinion, simply repeated:

- That's it, that's it!

Sometimes nearer and sometimes further away, the bitch could be heard splashing in the reeds, and the men followed her constant casting about in the morning silence, guided by the crash of breaking stems and the sound of undergrowth being shouldered aside by the powerful animal. After several long minutes of waiting, they saw her emerge from the reeds with a downcast expression and nothing in her mouth.

The older boatman smiled triumphantly. What had he said? But Tonet, seeing himself made to look ridiculous, swore at the hound threatening her with his fist to keep her away from the boat.

- Where away?! Find it, find it! he curtly ordered the poor animal once more.

She slunk off again into the reed beds dragging her tail disconsolately.

She would find the bird. Tonet, who had set her far harder tasks, swore by it. Again, they heard the animal splashing about in the watery jungle. She cast about indecisively from one side to the other, changing course every few moments, not really confident in her random searching, but not daring to come back defeated, for every time she turned towards the boats and stuck her head out between the stems she would be confronted by her master's fist and "Find it!" shouted as a threat.

Time and again she nosed her way along the track, finally getting so far away in her invisible search that her masters stopped hearing the noise.

A distant bark repeated several times made Tonet break into a smile. Hello! His old friend might take her time, but nothing got away from her!

The dog was continuing to bark in the distance, very far away, more and more desperately but without getting any nearer. The *Cubano* whistled.

- Here, *Centella*, fetch!

The splashing was beginning to be heard much nearer now. She was getting closer, snapping reeds, flattening grasses, and noisily churning the water. Finally, she appeared with something in her mouth, swimming with difficulty.

Tonet was still calling to her.

- Here, *Centella*, here.

As she passed close to his grandfather's boat, his customer raised a hand to his eyes, as if struck by lightning.

- Mother of God! he whimpered in terror, his

gun slipping from his grasp.

Tonet stood up, eyes staring, shaking from head to foot, gasping as if all the air had suddenly been driven from his lungs. Next to the gunwale lay a bundle of rags containing something pale, slimy, and bristling with leeches, a small head, swollen, shapeless and blackened, the sockets empty, but one of them trailing an eyeball, a sight so foul and repugnant that the air and water seemed suddenly to turn dark, as if night had fallen on the lake in the full light of day.

With both hands he raised his pole and so tremendous was the blow that the dog's head cracked wide open as, with a howl, the poor animal sank with its prey into the swirling water.

He gazed wide-eyed at his grandfather, who had no idea what was happening, at poor don Joaquín who sat frozen in terror, and then, poling robotically, shot like an arrow down the lead as if the ghost of remorse, which had lain dormant within him for a week, had suddenly come to life and was now digging its implacable claws deep into his back.

CHAPTER 10

It was a short trip. Emerging onto the Albufera he found several boats close by, heard shouts from their crews and had to hide, red faced like someone suddenly finding himself naked before strangers.

The sun seemed to hurt his eyes, the wide expanse of the lake to frighten him, he needed to curl up in some dark corner, to see nothing and hear nothing, so he turned and headed back again into the reeds.

He did not go far. The bow of the little punt buried itself among the stems and throwing down his pole the miserable creature let himself tumble into the bottom of the boat with his head hidden in his hands. For a long time, the birds were silenced, all noise in the reed bed ceased, as if all life hidden among the stems were stilled, terrified, by a single savage roar, a cry cut short like a dying gulp.

The miserable creature wept and wept. After the binge which had successfully deprived him of all feeling, the crime was rising again before his eyes, as if no time at all had passed, as if he had just that moment committed it. Just when he had thought the memory of that fatal deed was on the point of being wiped for ever from his mind, Fate had given it new life and it was there, passing before his eyes, and how!

Remorse renewed his fatherly instinct, dead since that fatal night. In horror he recognised his crime with cruel intensity. The flesh left for the reptiles of the lake was his own flesh, that bundle of cloth enclosing its writhing mass of leeches and worms was the fruit of his impassioned lust, his insatiable desires in the silence of the night.

The enormity of his crime completely overcame him. No more excuses, he didn't need to look for reasons to keep going as he had on other occasions. He was a miserable creature unworthy of life, a dry branch of the *Paloma* family tree which always grew straight, vigorous, wild, and rugged but clean and healthy in its isolation. The rotten branch had to come off.

His grandfather was right to despise him. His father, his poor father whom he now counted among the saints, was doing the right thing to cut him off like a wayward shoot. Poor unhappy *Borda*, despite her shameful origins, was a more worthy child of the *Palomas* than he was.

What had he ever done with his life? Nothing. The only thing he ever put any effort into was getting out of doing work. The much-maligned *Sangonera* had been a better man than he was. Alone in the world, with no family, lacking even the basics needed for his hard life as a vagabond, he had been able to live without working, as gently innocent as the birds of the air. But he, consumed by burning earthly appetites, selfishly avoiding all duty, had just wanted riches, a life of ease, meandering along, rejecting the advice of a father who could see danger coming, and had descended from a life of laziness and indignity to this crime.

What he had done terrified him. Now that his fatherly conscience was awakened, it clawed at him, but that was nothing to an even more terrible and bloody wound. His arrogance, that arrogant male desire to be the strongest and to dominate people with its boldness and daring, tormented him even more cruelly. He could see punishment approaching in the distance, prison, who knew, perhaps the hooded garrotting, that ultimate expression of the cruelty of man. He accepted all that, for in the end it was what happened to men, but for some cause worthy of a real man, for battling and killing face to face, bathed in blood up to one's elbows, in the savage madness of a human being transformed into a wild beast. But to kill a newborn with nothing but a cry to protect him! To have to confess before the world that he, the brave lad, the former soldier had, when he came to commit a crime, only dared kill his own son!

He wept and wept, beyond remorse, feeling only shame at his cowardice and despair at his own vileness.

One faint glimmer of belief in himself continued to burn in the darkness of his mind. He was not entirely evil. The good blood of his father ran in his veins. His only crime was to be selfish and weak-willed, which had made him lose touch with the struggle for life. It was Neleta who was depraved, that superior strength which had held him in chains, that steely self-interest which had crushed his will and moulded him to all the twists and turns of its own, like pliable wrapping. Oh, if he had only never met her! If only, on getting back from far-off lands, he had never encountered those pale eyes fixed on his, seeming to say: "Take me, I'm rich, I've achieved my goal in life and now all that's missing is you."

She had been the temptress, the force that had cast him into the shadows, the selfish greed behind the mask of love which had led him into crime. In order to save a few crumbs of her fortune she had not hesitated to give away part of her very self, and he, her unthinking slave, had finished her work by destroying his own flesh and blood.

How miserable his existence seemed! His mind swam with confused recollections of the old tale of la *Sancha*, the story of the serpent that generations had repeated on the shores of the lake. He was like the shepherd-boy in the legend, he had stroked and petted the snake when it was small, had fed it and even warmed it with the heat of his own body and when he returned from war, was astonished to see it so big and powerful, grown more beautiful with the passing of time, while it coiled around him in a fatal embrace, causing his death with its serpentine caress.

His snake was in the village, as the shepherd-boy's had been in that wild plain. That *Sancha* of El Palmar, since taking over the tavern, was the one causing his death with the unyielding coils of crime.

He didn't want to return to that world. It was impossible to live among mankind, he couldn't look at them, everywhere he would see that little deformed head, swollen, monstrous, with its deep sockets eaten out by worms. But when he thought of Neleta, a red veil passed over his sight and repentance was replaced by a homicidal urge, an urge to kill that which he now considered his implacable enemy. But what would be the point of a second crime?There in the solitude, out of sight of everyone, he felt better and there he wanted to stay.

At the same time, however, overwhelming fear surged through him with all the self-centred focus that had been the sole driver of his life. It was possible that news of the horrible event was at that very moment circulating around El Palmar. His grandfather would say nothing but that stranger from the city had no reason to keep his mouth shut. The patent leather tri-corn-wearing gentlemen from la Huerta de Ruzafa would come, searching, and checking. He didn't have the courage to face them down, he couldn't lie, he would confess, and his father, that pure hearted working man, innocent as God made him, would die of shame. And if he were, somehow, to succeed in maintaining the lie and saving his skin, what would that gain him? He would have to return to Neleta's arms and find himself once again in the reptile's coils. No, it was all over. He was the rotten branch and he had to come down, not just stand there, dead and dried out, but still clinging to the tree and distorting its future life.

Cañamel's shotgun lay in the bow. Tonet looked at it with a quizzical expression. The old innkeeper would have a good laugh if he could see him now! For the very first time the parasite that had grown fat in his shadow was going to make good use of something he had taken!

With robotic calm he took off one shoe and hurled it away. He cocked both chambers and, ripping open his jacket and shirt, bent over the weapon until the muzzle was touching his naked breast. His toe gently made its way up the stock, feeling for the triggers, and the double detonation shook the reed bed with such force that birds rose in a mad panic into the air on all sides.

Old *Paloma* did not get back to El Palmar until nightfall. He had left his shot in El Saler, swearing that he would never return to those parts, and just wanting to get off the lake and back to the city as soon as he could. Two catastrophes in two trips. The Albufera held nothing but horrors for him, the last of which was going to make him ill. The peaceable burgher, father to numerous children himself, could not get out of his mind the ghastly bundle that had passed before his eyes. When he got home, he would certainly have to retire to bed, pretending some illness. The shock had left him deeply shaken.

The same man advised old *Paloma* to maintain

complete discretion on the matter. Not a word must escape his lips! They had seen nothing! He ought to commend his poor grandson, no doubt still on the run after the terrible shock, to silence also. The lake had taken its secret back to its bosom and it would be naïve of them to say anything, knowing how Justice made innocent folk's heads spin when they were stupid enough to go looking for it. Men of honour ought to avoid all contact with the Law! After disembarking, the poor gentleman would not get into his coach until the old boatman, more pensive by the minute, swore repeatedly that he would remain silent.

When old *Paloma* reached El Palmar at nightfall, he tied up both punts in which they had left during the morning in front of the tavern.

On the right, behind the bar, Neleta was casting about vainly for Tonet. The old boy guessed who she was looking for.

- Don't wait for him, he said in a low voice, he won't be back.

In clearer tones he asked if she was feeling better, mentioning her facial pallor with a candour that made Neleta shiver.

She immediately surmised that old *Paloma* knew her secret.

- But what about Tonet? she again asked

anxiously.

Averting his gaze, as if he did not want to look at her, the old boy carried on talking in order to maintain his forced calm. Tonet would not be back again. He had fled. Run away, far away, to a country from which he would never return. It was the best thing he could have done. So, everything would sort itself out, although still wrapped in mystery.

- But you...? Do you...? groaned Neleta in anguish, fearful of what the old boy might say.

The old boy would keep his mouth shut, as he swore, striking his chest. He despised his grandson, but he had an interest in ensuring that no one knew that. After so many centuries of honourable service the good name of the *Palomas* was not going to be dragged in the dirt by a wastrel and a bitch.

- Cry, yes cry, why don't you! said the old boatman irritably.

She ought to spend her whole life crying since she was the cause of this family tragedy. Let her keep her money! He wouldn't be the one to come asking for it as the price of his silence, and if she wanted to know where her lover and her son were, she need do no more than look at the lake.

The Albufera, mother of them all would keep her secret as faithfully as he would.

Neleta was left stunned by this revelation but, even as the huge shock hit, was looking rather anxiously at the old man, fearing for her future, now she saw it was entrusted to *Paloma's* silence.

The old man struck his chest again. Might she live happily and enjoy her wealth! He would keep his silence forever.

The night was very dark in the *Paloma's* cottage. In the flickering light of the oil lamp, the father and grandfather seated face to face, talked for a long time, two serious beings separated by temperament who could only bear to be near each other when impelled to do so by misfortune.

Old *Paloma* used no circumlocutions in giving the news. He had seen the lad, dead, his chest ripped apart by two loads of shot, sunk in the mud of the thicket with his feet sticking out of the water next to his empty punt. Tono scarcely blinked. Only his lips moved, pursing convulsively, his clenched fists scraping his knees.

A long piercing wail broke from a dark corner of the cottage where the cooking area was, as if someone was being disembowelled in the gloom. It was la *Borda*, stunned by the news.

- Silence, girl, commanded the old man

imperiously.

- Quietly, quiet now, said the father.

The poor unhappy wretch sobbed, silently, her anguish stifled by the firmness of those two iron-willed men who could remain impassive while being gnawed alive by misfortune, without a trace of feeling in their eyes.

With many pauses, old *Paloma* told them what had happened, the appearance of the dog with it's horrible retrieve, Tonet's flight, and later, on the way back from El Saler, his careful exploration of the thicket, fearing the worst, and then the discovery of the body. He could put it all together. He remembered Tonet's disappearance on the evening before the shoot; Neleta's pallor and weakness, how ill she had looked after that night and how with the insights of old age, he had pieced together the evidence of that painful birth in the silence, terrified of being heard by the neighbours, and afterwards the killing of the newborn child, a crime for which he despised Tonet more for being a coward than a criminal.

The old man felt some relief in unburdening himself of his secret. Indignation now replaced his sadness. Miserable bastards! That Neleta had turned out to be bitch in heat who had put paid to their lad and pushed him to commit the crime to save her money. Tonet, however was a coward twice over, and more even than for his criminal act, he abominated him for having killed himself, mad with fear, rather than face the consequences. The "gentleman" had fired twice rather than face it, he had found it easier to disappear than pay his debts and suffer the punishment. Always fleeing his obligations, looking for the easy way out because he feared to fight for it. What times these were! Christ! What were these young folks coming to?

His son was hardly listening. He remained motionless, stunned by the enormity of the tragedy, and dropped his head as if his father's words were a mortal blow that had laid him out for good.

La *Borda* started whimpering again.

- Silence! I said silence! said Tono quietly.

In the immensity of his grief, it bothered him that others could find relief in weeping aloud while he, the hard man, was unable to unburden himself of his pain through tears.

At length Tono spoke, his voice steady but throaty with emotion.

That wretch's shameful death was a fitting end to the way he had lived. He had said before that it would all end badly. Laziness is criminal when one is born poor. That is how God ordained things and one had to go along with it. But he was his son after all, his own son, flesh of his flesh. The honourable man's steely rectitude might have appeared unfeeling in the face of such tragedy, but deep within his breast he was feeling a tight constriction, as if they had ripped out part of his innards which were at that very moment food for the eels of the Albufera.

He wanted to see him one last time, could his father understand that? He needed to hold him in his arms as he had done when he was a child, when he would send him to sleep crooning a lullaby about how his father was working hard to make him a wealthy farmer, the owner of lots of fields.

- *Pare! Father!* He said to old *Paloma* in an anguished voice. Where is he?

The old man replied angrily, things ought to be left as fate had left them. It was madness to change things now. No scandal and no light cast on the mystery. It was fine that way with everything well hidden.

When they didn't see Tonet, people would think that he was off in search of adventures new, and a gilded life, perhaps heading for America. The lake would guard its secrets well, and years would pass before anyone would find their way into the spot where the suicide lay. The vegetation of the

Albufera covered everything up. Besides, it they were to speak out and make the death public, everyone would want to know more, the forces of the law would come in to verify everything, and instead of one vanished *Paloma,* whose shame was known only to them, they would have a *Paloma* publicly dishonoured, who had killed himself in order to escape prison and perhaps the garrotte. No, Tono, and he was saying that with all the authority of a father. He was due some respect for the few remaining months of his existence and not to have his final days spoiled by a disgrace. He wanted to look the other boatmen in the eye and enjoy a quiet drink. It would all be fine. So, let's keep quiet…And besides all that, if they did discover the body, they would not bury him in consecrated ground. His crime and his suicide excluded him from the same patch of earth as other people. He was better to be in the water, sunk deep in the mud, surrounded by reeds the last cursed offshoot of a famous line of fishermen.

Irritated by la *Borda's* sobbing, the old man grew threatening. She should be quiet. Did she want to make them lose everything?

The night dragged on endlessly in tragic silence. The gloomy atmosphere in the cottage seemed denser than usual, as if the black wings of disgrace were casting their shadow over it. Old

Paloma was falling asleep in his wicker chair, a hard, selfish, unfeeling old man who just wanted to carry on with his life. His son spent the hours motionless, his eyes wide open, staring into the distance at the waving shadows thrown by the flickering lamp on the wall. La *Borda*, sitting hidden in the shadows by the hearth, sobbed softly.

Suddenly Tono shuddered as if to shake himself awake. He stood up, went to the door of the cottage, and threw it open to survey the starry sky. It must be about three o'clock. The night's calm seemed to sink into him and confirm the decision which had just stiffened his resolve.

He went over to the old man and shook him awake.

- *Pare! Father!* He said pleadingly. Where is he?

Half asleep, Old Paloma protested furiously. They should leave him in peace. There was nothing else for it. He wanted to sleep and, God willing, would never wake again!

But Tono continued pleading. He should remember he was his grandfather. He, his father could not live without looking at him for one last time. He would always be imagining him at the bottom of the lake, rotting in the water, eaten away by animals and fish without the simple grave which even the most wretched human beings were due, including that fatherless *Sangonera*. To have worked all his life to put bread on the table for his only son and then to abandon him without knowing where he was buried, like the dead dogs that got thrown into the Albufera! It couldn't be that way, father! It was too cruel! He would never be brave enough to sail again on the lake for thinking that the boat was perhaps passing over his son's body.

- *Pare! Father!* He implored, shaking the half-asleep old man.

Old *Paloma* sat up as if to strike him. Couldn't he leave him in peace? Was he going to look for that coward again? They should let him sleep! He had no wish to go back out into the mud and risk publicising the family's shame.

- But where is he? asked his anguished father.

He would go on his own, but, for God's sake, he had to tell him the place. If grandfather wouldn't tell him, he felt he would have to spend the rest of his life quartering the lake even though that would reveal their secret to the world.

- In Bolodró's thicket. You'll have trouble finding him.

He closed his eyes and dropped back into the slumber from which he had no desire to wake.

Tono gestured to la *Borda*. They seized their gravediggers' mattocks and punt poles, the sharp tridents that were used for spearing big fish, lit a torch from the lamp and crossed the village in the silence of the night to embark on the canal.

The black punt with the torch on the bow spent the night winding its way through the heart of the reed beds, like a red star wandering among the stems.

Near dawn the light was put out. They had found the body, after two hours of anxious search, just as the grandfather had seen it, head down in the mud with the feet sticking out of the water, the chest a bloody mess, torn apart, point blank, by the heavy shot of the two wildfowling cartridges.

They retrieved him from the bottom using their big tridents. As he sank his *fitora* into the pale bundle and hoisted it into the punt with a superhuman effort, the father felt he was sinking it into his own chest.

Later came the slow return, anxiously looking around, like criminals fearful of being taken unawares. La *Borda*, constantly sobbing, poled in the bow, the father aided her from the other end of the craft and between their upright figures, just two black outlines in the diffuse glow of the starry night, lay stretched the corpse of the suicide.

They landed at Tono's fields, that patch of reclaimed ground formed basketful by basketful, with the strength of their hands and a mad refusal to give up.

Taking hold of the corpse, La *Borda* and his father lowered it carefully to the ground as if it were a sleeping invalid who might wake up. Then, taking their mattocks, the two indefatigable gravediggers began to open a trench. A week earlier they had still been bringing earth there from the extremes of the lake. Now they were removing it in order to conceal the dishonour of the family.

Dawn was beginning to break as they lowered the body into the bottom of the grave which was seeping water from all sides. A cold blue light was extending itself across the Albufera, reflecting off the surface like hard polished steel. Above, in the grey void, passed the first V-shaped flights of birds.

Tono looked for the last time at his son and then turned away, as if shamed by the tears that breached his hardness and at last streamed from his eyes.

His life was over. So many years battling the lake, thinking that he was creating a fortune and instead, without knowing it, preparing a tomb for his son. With his feet he scraped the earth that now held the essence of his life. From the beginning he had invested it with his sweat, his strength, his hopes and dreams, and now, when it came to fertilising it, he was yielding it his own entrails, his son, his successor, the hope that brought his work to its conclusion.

The earth would complete his mission. The crop would flourish, and a sea of golden stalks would cover Tonet's body. But for him...what remained for him to do in this world?

The father wept as he contemplated the emptiness of his existence, the loneliness that awaited him now until he died, smooth, monotonous, and endless like the lake, glinting before his eyes with never a boat breaking its level surface.

And as Tono's wails of desperation rent the silent dawn, La *Borda*, seeing her father with his back turned, bent over the edge of the grave and placed a burning kiss on the livid head, a kiss of passion and of hopeless love which, face to face with the mystery of death, revealed for the first time the secret of her life.

Playa de Malvarrosa, Valencia, September - November 1902.

Printed in Great Britain
by Amazon

32373804R00215